12-17-11

<u>To</u>

Jim

Best Wishes

*This book is dedicated to all the
Confederate and Union Soldiers then and now.*

Three Came Home

A Civil War Trilogy

By
Edward Aronoff

Volume 1
A Third Edition

Lorena

The South cannot be understood by the mind
—Faulkner

Three defiant rebels captured at Gettysburg,
July 3, 1863

Three Came Home: Vol. I — Lorena

ISBN: 978-0-9772612-9-1

Three Came Home Publishing Co.
1858 San Mateo Drive
Dunedin, FL 34698

Other books by Edward Aronoff:

Betrayal at Gettysburg

Last Chance

The Pagliacci Affair

Three Came Home: Vol. I — Lorena

Three Came Home: Vol. II — Sam

Three Came Home: Vol. III — Rutherford

To order any book contact:
edwardaronoff@yahoo.com or write:
Three Came Home
1858 San Mateo Drive
Dunedin, FL 34698

Preface

The initial battle of the Civil War at Bull
Run was much like the first flakes of snow that
hint at the coming winter storm.

By 1865, four years of bloody civil conflict had
taken the lives of one million soldiers, and left
another million legless, armless or broken in
spirit. As the number of Rebel soldiers dwindled,
voices cried out to fight conservatively, behind
boulders and trees. But General Stonewall
Jackson said, 'The Rebel Yell from behind a tree
loses much of its impact.' And so they fought and
died as before.

This war between brothers drove the people of
Vicksburg underground to dine on rats and
horseflesh. It made the names of Fredericksburg,
Antietam, and Gettysburg a horror to the men
who fought there, and forced the Confederate
Congress to the unthinkable idea of enlisting
Negro slaves to fight for the lessening ranks of
the Southern Confederacy.

At the time of the siege of Petersburg, Generals Breckinridge and Lee cajoled and maneuvered the men of the Confederate Congress to stop the war. But in the end it was General Lee who was too proud to give in. And so the effusion of blood continued...

Three Came Home
Volume 1 — Lorena

I have ordered General Gerrard to arrest for treason all owners and employees, who work for the Confederacy, and let them foot it under guard to Marietta, whence I will send them by (rail) cars to the North...
　　　　　—William Tecumseh Sherman, 1864

Chapter 1

From the private journal of Lorena Boykins-Miller

January 15, 1852

From today forward, I will tell my story after a fashion of my own.

I, Lorena Boykins Miller, was raised by a grandmother, so old and gnarled, it seemed that she had evil forces within her that twisted her body into the shape of a bent tree.

Grandmother, her name was Mary Whitaker-Jones, always carried a switch made from a hickory branch, covered with the hide of an unlucky cow.

She never said much but when she did speak, she always backed it up with a few sharp blows of her "hider," as we children called it.

I discovered Grandfather's library when I was a young girl. I was too youthful to read but I loved to look at the words. One day my Grandfather saw me with an opened book. 'What are you doing, Child, you can't read.'

"I know, Grandpa," I said, "but I just adore looking at the letters." Grandfather decided right then and there to teach me to read.

It wasn't long before I learned to avoid Grandmother's hickory switch by hiding from her in the library, and gradually, when I learned to decipher the words, I began to spend long hours in that glorious place, reading the classics. I must admit that I spent not a few hours also devouring books that were forbidden to a young lady. My favorite author was Balzac.

Of course I started borrowing books from Grandfather's library and in due course Grandmother found them in my room. Not only was I immediately banned from my favorite place but Grandmother highlighted the discussion with a few whacks of her weapon.

Undaunted by her threats and whipping, I sneaked into the library at night when all in the house were asleep. Once a house slave, named Ravetta, discovered me while wandering the halls because she too couldn't sleep. But instead of betraying me to Grandmother she became my co-conspirator. My only cost was a promise to teach her to read. A small price for my freedom to peruse the books I loved. She was soon joining me in my nocturnal adventures.

Since Grandmother forbid me to use the library during daylight hours, I turned to writing. Thus, at the age of twelve, I began to keep this journal of my life. I take it everywhere I go.

Mother and Father are angels now. They died when their boat sunk in a storm on a trip to Europe for the United States Senate. When Grandfather heard that his only son was dead, he had a fit and died also.

To my great surprise, Grandmother began to mourn him. Her face, already looking like a baked apple, soon got creased and furrowed like an old leather purse. She followed him to Heaven three months later.

I wish I could die too.

I wanted desperately to cut General Sherman's throat, but I would have to touch him to do that.

Chapter 2

Lorena Boykins Oakwood was, in this fourth year of the Civil War, twenty-two years old. She had dark green Irish eyes and alabaster skin so valued by Southern women. Her face, an aristocratic legacy from her mother, was so pale one would suspect her flaming red hair had drained it of its blood.

Square of jaw, determined of mind, she wore large floppy hats with black veils, long sleeved dresses, and black gloves, which prevented the Georgia sun from otherwise marring her pale, blue veined complexion. A gentleman could span her tiny waist with his two hands, and her erect posture displayed a full bosom.

Her manner was composed and reticent. It came about through years of diligent training by

5

her autocratic grandmother, her black nanny, and a certain tyrannical, Madame Talvandes, who ran the *French School for Young Ladies* in Charleston, South Carolina.

Her features showed the handsome blend of her Portuguese mother and Irish father. However, it was Lorena's eyes that betrayed her. They burned with a lust for life, and exuded a willful sexuality that escaped her husband, but was readily discerned by other men. Although she was never unfaithful to John Oakwood, she was sought after and extremely popular with many military officers and statesmen at the highest level of Southern society for her wit and congeniality.

When Lorena married, she came from South Carolina to this place in Georgia soon after the railroad people named it Terminus. It was called by that name because the new, vibrant, burgeoning town was at the junction of three important train terminals.

As the town grew, a bright idea occurred to former Georgia governor Lumpkin and he, with a not inconsiderable monetary gift, influenced the city to call the new town after his only daughter, Martha. Thereafter it was called Marthasville.

As the city burst forth into a bustling metropolis the city fathers wanted a new name, something ambitious and exciting, in keeping with the new city's energy.

Jumping in to the rescue was Governor Lumpkin once more. After donating another goodly, but undisclosed sum of money, he recommended to the city fathers they call it Atlanta. They rejoiced and accepted the new name, thinking they had named it after the mythical kingdom, Atlantis. Little did they realize that his daughter Martha's middle name was Atalanta. Mr. Lumpkin and Martha kept their secret until they died.

Lorena Oakwood would never tell her age exactly, and even kept that little privacy from her husband. She was born into an aristocratic Southern family, her father being a United States Senator, and her mother, an accomplished violinist, all of them ruled by a martinet grandmother.

She married well at seventeen. But her father-in-law turned out to be tight-fisted. The old man was quite wealthy, and owned a thousand slaves on four separate plantations, but his only son had been given very little and had his name on nothing.

However, the son, John Oakwood, was a Harvard graduate and ambitious. He went to that prestigious New England school after spending a year at West Point. He was also a rising political star. Before the war he was an alderman in Atlanta, and planned, before the beginning of hostilities at Fort Sumter, to run against the incumbent, Joe Brown, for Governor of Georgia.

As most Southern women did, Lorena ignored her husband's penchant for drinking, riding, shooting, and clandestine whoring with slave girls.

After marriage she kept her charm and beauty, and he came early to a man's responsibility.

When the War Between the States began, John Oakwood dropped his political ambitions and joined a company raised by fellow Georgian, Robert Toombs.

Oakwood was voted captain of the company because of his popularity and also because of his year at West Point. On his father's plantation he had learned to be a good administrator and he quickly brought order out of chaos to his regiment. Noticed by the flamboyant cavalry chief, Jeb Stewart, Oakwood was promptly promoted to major.

By 1864, the third year of the war, people, who had an eye for talent and the ear of President Davis, whispered John Oakwood's name to him. Davis remembered Lorena Oakwood's flashing green eyes and John was soon promoted to the rank of brigadier general. In due time he became military attaché to Braxton Bragg, who had taken the place of Robert E. Lee as military advisor to the Confederate President. Late in the war Oakwood finally realized his dream of combat when he joined General Hood at the Battle of Atlanta.

Lorena

Lorena Oakwood was a perfect general's wife. Besides being a delightful hostess to their wide circle of friends, she was charming, witty, well read, and knew many important people, including not a few men who would gladly change places with John Oakwood.

When John was ordered to the capitol, Richmond, Lorena held court at the Spotswood Hotel where her eloquent voice and flaming red hair were only clues to a fiery temper and spirit that John Oakwood suppressed.

Her acquaintances and influence extended, through her large family, particularly her dearest friend and cousin, Mary Chestnut, to the highest offices of the South. It was whispered throughout Richmond that John Oakwood climbed to his military pinnacle, one foot on his wife's back and the other planted firmly on her cousin's.

We few, we happy few, we band of brothers
—Shakespeare

Chapter 3

Lorena walked up the creaking wooden stairs
to the second landing. Her steps were slow and
hesitant. She stopped at the top of the stairs,
sighed wearily, and listened. It seemed so strange
not to hear the steady buzz from the workshop
area, and the intermittent clanging of metal on
metal. It was almost as if the heart of a great
beast had been stilled.

Lorena closed her eyes and willed the
machines to be alive again. Nothing. She sighed,
walked a few steps and stopped at the first door.

She stepped inside and pulled the rope that
opened the transom to let air into the room. The
framed glass on the door read:

> *ATLANTA FOUNDRY WORKS*
> *QUALITY GUNS FOR THE CONFEDERACY*

Lorena laughed to herself silently when she thought about the first day she moved back to Atlanta and came to the foundry. *It was the first time I ever defied my husband, and it felt so good. I remember him saying, 'No wife of mine is going to work like a common Cracker.' He said it in that cold, infuriating way of his that told me he was very angry. But, I answered him, 'John, I have to do something for the cause, now don't I.'* She laughed again, this time aloud. "That stopped him." Still smiling she closed the door.

Lorena pulled out her hatpin and took off her hat and veil. She shook her head and a mass of dark, red hair spilled over her shoulders. She put the hat on the hat rack, went to her desk, smoothed her dress and sat down on her swivel chair.

Picking up a paper with the seal of the Confederacy she absently read the last part of an official letter.

—Generals Lee and Johnston are in desperate want of pistols and muskets, and the Tredegar works in Richmond cannot supply all they need. We pray your foundry can fulfill the balance. My armorer, Colonel James Burton, will be at your establishment on Friday, May 15th, to facilitate the purchase of the guns you have available.

11

Payment will be made in Confederate dollars immediately upon receipt of your invoice. Please send said invoice to, John B Floyd, Secretary of War, Confederate States of America, State House, Richmond, Virginia.
Your obedient servant,

Josiah Gorgas, Major, CSA
Chief of the Confederate Bureau of Ordnance

Lorena sighed. "There'll be no more guns from this armory, Major. You better hope Griswold and Grier at their Georgia armory, or the British Whitworth Ltd. can supply the weapons you need."

She put the letter down and looked up at the wall. All the different guns the foundry made used to hang on the walls in framed cases. Now only the outline of the cases remained. *The Confederacy must really be hard put when they confiscate our samples.*

Lorena shook her head, a sad look in her eyes as she thought of the Confederate soldiers from Jonesboro on the outskirts of the city, fighting and dying, defending their homes. "Rifles! Pistols! Why did anyone ever allow them to be invented in the first place? All they're good for is to kill." She looked back at the letter, shook her head then stared into space. In a few moments her eyes darkened giving her pale face a haunted look. Suddenly she crumpled the letter in her fist.

"Oh, God! Will I ever forget the sight of those wounded and dying men." Her face a mask of sorrow, Lorena laid her arm on the desk and put her forehead in the crook of her elbow. She squeezed her eyes tightly but could not shut out the sight of the horror she had seen earlier in the day. She shuddered.

This damned Civil War goes on and on, as if it has a life of its own. Will it ever stop? She lifted her head up and stared into space. *I remember when that crazy John Brown made his murderous way down here, sending a wave of passionate anger across the whole South. He awakened that horror of slave insurrection that lays dormant in the mind of every Southerner. Now, that the war is in full swing everyone I know is so sad and sorrowful. But they are only reflecting the fear they have for the sons they sent to war, afraid their precious flesh and blood will rot in some far off lonely grave.*

****

The morning had begun with Sherman's troops shelling the outskirts of Atlanta. Two of the missiles landed on Lorena's road, destroying the wing of one old antebellum home across the street, and the garden of another just two doors down.

After the bombing stopped Lorena came out of her damp basement with her maid, Ravetta, and the children. She heard a tramping of feet and a lone voice, echoing down the street, counting cadence.

Leaving her two children with Ravetta, Lorena ran upstairs, darted to the window and threw it open. On either side of her the sheer yellow curtains of the bedroom window billowed inward like the sails of a four master on the sea. She pushed them back and they wrapped around her clinging to her green and gold cotton dress.

Down the street came the boys of the Georgia Confederate Home Guard swaggering in their importance and their ability to march in step. They wore Confederate gray cadet uniforms with white canvas straps across their waists and chests. Their gray felt hats were pinned up bravely on one side with black cock feathers fastened at the brim. They were confidently heading south, toward Jonesboro and the distant muttering of battlefield artillery. If she did not know better the low distant rumble would, at other times, pass for remote thunder.

When the Home Guard saw Lorena they waved and began to sing:

We are a band of Brothers
  And native to the soil,
Fighting for the property

14

We gained by honest toil;
And when our rights were threatened
*　The cry rose near and far—*
"Hurrah for the Bonnie Blue Flag
*　That bears the single star!"*
Hurrah! Hurrah!
*　For states rights hurrah!*
Hurrah for the Bonnie Blue Flag
*　That bears the single star.*

Other windows on the street were flung open and Lorena's women neighbors were soon leaning out their windows, waving flags and shouting encouragement to the amateur soldiers. Hearing the stirring song, some of the more fervent women had tears rolling down their cheeks.

Lorena grimaced, *My, my, such shaking of flags, and handkerchiefs, and tears.*

The boys, overcome with the welcome, broke ranks and waved back behaving as if they were on a picnic.

Thinking of the wounded at the fairgrounds, lying on the ground, bleeding and dying, Lorena imagined these boys also lying dead and broken. She blinked back her own tears.

I don't think they yet know what's in store for them.

A regular army sergeant broke the mood, bellowing loudly, "You men get back into formation, *now!* The sergeant quickly ran along

the ranks bullying them back into line. When
they got back into step, he started up the cadence.
"Hup, two, three, four...."

When they got closer Lorena's eyes narrowed,
and she gripped the windowsill so tightly her
knuckles turned white. *This army is made up of
mere boys.* From where she was they looked pink
cheeked and, although they appeared determined,
they also appeared a bit frightened. *And their
uniforms, they're two sizes too big for them.*

A second company came up behind them.
These were older men and not all of them sang.
Mostly unsmiling and gray-haired, many of them
wore steel rimmed glasses. They were in route
step and every few strides some of them would
turn their heads and gaze back from whence they
had come. To Lorena, they had a reluctant look
about them, as if they had been dragged from
behind desks and counters and forced to become
soldiers. *I wonder if they volunteered or were
conscripted.* She muttered aloud; "To fight, and to
be made to fight are vastly different things."

Lorena silently prayed for both companies.

Suddenly a bomb came whistling overhead and
struck the next street. The women ducked back
inside their homes and slammed their windows
shut while the men on the street began to scatter.
The tough army sergeant bellowed a, "Halt," and
most of the men and boys froze. After a few
minutes of confusion, and a profane tongue-

16

lashing, he had both companies in columns of twos, double-timing sloppily toward the front.

Lorena watched them turn the corner with a sinking heart. After the last man disappeared, she began to close the window. A sudden cross breeze pulled the curtains out and they flapped against the side of the house. Lorena stopped, pulled the curtains in and quickly closed the window.

As she was turning around the bedroom door burst open and Ravetta came charging in, her eyes white and wide on her round, black face.

Ravetta Miller had been with Lorena's family since she was born. Even though they were near the same age, she became Lorena's nanny and confidante since the time Lorena taught her to read. Miller was her fathers name and she kept it.

A fondness for fats and sugar had put excess pounds on her strong frame and despite the rigorous work she did for Lorena, General Oakwood, and Lorena's two children, she could never seem to shed a pound.

"Oh, Lawd, Miss Lorena," she said her multiple chins trembling and her voice shaking with fear, "we gots to get de chillun and get outta here."

Lorena answered with a calm she didn't feel. "Now just settle down, Ravetta. The Yankees are still thirty or forty miles from here, and we have our best General between them and us."

Ravetta shook her head vigorously. "Mebbe so,

Miss Lorena, but dem shells the Yankees is shootin' is goin' over the sojers and comin' right on top of us. Dem Confedurate lil' boys and ol' men dat just passed cain't stop dem Yankee Devils nohow."

Lorena grimaced, shook her head and sat wearily on the bed. "You may be right, Ravetta, they didn't look very formidable. Let me think a minute." *The home guard won't hold the Yankees, but maybe General Johnston can stop them.*

While pondering her situation, a shell hit nearby and exploded, shaking dust from the ceiling. Lorena stiffened.

Ravetta's eyes widened and darted to her mistress.

The bomb made up Lorena's mind. "Ravetta, get the suitcases, pack a few things for all of us and put everything in the buggy. Then take the children to their grandfather's house. I need to go to the foundry to get some money. I'll join you as soon as I can."

"Go, widout you, Miss Lorena?"

The reluctant look she got from Ravetta did nothing to cheer Lorena's mood. She felt a spurt of anger but pushed it down and answered evenly. "You'll be just fine Ravetta. Just don't stop for anything or anybody."

"Yes'm," she said dejectedly, "ah'll sure go lickity split with all dem bombs fallin' 'round me," she said, not bothering to hide her sarcasm.

Ravetta waddled from the room, calling to the children to come and help her.

Lorena wished she knew more of what was happening so she could make the right choices. *If only I knew how close the Yankees were. What are the chances they would come to this street? Would they invade these beautiful old homes?*

From a distance she again heard marching men tramping and singing. Hope flooded her being. She went back, threw open the window again, and waited.

This time a brigade of regular Confederate soldiers came around the corner and abreast of her home, their sergeants calling cadence while the men lustily sang *Dixie*. Lorena opened the window and beamed at them.

I wish I was in the land of cotton,
Old times there are not forgotten,
Look away, look away, look away, Dixie land,
In Dixie Land where I was born, early on a
frosty morn',
Look away, look away, look away, Dixie land,
Then I wish I was in Dixie, Hooray! Hooray!
In Dixie land I'll take my stand and live and
die in Dixie,
Away, away, away down south in Dixie,
Away, away, away down south in Dixie...

These were seasoned, determined troops and it

showed. They were dressed in a mystifying variety of uniforms, some in homespun flannel shirts, others in brown uniforms and the rest in the familiar gray. Even though they looked like a ragged and dirty set of men, they moved smartly and their muskets were shiny and clean. Their spines were straight, and the guide flags snapped proudly in the breeze. At the head of each company was a color sergeant holding the company flag. Over all, at the head of the column was a fluttering flag of stars and bars.

Other windows opened and the shaking of hankies started again.

Little boys ran alongside the men playing soldier and shooting imaginary guns in the air. Young girls, appearing almost magically, stood by the side of the street and waved. Young men of military age who at first accompanied the girls melted into the side streets and disappeared to the derisive cries of, 'Shirkers', 'Bulletproofs' and 'Doughface,' coming from the marching soldiers.

Lorena leaned out the window and called to the nearest men. "Where is the front now, boys? I mean, how far away are the Yankees?"

A Lieutenant stopped and turned his face up to her.

Gracious, he looks no more than nineteen, she thought.

His face was clean-shaven except for a thin mustache. He had a head full of black wavy hair and, above a dazzling smile, a patrician nose topped by dark brown eyes. He put his hand over his eyes and squinted. When he saw Lorena he took his cavalry hat off and bowed gallantly. "Ma'am, General Johnston has made a brave stand at Kennesaw Mountain. They say he covered the mountain with blue corpses."

Hope sprang up in Lorena. *Maybe General Sherman will have to take his rabble back North after all.*

He shook his head as if reading her mind. "But a wounded trooper, we found staggerin' back to Atlanta told me, 'If Sherman went to Hell he'd flank the Devil and take the place.' Well, apparently Sherman flanked General Johnston, and went around Atlanta to Jonesboro. Our boys had to retreat south to face them. That's where we're all goin' now, to join General Johnston and see if we can help turn them Yankees around. Maybe we kin send 'em right the hell— 'Scuse me ma'am, right the devil back outta Georgia."

Jonesboro, that's only twenty miles from here. Lorena's smile hid her anxiety. "Thank you, sir."

The Lieutenant saluted, flashed a lover-melting smile and then, holding his sword to his thigh, ran to catch up with his company.

Now Lorena was torn. She knew that every day at eleven o'clock the Atlanta Intelligencer posted a list of the dead and wounded in the town square.

I have to join the children at their grandfather's, but on the other hand I'm desperate to know what's happened to my husband. Has John been wounded? Is he dead? Oh, God, I have to know.

The Seth-Thomas grandfather clock in the corner began to chime. *It's already ten o'clock.* Lorena's stomach tightened. *And, the closer to Atlanta the Yankee devils come the more feisty, Ravetta seems to act. I've always treated her like a member of this family, and I think she will be loyal to me. But maybe the other servants have filled her head with this freedom nonsense they're all talking about. It's all my fault, I've pampered her so much she's become a tyrant.*

Lorena turned and leaned back against the sill. *I don't want to leave Ravetta alone with the children, but John is with General Johnston—* "I just have to know what's happened to him!" she exclaimed aloud. Her face hardening with resolve she thought, *I'll just have to trust Ravetta.*

Her mind made up she bolted from the window and, holding her skirt in her hand, skipped down the stairs two at a time. When she reached the bottom she called to her servant.

Ravetta answered with an impatient shout then waddled to her mistress as fast as her fat legs would carry her. She arrived out of breath, one hand above her ponderous breasts.

"I'm going to the square to get the latest war news. You get the children and go to Father

22

Oakwood's. I'll join you as soon as soon as I can."

Ravetta rolled her eyes, but obediently replied, "Yes, Ma'am," in a cold voice. Then turning, and muttering just loud enough for Lorena to hear, "It's not enough I have to do everythin' 'roun' here but I also have to take..." Her voice faded away. Before Ravetta turned the corner, Lorena saw her shake her head, and force her lips into a pout as she went back to the children.

Hesitating for a moment, Lorena picked up her parasol and walked out of her house. There was a rivulet of people going towards the town square and Lorena joined them. Soon the rivulet turned into a torrent, and finally to a great crowd of milling, distraught humanity, all pouring into the square, wanting news of loved ones from the battlefields so close to them.

Lorena saw a few familiar faces but no one she knew really well until she spotted Dr. Garret. Lorena made her way to him, squeezing by people as best she could.

When she reached him, Lorena tapped him on the shoulder. "Dr. Garret, is there any news from the front yet?"

He turned and faced Lorena, his face reflecting so much anger, it made her stomach churn and her hands ball into fists.

If they will go on I will go on
— General Lee

Chapter 4

$\mathfrak{D}$r. David Robert Garrot, Senior was a tall,
slender man with a shock of white hair and a
short matching beard. He had an alert, intelligent
face and dark blue compassionate eyes. Walking
with his shoulders bent, it seemed as if he were
carrying a great load. He was always seen with
the same rumpled black suit, white shirt and a
matching black string bow tie that seemed to
have captured the droop of the man's shoulders.

The distracted doctor looked at Lorena with a
blank stare. "Damn these people, pushing and
shovin'. And damn the newspaper—" Finally
recognition came into his eyes. "Oh, Miz
Oakwood. No, I know nothin' 'cept that some
orderly keeps comin' from the make-shift hospital
at the fairgrounds, telling me to come with him
'cause we're gettin' lots more casualties."

He grimaced and shook his head, his white mane flowing just behind his movement. "About three times as many as usual, he says, so the fighting must be fierce." He smiled and shook his head. "Three years ago the only gunshot wounds I ever saw were young hotheads involved in duels. And now—" He shrugged his shoulders.

Garret looked back to the newspaper office. "I should be tending the wounded, but my son, David Garret is with Hood's division—" His chest puffed out and he said proudly, "He's a university trained physician, you know." Then his voice trailed off. "I'm torn, I have to get back to the wounded... but I have to know...."

Lorena was in the same predicament and felt his pain. David was the doctor's only child. She was going to say the boy was probably safe, far behind the skirmish lines, but she knew that artillery and sharpshooters left no one protected.

Suddenly Dr. Garret cocked his head and looked at her oddly. "Miz Oakwood, I know you're not a nurse, but the hospital staff surely can use some help. They have suspended classes at the Atlanta Medical College and the students and me have taken it over. With all the casualties comin' in, we also made an open-air hospital at the fair grounds. Could you come with me when we're finished here and help us for a few hours? We're so short of assistance— Maybe you could help some of the orderlies change bandages, or bathe a few wounds, that sort of thing." He looked at her expectantly.

Lorena thought about Ravetta and the children, felt a deep anxiety for a moment, then pushed them out of her mind. *For all the army has done for us I guess I can give the wounded a little time.*

"Of course, Dr. Garret," Lorena said absently, looking at the newspaper office, "If my John were hurt, I would want someone to help him."

He stroked his short gray beard and a hint of gratitude filled his eyes. "Good, it's settled then. After we find out the news here, we'll go to the depot." His face turned somber again and he pointed a bony finger toward a corner of the newspaper building. "They post the names of the wounded and killed on that bulletin board over there."

Just as he finished speaking a door opened and a small man with a hooked nose and pockmarked face stepped out. His sleeves were held up by two india rubbers and a green shade that covered his forehead. He came out of the building with a hammer and a rolled up paper. Without looking at the crowd he nailed up a list of names. When he finished he turned, gave a fleeting glance at the throng, and quickly went back inside.

For a moment nobody moved. Then one man made a step toward the board and the crowd came alive again, surging behind him and taking the doctor and Lorena with them. A great deal of pushing and shoving to get to the front began for people desperate for news of loved ones.

When Lorena saw the length of the list she sucked in her breath. Quickly read by those in front, the people either left with a grateful look, or broke down in tears and despair.

When Lorena finally pushed her way to the board, her eyes scanned down the list to the O's. She went up and down the names looking for John. *O'Hara, O'Malley, Osteen.* Nothing. She breathed a deep sigh of relief. *No Oakwood. Thank God.*

She turned to Dr. Garret to share her joy but was stopped short. The doctor's face looked as white as his hair. He appeared to be in shock, like a man that had been struck by a bullet, his look incredulous, his body tremulous.

"Dr. Garret! What's wrong?"

Dr. Garret stared at Lorena with watery blue eyes. "It's David— dead at Kennesaw—" he said mechanically. His legs gave way and he went to the ground on his knees, oblivious of the crowd around him, then he closed his eyes.

Lorena kneeled down next to him.

People stumbled around them muttering and cursing.

Lorena put her hand gently on his shoulder. Garret opened his eyes and looked at Lorena with eyes so full of pain it hurt her heart.

He hesitated and tried to speak. His mouth worked but no sound came out. Finally he shook his head slowly and spoke in a voice so low Lorena had to bend forward to hear the words. "What will I tell his mother? This will kill her..." His voice faded into nothingness as he stared into space desperately trying to conjure up his son's face.

This damn war goes on and on, Lorena thought. *There are wounds that won't show but will need healing just the same.* She took his hand gently in hers. "We'll go together. I'll tell her."

He jerked his hand away and an air of authority came back to him. He got up quickly as if he were ashamed of showing so much emotion.

"No! I must get back to the wounded. Mrs. Garret can wait." He looked at her sternly. "And you must come with me." Dr. Garret took her hand and forcefully led a confused Lorena through the crowd toward his buggy.

Now Lorena began to see other people she knew. Friends and neighbors with bowed heads and faces etched in pain. Elderly men holding protective arms around frail women their thin shoulders shaking. It was too much. She looked away avoiding the pain in their eyes.

Lorena felt the heat from the sun bearing down and the closeness of the crowd. Dr. Garret was moving her too fast for her to open her parasol. The corset she wore had staves made of bone that pressed in on her ribs and interfered with her breathing. She felt faint. Shaking off the nausea and vertigo, she quickened her pace to keep up with the doctor. She wished fervently she were home, the corset off, and a glass of cold sun tea in her hand.

Maybe I need something stronger than tea. By the size of that list there will be many, many women dressed in mourning black tomorrow. No one will soon forget this day.

Lorena noticed a small group hugging and laughing. *Their sons must not be on the list. Don't be so happy, friends, there will be lots more fighting to come.*

Dr. Garret and Lorena forced their way through the still gathering crowd and finally reached his buggy. The carriage was a one-horse covered rig that the doctor used to make his rounds of the sick throughout the county. It once belonged to the doctor whose practice Dr. Garret had taken. Garret had hoped to one day to give the horse and carriage to his now dead son, David.

Dr. Garret helped Lorena up onto her seat. While she waited for him to go around and get aboard she watched more people streaming toward the square with mixed looks on their faces.

Garret slid in next to Lorena, took the whip out of its slot and slapped the horse on its rump.

With a small jerk the animal started through the crowd shying and snorting, making his way down the street.

It seemed to Lorena now as if all of Atlanta was coming to the square, and the horse had difficulty moving through the mass of people. After a difficult few minutes the crowd began to thin out, the people, at first an eddying throng, were now a sluggish stream. Soon they rolled into almost empty streets and clipped along at a steady pace.

When they got close to their destination traffic picked up again. But now the vehicles were ambulances and the people, soldiers. Finally they were one street away from the fair grounds. They turned the corner and rode along a section of high tents separating the medical grounds from the street.

From and behind the tents came a foul stench and unearthly sounds that made Lorena apprehensive.

In a few moments they reached the brick entrance to the fair grounds. Dr. Garret put the reins on the horse's neck, turned him, and entered the grounds. The animal, his senses alert, shied past the first tent. Ten yards after entering the grounds the doctor pulled on the reins and the horse stopped short before an open field, breathing heavily.

Lorena stood up, stunned. For a full minute

she just gaped at the macabre scene with a slack jaw. Slowly, uncomprehending, she sat down her eyes wide with astonishment. Then she turned to the doctor, shock and dismay imprinted on her face. She felt herself an intruder upon a mountain of grief.

Stretched out on the field in front of Lorena, in bloody and bandaged rows, were the results of the Confederate fighting from Dalton to Kennesaw Mountain.

The Rebel wounded and dead lay crowded together in haphazard rows and, for the most part, left untended. The injured assaulted the ears with screaming and moaning and cries for water. Others, with wounds that were not visible, curled in fetal positions. The dead were silent.

A light breeze brought the mixed stench of gangrene, blood, sweat and dying to the buggy. Lorena turned a shade of green, gagged, leaned over the side and vomited.

Dr. Garret patted her heaving shoulder. "You'll get used to it, my dear.

Lorena turned her head, wiped her mouth and gave him a baleful look.

Ignoring her stare he said with authority, "Let's get to work." Dr. Garret got out of the buggy, absently patted the horse's rump and yelled to an orderly who was closing the eyes of a dead man. "You there, orderly, take this lady and show her what to do." He turned to Lorena and

made a sweep with his arm over the dead and
dying. "You stay here with us, Miz Oakwood, we
need your help."

This pestilential day became the prelude to the
longest year of Lorena's life.

****

The blazing southern sun made the depot a
nightmare. It baked the injured and the maimed,
and like the biblical sun, stayed in the middle of
the sky refusing to move.

After a few minutes with the dying, Lorena
was soaked with sweat from head to toe. Her
dark dress, made for visiting and teas, clung to
her clammy body. Bewiskered men covered with
lice, their clothing stained with blood, lay
helpless at her feet. Flecks of blood soon speckled
the white ruffles of her garment.

The orderly walking beside her grabbed her
arm and stopped. He picked up a bucket filled
with water and put it down in front of her. He
cocked his head and looked at her strangely. "You
sure you want to do this in that dress, Ma'am?

Lorena gave him a withering look. "I didn't
plan on spending my day tending wounded men.
Can we get on with this?" she said with impatience.

The orderly shrugged his shoulders and gave
her a nasty smile. He looked over the vast array
of wounded. "Why the hurry?" With that retort he

32

bent down to a nearby wounded man and began to sponge his maggot covered wound. Lorena was revolted when she noticed the water was already dirty and tinged with red.

She was soon tearing ragged cloths, and washing and dressing open wounds. Gritting her teeth, she went from man to man wiping feverish brows. She noticed most of the bandages were made from strips of coarse, unbleached homespun cotton on which the blood had congealed. The blood stiffened the bandages making every crease cut into the skin like a knife.

Lorena got busy changing bloody rags for clean ones, exchanging soft bandages for the coarse ones when she could. When she ran out of bandages she ripped strips from her own petticoat. She rested only when she held the hands of men, watching them die.

Even in the open air the smell of gangrene was oppressive. The sicky-sweet smell was worse up close and she would have vomited again if she had anything left. Swarms of fat green flies, and gnats so small they were almost unseen, hovered around wounds and mouths, making it hard for the men to breathe.

As she made her grisly rounds grizzled veterans looked at Lorena longingly, many too weak to want nothing but the sight of her. Others pleaded with her to write a line or two to their wives. One man told Lorena, "Please write my ol' woman, and tell her I'll be home fer spring plantin'." Then he died.

Lorena scurried from one wounded man to the next, ministering to each from her limited knowledge of nursing. It wrenched her heart to hear some of the wounded screaming in their delirium calling for wives and mothers. Other men in shock were quiet and pale. In back of the surgical tent, which she passed often, was the morbid debris of the day before. Put there were men who were no longer men, stacked like cordwood; a cold reminder of her own mortality.

In the midst of her going from man to man, Lorena suddenly stopped short. Lying in front of her, resplendent in his Federal blue uniform, was a Yankee officer. Lorena froze then recoiled back, hating the sight of the wounded Yankee. *He and his kind are the cause of all this misery.*

The Union officer was lying on his back between two raggedly dressed Confederates. She looked more closely at his lapels and saw the two USA insignias of a captain. A rush of anger filled her heart and then spilled over into her body. She began to shake as she stared at the wounded man fighting the urge to strangle him.

When he saw her he smiled. His smile disarmed her. It was warm, and when their eyes met, to her dismay, his was full of intelligence. His eyes also reflected the deep pain he was in. She tried to turn away but couldn't.

The orderly was passing by and took in the situation. He leaned toward her and whispered in her ear, "We have to treat them too, Lady, doctors orders." The sarcastic look on his face dared her to do otherwise.

She stared down at the officer. The Yankee captain seemed to be near her age. She guessed about twenty-three or so. He had hair the color of corn silk and eyes of blue so pale it looked as if he were blind. Lorena lost her anger as suddenly as it had come, and kneeled down beside the Federal officer. She quickly looked him over for wounds, and saw his right pant leg was shredded and stained red.

If my John were hurt and some Yankee nurse were near him I would want her to care for him. Lorena's heart went out to the captain. She loosened the tourniquet around his thigh, deftly cut away the pant leg and stared at his shattered knee. It was caked with dried blood, pieces of bone and dirt. Gritting her teeth, Lorena went right to work cleaning the damaged tissue.

As gently as she could she washed and debrided the painful wound. The captain stiffened and groaned, but never cried out. When she finished Lorena stood up. It was then that she noticed how mottled and dark the Yankee captain's foot was. Lorena shook her head. She knew it would have to come off.

He noticed her staring at his foot. "Will I lose

the leg?" he said in a hoarse whisper.

"I hope not, Captain. I'm sure our doctors will try to save it."

"You're an angel, Miss. I'll never forget you."

"No offence, Captain, but I'd like to forget you, and everyone else here—"

"Mrs. Oakwood." It was Dr. Garret calling her. "Come quickly, I need you."

She reached down and held the captain's hand for a moment. He squeezed and she felt his strength radiate into her arm. She quickly laid his hand down at his side. "Sorry, Captain, I have to go."

His eyes were bright with thanks. "God bless you, Mrs. Oakwood."

Lorena smiled. "Good luck, Captain." Her eyes were moist as she turned away. She could not help seeing the surgical table around which amputated arms and legs were strewn.

The day ground by slowly. Wounded men cried pitifully for water and young boys, their eyes filled with the fear of death, clung to her. Some of the delirious ones cried out and called her, 'Mother.' There were so many wounded lying in uneven rows Lorena would sometimes trip over legs provoking hoarse shrieks of pain.

During the arduous work Lorena looked at the men in wonder. *Lots them are just boys. Some look even younger than sixteen. So many of them have bloody feet and no shoes.*

Later in the day as Lorena passed near Dr. Garret, she wearily turned as she heard the doctor call out to her. As she approached him she noticed his eyes were watery and the corners of his mouth pulled down so tight it made his mouth an inverted U.

"Miz Oakwood, I think you will want to give some attention this man over here."

Lorena was puzzled but she followed him to a wounded soldier. Dr. Garret stayed beside her.

As she looked down at the bloody man she uttered a cry of dismay.

"Courage," Dr. Garret said and put his hand on her shoulder for support.

Lorena instantly recognized the man on the ground. It was Josiah Buchanan, the owner of the Atlanta Foundry. His skin was a rusty bronze from too many days in the sun and his uniform was torn and dirty. Across his abdomen spread a dark and ugly scarlet stain.

His eyes met hers, and in them she saw emptiness and confusion. In a low, pitiful voice he mumbled to her, "Water, water."

She knelt down and looked up at Dr. Garret hopefully.

Dr. Garret's brows knitted in a severe frown, he pursed his lips and shook his head slowly. "The water is not good for him, but—" He shook his head, turned and left for the next patient.

Lorena looked around her. Nearby a dead

trooper in rigor mortis clutched his canteen to his chest. She went to the soldier, and, avoiding his staring eyes, with difficulty, wrenched the wooden canteen from his clamped fingers. She came back to Buchanan, kneeled down and opened the spout. She brought it to Buchanan's lips. He felt the canteen, opened his eyes and grasped at it. Lorena jerked it away spilling some of it over her grimy, bloody hand. She berated herself silently and waited for Buchanan to calm down. When he lay still again, she brought the canteen more carefully to his mouth.

As he drank, Buchanan stared up at her with indifference.

Lorena realized he was so mad with fever he didn't know who she was. She sat down on the warm ground, cradled his head in her lap and gently tippled water into his mouth, ignoring the bedlam around them she stayed with him, trying to comfort him.

Suddenly his eyes changed in a way that frightened her. He began to gurgle bringing foaming frothy red bubbles around his mouth. He grabbed Lorena's sleeve and hauled himself upright. Now his eyes were saucer wide and feverish. He turned his head and looked wildly to the right and left.

Lorena shrunk back but he held her in place by his strong grip.

Hanging on to her sleeve he cried out, "Look,

General Jackson, they're running." He turned to her, his eyes bright with delirium, and focused directly on the face of the frightened Lorena. Then he looked past her, tightened his grip on her arm and yelled, "Sergeant, quickly, get your men and follow me." He stared into the past for a moment, and slowly eased back down. After a few moments he bared his teeth in a mirthless grin, and the feverish light in his eyes went out. He was dead.

Lorena looked at his wide innocent eyes, his kind face, the fringe of white hair at the back of his head, and his potbelly now marred with a ragged wound. Tears made a path down the grime on her face as she smoothed down his wild hair.

His daughter is the most beautiful debutante in the entire South, but I'll wager she'd give up her beauty and all her beaus to get her father back.

She shook her head slowly. *He belonged home, bouncing grandchildren on his knee in front of a fireplace, not on a battlefield. But he said he would die defending his home and he did.* She reached down and closed his staring eyes. *Goodbye Mr. Buchanan.*

Lorena didn't realize it, but as she worked for the rest of the afternoon, tears rolled down her cheeks.

****

39

The day wore on with a maddening sameness. Finally, riddled with worry and guilt over her children, Lorena decided she must go home. She made her way to Dr. Garret.

When she found him the doctor was bent over a Confederate soldier, surgical saw in hand ready to amputate his leg. The soldier had a desperate, frightened look in his eyes.

The doctor's face was soaked with sweat and his shirt and vest were covered with dark, dried blood. Flies buzzed around the patient's blackened leg. The orderly that got Lorena started in this macabre business indifferently brushed them away.

"Son," Lorena heard the doctor say to the wounded man, "we have no chloroform left but this will only take a few moments. This orderly will help hold you down. Now you be brave." He handed the wounded man a small stick of wood. "I want you to bite down on this stick. It will help."

The orderly stopped fanning, moved to his head, and gripped the trooper's shoulders. The frightened soldier let a small animal cry escape him as he reached for the stick with a trembling, dirty hand. He nodded his head dumbly. Beads of sweat rolled down his cheeks over the grime on his pallid face. His eyes were deep set in black sockets wide with fear and pain. His skeletal face showed a confused grin and then a frown in quick succession. "Cain't you just bandage it Doc? Ah heals real quick-like." Then he laid his head back, dropped all pretense and howled, "Ah cain't plow with jes one leg!"

Garret shook his head. "No, Son. If I leave the leg on, the gangrene will kill you. Better for your family to have a one-legged man than no man at all." Dr. Garret shook his head slowly, a redness spreading up from his neck to his face, belying his calm. He mumbled angrily. "This goddamned war..."

Garret turned to the orderly. "Now you hold on to him tight."

The orderly shook his head dumbly, exhaustion and fatigue making him more detached than usual.

Garret brought the surgical saw down just above the blackened and dying flesh. Lorena momentarily turned away and fought her nausea.

Trying desperately not to be ill, she retched. All that came up was bitter bile. Lorena wiped her lips with the hem of her dress, and turned back to the ghastly scene. She stepped up to the surgical table.

"Dr. Garret, I can't stand it anymore. I have to go home and find my children." She hated that her voice was high and whining.

Dr. Garret lifted the saw and turned to her, his eyes flashing.

The soldier on the table groaned with pain and

apprehension and tried to sit up. The orderly pushed him back down.

Garret fought to control himself and wiped his brow with the back of his arm leaving a streak of blood on his forehead. "Leave? You can't leave, Miz Oakwood. We need you here."

The soldier took the stick out of his mouth, forced his way up on one elbow. He looked at Garret imploring. "Doc, jes bandage it and let me go. I'll be okay."

Dr. Garret's fists balled and he whirled to the soldier. "Shut your mouth, you damn Swamp Cracker."

The boy fell back, defeated.

Garret turned to the orderly. "Hold on to him, dammit!"

The orderly bristled.

Garret pivoted back to Lorena. "Your slave will take care of your children." He shook the surgical saw at the rows of groaning and dying men. "They need your help more than any children." He swung his arm around them in a wide arc. "Just look at us. We're out of Chloroform, iodine, quinine, everythin'. The little opium we have, I have to give to those who are dyin' and in desperate pain." He shook his shaggy head and looked down at the gangrenous leg and absently brushed away the flies. "Worst of all we haven't got any help. No, Miz Oakwood, you *must* stay."

Lorena turned her head and looked behind

her. The fair grounds had more dead and dying soldiers than before. They lay as far down the field as she could see, and beyond. *Is there no end to this nightmare?*

Lorena squared her shoulders and turned back to Garret. "No, Dr. Garret, I *will* leave. I must see about my children and," she looked at the leg of the future amputee on the table and sobbed, "I've had enough of this—"

Dr. Garret's eyes narrowed and his hands shook. He raised his voice to a shout. "Miz Oakwood, you are one of the spoiled women of our generation. As long as you women feed your men with delusions of knightly grandeur, they fight for you, coddle you, put you on pedestals, and give you slaves to do the real work. Your mothers helped carve cities and towns out of the wilderness, but all you pampered ladies want to do is have teas, go to gossip parties and have black nannies raise your children." He turned and looked at the rows of mangled men. "I hope you spoiled matrons can keep hiding from reality, but I fear the Yankees will waken all of you when they descend upon us like a plague from old Egypt."

Shocked at his own behavior, he stared at Lorena's stunned face. His face softened for a moment, and his rounded shoulders sagged.

"All right, all right," he said, his voice returning to normal, "If you must go, you must." Something like anxiety came into his eyes. "But come back the moment you can."

She turned to leave.

Garret stopped her with a touch on her shoulder. Miz Oakwood," he said abruptly, "stop by my house and tell Mrs. Garret about Dav—" His face reddened and his hand gripped the surgical saw so tightly his knuckles turned white. "No, maybe I'd best tell her myself. Thank you anyway."

Lorena nodded her understanding and started to walk away. The scream from the man under Dr. Garret's saw pierced her brain and she began to run.

Stumbling over legs and her own tired feet, she ran out of the depot past wagons carrying dead and wounded soldiers, past the people rushing to claim dead relatives, away from all the hunger and dirt and pain until she could no longer see the dreadful sights.

Winded, she leaned against a tree, and took a deep breath. The air was sweet and clean, and the cooling summer breeze refreshed her. Despite the help she knew she gave, Lorena was glad to leave that terrible place.

When she recovered her breath, Lorena again started toward home. Soon she entered avenues that had been shelled. Bomb craters left deep gashes in the ground.

Lorena suddenly came upon a macabre scene. Dead soldiers and mangled horses lay scattered like broken children's toys on the street. *There must have been a cavalry company caught in a bombardment here.* She felt alone and afraid. *Can this really be happening, to me, to Atlanta, to the South?*

Suddenly she felt weak. Her legs went numb and gave way. She clutched the iron fence of one of the untouched houses and hand over hand made her way toward home, bent and shuffling, like an ancient crone. She stared at the ground turning her head away from the death in the gutter. *Will this day never end?*

After a few moments, visions of her children danced in her head and she straightened up and began to run toward home again. Lorena felt dirty and desperately wanted a bath, but she knew that no amount of soap and water could wash away the memory of what she had seen. She looked down at her bloody dress. *This will never come clean.*

Lorena stopped short. On the walk in front of her was a lone body. She moved away to give the dead soldier a wide berth, but something about him drew her.

She went to the dead Confederate lying face up in the street. Looking down at him her heart wrenched. The lad was young, too young. His dull blue eyes stared sightless at the branches of the sycamore and elm trees, meeting in arches over their heads.

Lorena looked at him with pity then kneeled down, smoothed his unruly blonde hair and closed his eyes as she had done so many times that day. *Oh, God, what a waste.* She studied his serene face. *Is this what we have come to? Dead children lying untended in the gutter?*

Fighting her revulsion, she searched his body looking for papers, documents, anything that might give the boy a name, or a family she might comfort. She found nothing but a few acorns in his jacket pocket.

All at once she stood up, ashamed. *Someone might think I was robbing this poor dead boy.*

She thought of this young soldier being dropped into a nameless grave, and almost cried. She turned her head to the sky, balled her fists, and said loudly through gritted teeth, "You Yankees won't be able to wash the blood of Georgia off your hands for a thousand years."

She turned and stumbled away from the body toward home, feeling a bone chilling weariness she had never felt before.

When she first started nursing the wounded men, she was appalled by the death and the kinds of wounds inflicted by the war. Gradually she got used to it, and finally it became commonplace, almost normal.

Normal? She thought to herself stumbling toward home. *Is it normal to have a leg or an arm off? Is it normal to have your intestines spill out on your hands while the sun bakes your brains? If the Yankees want to free the slaves so badly they can have them, all of them. This death and destruction is not worth any slave.*

Finally she turned the corner of East Ellis Street onto Ivy Avenue and stopped short. She stared at the house on the corner. This ruin was once the stately, dignified Ponder house. She shook her head slowly looking at the old place first in awe and then in dismay. A third of the upper floor of the antebellum home was a gaping hole made by an errant Yankee bomb.

Lorena took a few steps toward the building and peered inside the damaged wall. She saw splintered beams in the master bedroom, hanging down like Zulu spears stuck into the heart of the grand old mansion. Her eyes moved slowly along the remaining outside wall where she saw smaller holes and pockmarks in the brickwork. Not one windowpane had survived the ferocious assault.

Are our homes now the battlefield? Where is the army to protect us? Where is General Johnston? Where is John Oakwood?

Lorena looked around her at the Ponder garden she was standing in. At her feet was the trunk of an old oak tree that used to supply shade to the front of the house. It lay on its side, the victim of another wayward bomb. The old majestic oak's leafy arms stretched out covering

the flowers and plants that were crushed by the
Ponder family's rushing feet, escaping the
Federal fury.

Fear clutched at Lorena, when she thought of
her own home and children just a few blocks away.
With a cry of alarm she started running down Ivy
Avenue. When she got to her house she breathed
a long sigh of relief. The Oakwood residence had
escaped the violence and never looked better. The
familiar green vines that crawled up the sides of
the pristine white walls and the burst of color
from the garden gave her hope.

Suddenly the whole frightful day caught up
with her. Lorena's body trembled and her steps
became unsure. She made her way shakily up the
three stairs to the front door.
Just as she put her hand on the front door knob a
flash of black caught Lorena's attention and she
stopped and turned around.

An odd sight appeared. One of her neighbors
was walking aimlessly down the middle of Ivy
Street.

"Nellie, what's happened, why are you dressed
in mourning clothes and why are you outdoors
with all this shelling?"

Stomach tightening, Lorena realized
something was very wrong. With her black
clothes and pale skin, Nellie looked as if she were
drawn in charcoal. Her face was colorless and
outlined in gray. She seemed a cardboard figure,

empty and two-dimensional. Lorena focused in on her hands. Nellie was carrying a headless doll. Lorena shuddered.

At the sound of her name the young woman turned and came mechanically toward Lorena. As she got closer Lorena could see this was not the Nellie Spencer she knew. This Nellie looked gaunt and cold, her ice blue eyes focused in another time, at another place.

Lorena's heart constricted.

Without invitation Nellie sat down heavily on the second step. After a few moments she turned and stared at Lorena, a face without life or expression, empty eyes staring at nothing. Lorena understood. Nellie had lost touch with reality.

She looks just like one of the wounded, their deep sunken eyes following me from man to dying man... Her face will haunt me....

Suddenly Nellie turned away and began to speak in a low monotone. "My Sally is dead, torn apart by Yankee guns."

Lorena put a fist to her mouth and sucked in her breath. "Sally? Six-year-old Sally?"

Nellie shed no tears. She looked old beyond her years. She was cold, and hard, and moved with a rigidity of manner so unlike her.

Where is my young neighbor who used to be so full of life, so full of love? All of our used to be's, gone....

"She was wounded so badly..." Nellie shook

her head sadly. "Just before the end I put my hand on her little knee and she said, 'Oh mamma, my feet are so cold.'" Nellie looked at Lorena blankly. "Her legs had the chill of death."

Lorena stared at her friend. *The most frightening thing is the impersonal manner Nellie has as she speaks of her daughter's death. Almost as if it were some inconsequential article from a newspaper she was reading.*

Lorena tore her eyes away from Nellie and looked across the street at Nellie's house, still smoking from the bomb.

The house looks twisted, gray and remote, like a graveyard in a nightmare. It was once the scene of gay socials. Now it's a home of drawn shades and heartsickness, a place of the dead.

Nellie put her head down and began crying.

Lorena wept too. *Finally she's weeping human tears.* Lorena started to reach out to her.

Suddenly Nellie looked up and her appearance froze Lorena. Her face turned from gray to white, as if all the blood had drained away and she began to twist the leg of the doll.

Controlling her fright for Nellie, Lorena spoke soothingly as she reached for and tried to pry the doll from her grasp.

Nellie stopped pulling, let the doll go and stood up, her eyes darting right and left. Without warning she leaped to the ground and started running down the street.

"Sally," she yelled to the phantoms around her, "Sally, come home, it's time for your nap. Come home…"

Lorena made a start to run after her but was overcome by exhaustion and futility. She sat back and merely watched Nellie disappear around the corner, yelling for her dead daughter. Lorena stayed and listened until Nellie's voice faded to oblivion.

When she could no longer hear her, Lorena got up wearily to go into the house, still holding the dead doll by one leg. Before she could grasp the door handle it opened and there was Ravetta, her jowls shaking with fear and effort. She reached out, took Lorena's hand and fairly dragged her inside.

"Oh, Miss Lorena, ah nevuh bin so glad to see someone in all mah born days. We thought you done got kilt by de Yankees." Her eyes focused on Lorena's bloody dress and she fell back. "Mah God, you *is* hurt, jes look at you."

Lorena ignored her concern. "It's not my blood," she said laconically.

Ravetta stopped and eyed Lorena critically. Not your blood, well who…?

Lorena ignored her. "I thought I told you to take the children to their grandfather's house," she said, starting to get angry.

Ravetta's petulant lip stuck out so far the pink showed. She looked down, smoothed out her dress, and began to sway. "Ah couldn't, Miss Lorena, de confedurets came and took de horse away. Dey laughed at me when ah tried to stop 'em." She mimicked the soldier. "We am conscriptin' dis mule into de Rebel army."

Lorena fought the anger that was overtaking her. She pushed it down with a will and absently brushed at her dirty dress.

She looked intently at the homely, round face of her servant and instantly forgave her. She smiled wearily. "It's all right Ravetta, you did just fine. We'll go there together." She handed the broken doll to her servant.

Ravetta's brown eyes shown with relief and she pulled in her lip.

"Mama, Mama." Lorena turned and opened her arms for her daughter. The child ran to her, leaped into her arms and they hugged each other fiercely.

As Lorena smoothed her daughter's curly red hair a small, grave voice came from the staircase and brought a smile to Lorena.

"I'm glad you're home too, Mother."

Joy came into Lorena's heart. Both her children were safe. Her son, Zachery, was standing on the stairs, cool and dignified, his hair combed precisely, his shirt and pants creased and immaculate.

Just like his Father. Sometimes I wish he were more like a child than a little man. She smiled warmly at him. "So am I, Zack. So am I."

Lorena put the girl down and turned to Ravetta. "After my bath, we're going to take the children to their grandfather and stay there with him. I think his plantation is far enough away from this war that the Yankees won't bother us there. For a while at least."

The servant's eyes got big and the kerchief on her head trembled. "Lawd a mercy, Miss Lorena, if we's goin' den let's us get gone 'afore dem Yankees comes and gits us."

Lorena smiled. "You get the children ready. I'll wash up and go to the office to get some money from the company safe." She thought of smoothing the old man's hair as he lay dying in her arms. "Mr. Buchanan won't mind me taking it now."

The whole of the Confederacy could not atone for the sacrifice of McPherson.
— *Sherman*

Chapter 5

𝕬 huge bomb blast shook the factory building and shards of plaster hit the floor. Fine dust floated down and settled on Lorena at her desk. She lifted her head off her arm, got up, dusted off her dress, bent over and shook the plaster dust out of her hair. "Damn Yankees!" she muttered.

Lorena dropped the letter from Major Gorgas into a trash basket then went to the office safe. With a practiced hand Lorena turned the tumblers until she heard a large click then pulled open the heavy door with both hands. She quickly glanced at the various cubbyholes. Shaking her head impatiently she began to pull the various stacks of documents off their shelves looking for a pile of greenbacks Buchanan usually had in the safe. Nothing!

"Acrimonious fiddlesticks! Not a dime here."
Lorena said, standing among the papers in
disarray on the floor. She angrily pushed the safe
door shut and sat down.

Suddenly she felt apprehension without cause.
Then a jolt of fear coursed through her as she
heard the front door of the foundry open and slam
closed. She stood up, cocked her head and, barely
breathing, listened to the loud footsteps running
up the stairs.

Who could that be? Her eyes flashed around
the room for a weapon. Nothing. She waited
without breathing.

For a few moments there was silence, then
suddenly the office door flew open and Richard,
the office boy, dashed in. Lorena put her hand on
her chest, let out a sigh of relief, and fell rather
than sat down on the desk chair.

"Richard, you scared me out of three months'
growth."

"Oh, Miss Lorena, are you still here? You
better get on outta here and go home." His face
took on a worried look. "Joe Johnston is gone—"

Lorena's eyes flew open in surprise, felt her
heart start to pound and her blood go cold.
"Gone? Dead?"

"No, not dead, replaced! General Johnston was
fired by President Davis, and old pegleg Hood
done took his place—" Richard gulped hard,
trying to catch his breath.

"Johnston, gone? General Hood, in charge?"
Another jolt of fear went through Lorena. "But
my husband is with Hood."

Lorena reached out and touched the boy's arm.
She thought about the sad, hound-dog-faced
General Hood who looked so much older than his
thirty-odd years. *His right leg, lost at Chickamauga,
and a useless arm, maimed at Gettysburg. He's an
impetuous, stubborn, headstrong man who'll
charge right at the Yanks. And my husband is his
adjutant.*

"Try to calm yourself, Richard, and tell me
exactly what's happening."

Richard brushed his mop of black hair away
from his eyes, absently touched the pimples on
his freckled face and smoothed the peach fuzz he
was just beginning to raise on his cheeks. He
began to give an account of the battle while
walking up and down the room, occasionally
stopping and sitting on the window sill, but too
restless to stay there for any length of time.

"What's happened, Miss Lorena, is that
Sherman went south to Jonesboro and cut the
Macon line. That cut off the army from its
supplies so the whole Confederate army has to
leave. An' you better get on outta here too. The
Yankees are comin' sure 'nuff. They've already
given us a whippin' at Peachtree Creek." His eyes
narrowed. "They're like a plague of locusts, Miss
Lorena. Everywhere they go they leave ruin.

56

They been burnin' and lootin' as they go along. I went to my house on Peachtree and fires were ragin' everywhere." His face took on a forlorn look. "My Daddy's gone, an' Mother says she doesn't know where to. Even old folks were bein' stopped by the Yank soldiers from takin' anythin'. They mostly laughed when folks pleaded with them. An Atlanta fire wagon came to battle the flames but the Yankees just chased 'em off." His eyes reddened. "My mother tried to take some blankets—" Richard stopped suddenly and turned away.

This boy has seen things no lad his age should see. "Richard, my husband, John is with General Hood. I have to know what's happened to him." Lorena turned to leave.

Suddenly her face turned gray, the color of ashes, as a greater realization dawned on her and she put her fist to her mouth. "Peachtree Creek. Oh my God, Yankees there already— My home— The children— I was told they were still twenty miles away." Lorena trembled and her hands shook.

Richard's face screwed up as if he were in pain, distorting his bad complexion. "Hood's men have already left, Miss Lorena— Lots of 'em have jes given up, deserted the army, and gone on home— An' the men still under Hood's command, well, they're marchin' right on outta Atlanta." Richard was so nervous he blurted out his speech in disjointed sentences.

He shook his head and Lorena could see fear behind the scowl on his face.

"Now it's up to the boys and me to stop 'em. We *gotta* stop 'em." He shook his head rapidly; his eyes looked far away under a wrinkled brow. "They've all but destroyed Atlanta with their bombin' and settin' fires and such."

He came back to the present moment, bolted to the closet, and rummaged for a moment, then pulled out an ancient Revolutionary War long musket and held it slantwise across his body. "I would escort you home, Miss Lorena," he said proudly, "but the Georgia Militia needs me. Governor Brown says he is dependin' on us to stop them Yankees. He said he was savin' us for defense an' now's our time."

Suddenly his chest puffed out in pride. "Every one of our boys kin shoot out a cat's eye at a hundred yards. Let's see any a them bluebellies do that."

Richard looked into Lorena's eyes intently searching for something. "We'll stop 'em Mrs. Oakwood, don't you worry." He nervously brushed his hair back again and turned to leave.

Lorena's sharp tone stopped him. "Richard Morgan," she scolded, "you're not but fifteen years old. You need to go on home, even if it's burned, and take care of your family. Your Mama would have a fit if she knew you were going out to fight Yankees. And with that thing." She pointed a shaking finger at the ancient rifle, intending to shame him.

Richard started for the door, stopped, looked down at the ancient smoothbore musket then turned and stared at Lorena. For a moment he looked as if he were going to cry, then his cheeks turned pink, his childish face filled with resolve and, without another word, he whirled about and bolted out of the room.

"Richard, Richard, stop! Don't go!" Lorena said to the closing door. "Stupid boy," she said, torn between admiration and anger for him at the same time. *I guess this is the day Richard leaves his boyhood behind.*

Another bomb blast shook the building again. Lorena gave a frightened glance upward and saw a fault line creep across the ceiling. *I better get home. With all these bombs falling— Ravetta! There's no telling what she'll do. The closer the Yankees get, the more peculiar she behaves. She's probably just up and left the children, and ran off to General Sherman's army, just like the other Africans have.* She thought about all the trouble her friends had recently with their slaves, and shook her head. *If she did that, he can have her. I better get home.*

She started to leave, then stopped, opened a drawer and picked up a small leather bound book from her desk. *Can't leave my journal.* She put it in the pocket of her dress and rushed to the door.

Anxiety showed in Lorena's face as she gathered up her skirt and flew down the stairs, two at a time. On the ground floor she opened the door took a step out and stopped. She shaded her eyes and looked up at the sky. The sun had just started the downward path from its zenith and there were few shadows on the street. Lorena was amazed at the quiet. After the din of the thirty-six days of siege, and the shelling of Atlanta, the silence was unnerving. She thought there would be fighting in the city, with Confederate soldiers defending every street of the city to the end.

Where's our army? Maybe Hood has stopped the Yanks at Peachtree Creek. Oh, God, please help him stop them. And also Lord, keep my children safe, and our home too.

Lorena looked right and left up and down the street expecting the worst. All month long she had been seeing the results of the Union bombing. Old stately homes reduced to ashes, and dreary dark hearses with their pairs of ebony horses wearing black plumes that danced and shook stiffly as the animals plodded along to the cemetery carrying their hated loads. What she despised most was the small white caskets. The Union bombs did not discriminate between adults and children. *God I hate those Northern people.*

As Lorena stepped down the remaining two steps into the street, out of the corner of her eye she saw a blur of blue. A soldier, dressed in a

Federal uniform turned the corner, stopped and snatched his rifle to his shoulder, the muzzle pointing right at Lorena's chest.

Lorena stopped short, her heart pounding. *God, Yankee soldiers, right here, in Atlanta!*

Recognition came into the soldier's face when he realized Lorena was a woman. He sheepishly lowered the weapon and touched his cap.

"Sorry Ma'am," he said politely, "but you ought not to be on the street just now."

Lorena blushed, surprised but delighted at his pleasant manner. "I was just goin' home, sir."

Lorena turned to leave when she heard the sounds of horses' hooves echoing on the cobblestone street and a strident voice ring out from the end of the block. "You there, Sergeant, who is that woman?"

For a moment Lorena froze, then she whirled towards the voice as the Sergeant snapped stiffly to attention.

"Don't know, Gen'ral Sherman, I was just about to question her."

The general spurred his horse from under the trees lining the street, and rode toward Lorena and the Sergeant. His staff, their uniforms rife with the gold braid of their rank, trailed a few paces behind. When he reached Lorena and the sergeant he stopped and slid down off his horse. The sergeant stayed at attention.

*So this is the famous General Sherman. Let's
see what kind of a man this is this who makes
war on women and children.*

As she looked at him a dark hatred started in
the pit of her stomach and rose upward quickly
clouding her mind. She curled and uncurled her
fists to ease her anger.

Lorena stared hard at General Sherman as he
approached her. To the end of her life she would
never forget the sight of him. His rumpled blue
uniform, with no epaulets, covered a body that
was spare and tall.

His black slouch hat had holes in it, not from
bullets or battle but rather from the extreme
habit of banging it against his thigh to knock the
dust off, real or imagined. He had a high,
intelligent forehead, with reddish hair. His beard
was of the same color as his hair except for
strands of gray throughout. His manner was
abrupt and his movements quick and jerky. His
hands were never still, always fumbling with his
gloves, his hat, the buttons on his blouse, or the
hilt of his sword. The only display of his exalted
rank was the three stars confined in a wreath on
his collar.

There was a certain look of ruthlessness about
Sherman that made Lorena feel uneasy. A cold
fear crept over her anger.

The general pulled off his gloves, one finger at
a time. He put the gloves in his left hand and

tapped them nervously on his right palm as he eyed Lorena.

Lorena squirmed under his glare, felt her face get warm, and she began to perspire. *I wish I had left before this most unkind man came.*

The general turned to the sergeant, took off his battered hat and slapped it on his thigh, raising dust. His hair straggled in several directions and he attempted to smooth it with an abrupt move of his hand. He nodded toward the foundry entrance and spoke to the sergeant, still keeping his eyes on Lorena.

"Did this woman come out of that building, Sergeant?"

"Yes, sir, I think so, sir." the sergeant snapped back.

"Obviously she works for this Rebel foundry, you should have arrested her at once, Sergeant." He pointed his finger down the block. "You get back to your unit. We'll handle this."

Lorena's brow furrowed. *The General displays in this matter a smallness of mind, scarcely in accord with his commission.*

The sergeant gave Lorena a sympathetic glance, then stood up to his full height and snapped a salute. "Yessir, Gen'ral." He moved off quickly in an infantryman's crouch, turned the corner and was gone.

Lorena felt her face get warm again as Sherman, still tapping his gloves in his free hand,

walked completely around her, his face and eyes
showing contempt. When he completed a full
circle he stopped, faced her and pointed to the
foundry door.

"Do you work here?"

Lorena looked at the general, clearly puzzled.
She cleared her throat. "Yes, sir," she said, a little
indignantly.

"Do you realize they make guns here?" he said
angrily, his voice rising.

Lorena looked the general straight in the eye
and answered pointedly. "Yes, sir, they make
guns to protect our homes and children."

Sherman bristled. His voice got louder and his
eyes blazed. "Madam, do you know how many
men I lost at Kennesaw Mountain—" He half
turned away and then whirled back again, his
face red and his eyes narrowed and sparking with
outrage. "—Or how many of my boys are lying
dead right over there, at Peachtree Creek? Do you
ever think that you might have made the guns
that killed them?"

A spurt of anger and adrenaline made Lorena's
face turn crimson. She began to sweat profusely.
*No man has ever spoken to me like this. You damn
Yankee!* A picture danced in her head of her
grandmother whipping her. She felt her
combative Irish heritage surging up. She forced
herself to try to put a guard on her tongue, but
impulsively both of her hands balled into fists.

64

"General, do you realize you have been shelling innocent children, women and old folks for more than a month? And we've lost lots of soldiers too—" she rejoined, remembering the wounded and dead at the train depot.

Sherman stopped her short. "Madam," he sputtered and shook his fist at her, "you southern women are more guilty of treason than the men are. You ladies urge them on, putting fearful pictures in their heads of Negroes and Union soldiers taking advantage of you."

He turned away and slapped his glove on his free palm, the gesture of a man who has made up his mind. "I have declared that any woman who gives succor to the Rebel army is guilty of treason." He started to put his gloves on. "Those who join in the insurrection will have to pay the penalty."

Lorena's eyes went wide and she put her fist to her mouth then quickly dropped it to her side. *Penalty? What penalty?* "General, I have children at home waiting for me. I have to leave."

"Madam, you'll leave when I tell you to." Sherman put his foot in the stirrup, lifted himself up with a grunt, and slid into the saddle. He looked down, staring at Lorena, his dark eyes two burning coals, his face a picture of contempt. The General's horse picked up his anger and pranced, his iron horseshoes thumping on the cobblestone street, sparking and making a dull metallic sound.

Sherman reached over and patted the horse's neck gentling him. "Whoa, Lexington, whoa," he said, his voice soft and tender to the horse. In a few moments the large black animal stopped moving and stood still, air blowing in short intervals out of his nostrils. Sherman jerked his head back to Lorena, his eyes again darkening with anger.

"We didn't start this war madam, you did, but, by God, we'll finish it. And to do so I will make Georgia howl. You should have thought of your children before you aided the Rebellion." He half turned in his saddle. "Colonel Hitchcock!"

His aide spurred his horse and came forward. His hand touched the brim of his hat in salute. "Sir?"

"Colonel Hitchcock, I want you to put this woman on the first north bound train with a man to guard her. He is to let her off when the train reaches its final destination." He looked back at Lorena. "And I hope it's in Canada."

He turned back to the Colonel. "She is to take no money and no extra clothing. Above all she is not to go home. This woman is to have no communication with anyone save you and the guard on the train." He laid the reins on the horse's neck and turned him away from the colonel. Suddenly he stopped his face wrinkled in thought. "By God," he muttered, "after we chase Hood out I think I'll make all the civilians leave

Atlanta and then burn the damn place. We'll teach these Rebels what war is like." Sherman dug his heels in the horse's flank and the animal shied a few steps sideways.

Fear, astonishment, and disbelief were written plainly on Lorena's face. She ran to Sherman, reached out and touched the neck of his horse. The beast tossed his head at her contact. Tears coursed freely down her cheeks. "General, my children—"

The general's small red beard bristled again as his eyes flashed and lost their reason. "Madam," he said, his voice this time low and menacing, "this war has changed us all. I have reached the point where I could have a woman and child shot without winking an eye. You have blood on your hands. You are an enemy to peace, a betrayer!"

Sherman looked away. "According to the Provisos of War, the Commanding General may send the captured enemy back to prison camps. Therefore, Madam, this general is going to ship you back, but not to a prison camp. You'll be sent as far north as possible and by the time you make your way back to Georgia, this war will be over, God willing, and you won't be the enemy no more."

My God, he's serious. Lorena's face turned ashen and she fell back, weak and confused.

Colonel Hitchcock stared first at the white-faced Lorena, then at the General. There was an incredulous look on his face. "General Sherman, are you sure you want to do this? We'll have to deal with these Rebels later, in peacetime."

Sherman whirled to the colonel, his face coloring a deep angry red, his eyes twitching and his head jerking. When he finally spoke he made a nervous motion with his left arm as if he were pushing something away. "Colonel Hitchcock, are you choosing this time in your career to be insubordinate?"

The Colonel's face hardened, and he braced in his saddle. "No, sir!"

"Then do what I ask, and be damned quick about it."

General Sherman reached over and patted his horses' neck again. "Let's go Lexington, we've got lots to do." Then he sat up again as straight as a ramrod, adjusted his battered hat and patted it down. He reached into his pocket, took out his watch then looked up at the sun emphasizing the time element. He half turned in his saddle and said to the rest of his staff, "Let's get back into the war. That Hood's a fighter. He may be running, but he's not beaten yet."

Lorena stared in disbelief at the back of the general, as he and his staff cantered off. When they were gone she turned to the colonel, but met a stony stare.

"Sergeant," the colonel said to his orderly, "arrest this woman and bring her along." The

sergeant trotted over to her, got off the horse and
cupped his hands. Lorena reluctantly put her foot
into his make-shift stirrup, and he lifted her
easily onto the saddle.

She tried to sit sideways but the sergeant forced
her leg over and she had to straddle the horse.

"Sorry, Ma'am," he said as he put his foot in
the stirrup and lifted himself easily into the
saddle behind her, "but this here is a McClellan
saddle, and you can't ride sideways with me on it
too." The saddle was small and Lorena sat almost
in the sergeant's lap. Before they started off the
sergeant took a plug of tobacco out of his pocket
and bit off a chew.

Lorena rode double with difficulty. She sat
uncomfortably in front of the sergeant, the colonel
following close behind. Forced to straddle, she
had to pull her dress above her knees. The
sergeant smelled of sweat and tobacco and had
his arm around her waist, which was distasteful
to her. She prayed that none of her friends would
see her in this humiliating predicament.

At first Lorena was confused, then she thought
of nothing but escape. She glanced back. It
appeared the colonel, anticipating a desperate
move watched her carefully.

*I suppose I could drop down and make a dash
for it. But, this Yankee sergeant would like nothing
better than to tell his grandchildren how he
dropped a southern witch in her tracks. Besides,*

who would care for my son, and daughter?

The munitions factory was in a suburb of Atlanta, as yet relatively untouched by the war. As they neared the center of the city, Lorena began to see what Richard had meant about the devastation the Yankees had brought. Her eyes moistened as she surveyed the damage.

Smoking and gutted buildings lined both sides of the road. On some streets, the only thing left, of formerly stately homes and businesses, were piles of rubble and blackened chimneys. Incinerated wagons and buggies lay over on their sides and the horses that used to pull them were sprawled in the street, horribly wounded or dead, their four stiff legs pointing to the sky. Men in all the positions of death lay among the wreckage. Homeless people and slaves wandered about or sat dazed and hurt in front of what were once their homes. Lorena slowly shook her head in disbelief at the ravaged plantations and burned out sugar and saw mills.

As they passed open fields, Lorena was equally horrified. The dogwood trees with their masses of white blossoms were gone. The profusion of waddling ducks and graceful geese had disappeared from the fields and streams, both species consumed by voracious armies. In their places she saw serpentine trenches with sharpened tree branches in front. *Chevraux de Fries, John called them.*

In the distance she saw blue and gray bundles that, as she got closer, proved to be dead soldiers. Here the ground, composed of red clay, was infinitely redder with the spilled blood of unburied men. In a profusion of color, the men of both sides looked like rows of damaged blue, brown and gray toy soldiers spilled over on the floor of a boy's room.

The artillery, firing loads of cannister at point blank range, had done its work well. The torn men lay dead in the fields, in the trenches, and sprawled over the sharpened branches. Some of them had limbs gone, some decapitated. All lay quietly in their last poses of death. Around them there were giant holes gouged out of the earth by the lethal bombs that tore at men's bodies.

Yankee soldiers were burying the dead while Southern women walked among the Confederate corpses, looking for husbands or relatives.

Who will look for the dead and dying by unknown rivers and streams far, far from home?

At first the Civil War was a nameless terror before, a sheet of paper with a list of the dead and wounded soldiers. Now, for the second time, Lorena saw the real horror of battle up close, a field of mutilated men, and women and children wandering the streets homeless and hungry.

Around the dead men of both armies were canteens, rifles, broken cannon, and all the other flotsam of battle. Lorena had to turn her head from the sights. She put her hand over her eyes and sobbed. Finally the stench of death was too much, and she took her handkerchief from the sleeve of her dress and put it over her nose.

My God, what have these people done to us?

The colonel stopped his horse and looked at the breastworks. "There was a great battle here," he murmured. "We lost a good many fine men this week... General McPherson... dead."

The Sergeant leaned over and spit a long brown stream then tapped Lorena's shoulder. "That's probably why General Sherman was so angry with you. General McPherson was like a son to him. Why when I tol' him General Mac was dead, why he started cryin'. Right off he jes started cryin."

Lorena stared at the multitude of brown bundles. *It looks like we lost a lot more men than you did.*

Lorena sat up suddenly and half turned back to the officer. "But Colonel, I didn't have anything to do with this."

The colonel smiled at her wanly, then turned back and looked over the carnage. "Didn't you, Madam? Didn't you?"

Lorena sat back in despair, and the colonel took his refuge in silence.

Let me go!

Chapter 6

𝕿he transfer of the prisoner was made without incident. The colonel explained the situation to the guard on the train, and the sergeant held Lorena's arm as she slid down off the saddle.

With a sinking heart Lorena stood on the steps of the train and watched the colonel's back after he exchanged salutes with the guard.

With a sigh that appeared to her to be of misgivings, the colonel walked to his horse and started to mount up while his sergeant leaned on the raised part of his saddle, his wad of tobacco sticking out of one cheek. He looked away, spat a brown stream, then turned back and stared stoically at Lorena.

Suddenly the colonel stopped, one foot in the stirrup, the other in the air. Slowly he got down and went back toward Lorena.

Her heart leaped in her chest and she took a step forward. The guard stirred and gripped his rifle.

"Madam," the colonel said, his face obviously pained, "if it were up to me... The General thinks by doing things like this he can shorten the war. I think the opposite...." Backing away, red faced, the colonel reached his horse, and quickly mounted. The sergeant followed suit.

Nodding to Lorena, the colonel touched the brim of his hat, then laid the reins on the horse's neck and turned the animal towards the embattled city. The sergeant kicked his horse lightly in the flanks and moved after the colonel.

Lorena followed them with her eyes, twisting her hands nervously.

After a few steps the colonel stopped, turned back and stared at Lorena, an undecided look on his face.

Hope leaped in Lorena's breast, and she leaned forward, alert as a cat, ready to run to him.

Suddenly a hissing cloud of white steam billowed up and blocked her view. Just at that moment the guard took her arm roughly, and pulled rather than led her, into the train and down the aisle. She dragged her feet and said, "Stop! I think the Colonel wants me to go back with him."

The guard looked at her oddly then forcibly took her with him. When they got to the seat he wanted her to sit in he pushed her down.

"Let me go!" she yelled, squirming to get loose, "I have children I must go to..."

The sergeant held her down firmly as the rail car made a jerk forward.

Breaking away, Lorena scooted across the seat to the dingy, barred window and looked anxiously for the colonel through the bars. Her heart dropped. She saw only the backs of the two soldiers moving away. Another cloud of steam and they were gone.

Fighting off her despair and rage, Lorena looked about, her eyes darting to both ends of the car. She was still hoping to escape from the madmen who had captured her. She realized the railroad car was empty except for her and the guard.

The car jerked forward again then stopped, and the cars came together in a grinding bump. After another great hiss of steam the cars began to move slow and jerkily out of the station. Suddenly the door to the next car slid open and another soldier joined them. Lorena's heart sunk, now she had two guards.

She stared at them. The older one, a barrel-chested sergeant who dragged her to the seat, and a younger man, a sandy haired corporal with a pock marked face, wide ears and a long nose.

Lorena remembered, with dismay, what the colonel had told the older guard. "General

Sherman's orders. This woman is to go nowhere except to the lavatory. The window is barred so she can't escape that way. The door is locked and bolted so she can't get out. One of you will bring meals to her from the dining car." He turned to leave and then stopped as if he just remembered something important. "Sergeant, she is to have no visitors." He stared hard at the soldier. "And especially, no fraternization. That's by order of General Sherman. You understand?"

The stout guard nodded stiffly and saluted, the colonel returned his salute and turned to leave.

The colonel stopped suddenly and pivoted the horse back around. "Also, Sergeant, when you reach the most northern terminal that this train goes to, she is to be let off. She is to take with her nothing other than what she now has on her person. No money and no extra clothing. Nothing! Understood?"

Lorena did not know it but at that moment her face changed. There was a hardness taking shape there, and a bitter hate lurking behind her eyes that would never leave.

The train lurched forward again in a series of jerking movements, and with it her last hope of escape. Later, as the train sped through the countryside, Lorena stared out the window and watched the rolling red hills blur through the tears streaming down her face, her sobs almost keeping time with the clickety-clack of the wheels.

Atlanta is bleeding in the grip of the beast.

Chapter 7

From the private journal of Lorena
Boykins Oakwood

August 28, 1864

It seems General Sherman blames me for
his men being killed at Kennesaw,
Jonesboro, and Peachtree Creek. Who
shall we blame for our boys' deaths?

Hood has run away, or to use military
excuses, beat a strategic retreat. With no
soldiers to protect her, Atlanta is
bleeding in the grip of the beast.

The North has so many soldiers and we

so few. Hood recklessly spends our soldier's lives by the thousands and we are almost out of men. Now he is robbing the cradle and the grave, using old men and boys, like Mr. Buchanan and Richard, to stem the tide of aggression. Most of them will soon be gone, and then nothing will remain except for the old and infirm to fight on and wait for another generation to grow up and take their place. I now think, "The Cause", is a lost cause.

I believe General Johnston was right. To stop the Yankees from taking Atlanta, you had to bloody their nose at every turn and conserve your fighting strength for the last. If I could see President Davis again I would tell him so. Firing Johnston and putting in Hood was a terrible mistake. I know Hood; he is too rash by far.

I remember General Hood well from our socials. I was at several parties when he courted Miss "Buck" Buchanan.

A Kentuckian, Hood is tall and thin,
with sad quixotic blue eyes. He has a full
tawny beard that covers the lower part
of his face giving him a look of a
biblical prophet. He was so reserved and
shy when he came to parties at my
house, he would practically hide
himself. Except for his missing leg and
useless arm, one would hardly know he
was there. But my husband, John, told
me, 'On the battlefield Hood is
transfigured. His mild eyes burn bright
like that of a Christian Crusader. And
you can always find him at the hottest
part of the fight. Yet with all that, there
is something strange, some small facet of
deviousness about the man.'

My husband is with Hood and I fear for
him. And what about my children? I
pray that Ravetta got them away before
the Yankees descended on our home. My
house, my beautiful home, I miss it so.
On my way to the train I have seen what
those minions of Sherman have done to
Atlanta. Those Yankee Bummers have no

respect for anything. I fear my home will
be destroyed.

I can see the end of the war coming
now, and if these people are a
representation of our conquerors, I fear
that our velvet life of midnight rides
and mint juleps during silky afternoons
are gone forever. The soft, gentle ways of
life in the South is dead.

Oh, God, I pray to you that General
Johnston will get his army back. And
also that he and General Lee will join
together their gallant troops. Together
they can perhaps lift this heavy yoke of
oppression off our necks. Help them Lord,
help them turn those people around,
and send them running back to that
blackguard, Father Abraham, from
whence they came.

I'll help you go straight to Hell!

Chapter 8

𝕿he rail car was old, with boards of pine making up the hard wooden seats. It had been converted from a passenger train to a prison car for the transfer of captured Rebel soldiers. The rail car was grimy and unpainted and badly in need of repair. The floor of the car was carpeted, but many thousands of scuffling feet had worn it almost bare. In some places the exposed wood flooring could be seen.

The hard seat made a poor bed and Lorena slept fitfully. She was awake long before the sun shone through the grimy, barred window. She sat in the darkness, depressed, listening to the monotonous click of the train wheels on the iron rails broken only by the occasional mournful whistle announcing their slowdown or arrival at a station.

As the day wore on, the heat in the enclosed

box became stifling. When it finally became unbearable, Lorena stood up and stared at the guard.

He sat like an unmoving eunuch, sweat forming under his blue forage cap and trickling down his face and over his bibulous nose. The butt of his Springfield rifle sat on the floor, the trigger guard resting against his knee and the barrel extending above his head.

Lorena put her hands through the bars and tried to pull up the window. Grunting and pulling with all her strength, she couldn't budge it. She turned and glared at the motionless guard. "You, sir, would you help me lift this window?"

The guard had a round face, a thick neck and creased skin the color of burnt copper. He looked like a man of forty, old for a soldier and, Lorena thought, glad to be away from the front. He had thick lips and dull brown hair that stuck out in places beneath his forage cap. His wrinkled dark blue wool uniform covered a full chest and a rotund belly that was too large for the rest of him. It gave him an absurd appearance that would have made Lorena laugh when she first saw him, if he weren't the keeper of her private hell.

At first the guard just grunted, ignoring her entreaty. When Lorena asked a second time, he spoke in a gutteral Northern tongue.

"The Colonel said no talkin', lady. This is the last time I'm gonna say anythin' to ya 'bout it."

Lorena flushed, sat down and suffered the heat. She was left to brood in solitude.

The train moved along in fits and jerks and stopped periodically to let off and take on passengers. Lorena prayed someone would come to her car. No one did.

Days passed and Lorena began to lose track of time. She tried to while the time away by drawing pictures of the changing landscape and writing in her journal. She thought often of her family and home. Images of Ravetta leaving the children and deserting to the Union army danced in her head. Those thoughts became more unbearable than the heat.

The train picked up speed when it reached farm country and began moving at a steady clip, each mile further from home filling Lorena with more despair. To keep from dwelling on dismal reflections, Lorena turned her attention to the landscape hurtling past her. The freshly plowed fields brought to her mind the smell of newly turned earth on the family plantation. She stared at them glumly.

At the end of the second day the sun was low on the horizon and cast long shadows on the land. Everywhere she looked she saw endless miles of cotton fields, growing in brick dust colored soil that eventually gave way to rolling hills and tall, gaunt pines, their tops bending in the wind. Spaced erratically between the trees were the heads and shoulders of granite rock that had been thrust upwards from the blood red earth during the volcanic age.

Soon the train was making its way through cool, dark virgin forests, making Lorena wish she could open the window of the rail car and let fresh air in.

Time and the days dragged on interminably. There was little change in her tedium and the only exercise she got was the walk to the foul smelling privy. She remembered having bought, *Augusta Evans* new book, *St. Elmo,* and wished to God she had it with her when Sherman had her arrested. She tapped her dress pocket. *At least I have my journal.*

In strict accord with army protocol, the sergeant was relieved every four hours by the younger guard, the corporal. He brought food to Lorena, was congenial and spoke to her, temporarily easing her monotony. But, though the corporal was pleasant to her, it seemed that only too soon the sergeant would return and the hateful silent treatment would begin again.

At first Lorena would not touch the meals the corporal brought. The young man would urge her to eat, and when she would not, would shrug and take it away. But after two days hunger overcame her depression and she began to eat, though sparingly.

By the third day Lorena began to have wild

thoughts. She thought about her children all morning. *Sarah, five-years-old, all ribbons and blonde pigtails, sweet as sugar on pie. Seven-year-old Zack, the spitting image of his father, cold and straight and getting tall, like the pine trees surrounding our home.*

Home, will it ever be the same again? Is John Oakwood still alive? Shall I ever see the dogwoods near the house bursting with pure white buds? The hens busily pecking at the ground while the cock struts around letting everyone know that it's his harem they're looking at.

Oh, God, guide the children to Grandpa's, and let them stay there 'til I return.

Return. How will I ever get back? Where will they leave me? Canada? Oh, God, help me. God, help me— Lorena put her head in her hands and sobbed.

After a few minutes she sat up. *Stop it Lorena! Get yourself some backbone. Show at least a little of the spunk our boys show on the battlefield. Think! Think! The sooner you get off this train, the closer you are to Atlanta.*

She dabbed her watery eyes and looked at the sergeant. *No, he doesn't look as if he has any compassion. Maybe the corporal... Maybe my best hope is that they'll get drunk and shoot each other. Fat chance—*

Suddenly the train braked making a loud metallic squeal, and Lorena had to throw her hands out to the seat in front to prevent a fall. After it stopped the train lurched forward a few times more throwing Lorena backward then came to another sudden stop forcing her to slide forward on her seat. When she recovered she stared out the barred window. In a few moments three men on horseback came into view, dressed in Federal Blue. Just before they got to the train they stopped and began to discuss something. The eldest shook his head and dismounted. The two others followed suit. All three walked toward the rail car through the fog-like steam rising from the underside of the train.

The sergeant ran to the window, looked out then stepped back, his rifle at present arms.

After a few anxious minutes the rail car door to the main train opened and the three new soldiers stepped in followed by the corporal with the bad complexion. When he saw the officers the sergeant's rifle butt hit the floor and he snapped to attention.

Lorena came to the edge of her seat and her heart began to thump.

The officer leading the others was an enormous man sporting a great handlebar mustache. A robust person with sandy hair, he was seemingly stuffed into the blue uniform of a high-ranking Union officer. He had an immaculate white shirt under his long waistcoat and his face was clean-shaven, except for the large mustache that came down on both sides of his mouth making an inverted U. On his collar was the single bright star of a brigadier. For a large man he moved with surprising grace and agility. The two men in back of him, one a lieutenant, the other with the chevrons of sergeant on his sleeve, appeared to be his aides.

The general stared at Lorena and then glared at the sergeant. "What's goin' on heah, Sergeant?"

The general's New England Yankee brogue grated on Lorena's ears.

The sergeant stayed at attention staring straight ahead. "Nothing, sir, ah, I mean it's all official. This here woman is General Sherman's prisoner, sir. I have orders to take her as far north as the train goes and drop her off to fend for herself."

The general's eyes narrowed. "What are you talkin' about, Sergeant? For what crime was she imprisoned?"

This time the sergeant turned his head and looked at the general. "Near as I can gather, sir, she worked in a foundry that made weapons for the enemy."

The general's face turned incredulous. "Whaaat! That's ridiculous. Why my own sister works in—"

Hope sprang up in Lorena's bosom and she sat up expectantly.

The general caught himself and his face turned stoic.

"Never mind that. There's a big push on by General Grant to end this blasted war, but he needs more men. We're combing this train for deserters, and shirkers who would be better served at the front." He looked at the sergeant and then the corporal. "You two, when you're finished with your duty, return to your outfits immediately. For the time being carry on."

Lorena's heart dropped and she slumped back down in her seat.

The general turned and for the first time acknowledged her with a small smile and a touch of the brim of his hat. He seemed surprised at something he thought of, stopped and stared at her for a few moments. Then he shook his head and started toward the door again. Once again he stopped and turned back to the sergeant. He absently combed his mustache with his fingers, his brow wrinkled in thought. Then he looked at Lorena. "You know, Sergeant, I can't countermand General Sherman's orders, but because of circumstances I can sure modify them."

Lorena sat up again.

"There's a new prison camp next to the arsenal at Rock Island. A lot of rebels captured from the battle at Chattanooga are being sent theah." He nodded toward Lorena. "I'm sure this woman would serve the Union a lot better by helpin' out her own countrymen at the prison rather than wanderin' around loose at our northern border."

He nodded his head once firmly and squared his shoulders. "Yes, a lot better."

Lorena stood up, her eyes blazing. "Sir, I am not a maid."

The general stared at Lorena his face showing the first signs of contempt. "Madam, you're fortunate I don't let them have you for other comforts."

A shocked Lorena, her face getting warm sat down slowly.

The sergeant snickered and turned his head to hide his amusement.

The general tuned back to the sergeant with a look that stopped his mirth. "The next stop of this train is St. Louis. I want you and the corporal to get off this train with the prisoner, board the Rock Island Line and take her to the prison camp. I'll take the responsibility with General Sherman." He sat down on one of the pine board seats, pulled a notebook out of his coat pocket and began writing. When he finished he tore off the page and handed it to the Sergeant. "Give this note to the commandant of the prison and then both of you report to General Rosencrans in Cincinnati."

He turned to Lorena. "Madam, I'm sorry I snapped at you. Actually I believe the camp will be better for you. The war is almost over and I think you will be safer at the prison until the end. In any event, Illinois is a lot closer to Atlanta than Canada."

Lorena nodded dumbly.

The general turned and started toward the door. The sergeant and the corporal came to attention and saluted. The general and his lieutenant returned the salutes and left.

Lorena was lost in confused thought the rest of the way to St. Louis.

****

At the transfer in St. Louis, Lorena saw a line of Southern prisoners boarding a train. Many of them were wounded and all of them looked haggard. The long line of bloodied and bandaged young men and boys shuffling and stumbling along in ones and twos brought the imminent defeat of the South to Lorena as no other scene had. Not even the moaning and dying at the fairgrounds was more telling.

When she got aboard the new train, Lorena was disappointed to find the new rail car was no better than the old. In fact it was worse. It also had bars on the windows but in addition, its wicker seats pushed uncomfortably into Lorena's back. The windows were also stuck shut, as they were in the other car, and there was a lingering odor of decay in the air. The heat reminded Lorena of a stifling oven.

The corporal had the first watch and chatted so steadily Lorena's head began to ache. Finally his duty was over and the sergeant took his place. *The bigger of two evils*, Lorena thought.

Lorena felt the urge to relieve herself and held up her hand like a schoolgirl.

"Sergeant, I have to, uh, use the toilet."

The sergeant grunted, shifted his rifle, and nodded his head.

Lorena slid out of her seat and started toward the bathroom at the end of the car.

This toilet was no better than the one in the previous car. As always, when she opened the door the stench hit her like a fist. Lorena shook her head and held her breath as she walked into the small, odorous room that stunk from the improper waste disposal of a too many previous users. She reluctantly lifted her skirt, dropped her pantaloons and straddled the hole of the privy. She could hear her urine hitting the waste below and shut her mind as well as her nose.

Finishing as quickly as she could Lorena got up, adjusted her clothes and smoothed her dress. She poured dingy water from a pitcher over her fingers, into a washbowl. There was a dirty towel on a hook next to the door. Lorena reached for it, thought better of it, and wiped her hands on her dress. Then she absently primped the loose ends of her scarlet hair and walked back into the railcar.

Even though the car was hot, the first breath she took away from the privy was deep and felt cool and sweet.

Lorena stepped into the aisle and stopped short. *Wait a minute, something's wrong.* She looked about the car and immediately realized the sergeant was not in his usual place. When her eyes found him, she felt something inside stab her. He was sitting in her seat near the center of the coach his ever-present rifle beside him.

Lorena hesitantly sat down where she was.

The sergeant cocked his head and grinned a twisted, tobacco-stained smile.

Lorena suddenly realized she left her journal on her seat. *I have to get it.* She felt a knot form in her stomach but forced herself to get up and warily start toward the sergeant.

His smile got broader.

When she reached the sergeant she stopped in mid-step, then gingerly put her booted foot down and stared at him. The hackles on the back of her neck stood up and she felt a cold chill of fear.

The sergeant leaned back with the magnanimous demeanor of a man about to deliver a favor.

A spurt of anger hit Lorena when she saw her journal in his stubby, tobacco stained hands.

The sergeant pursed his lips and spoke, his gravely voice and Yankee accent had a dismal effect on Lorena.

"I was just thinkin', dearie, you'll be gittin' off this here train in a day or two, with no money and no way ter get none."

Lorena's eyes narrowed. She could feel the evil

ooze from him, like poisonous gas seeping into the rail car.

Lorena's voice had an edge. "What do you want, Sergeant?"

His smile broadened, not with friendliness, but rather as a shylock who has just gained an advantage. He patted his bloated stomach. "Well, dearie, I think maybe we could make a trade. You know!"

Lorena's face hardened to granite.

He continued. "Well, here's the way it is. You see, I still would have to take you to the prison camp, but," he reached into his shirt pocket and pulled out a fistfull of dollars, "I could give you some greenbacks, good in the North and absolutely vital in the South. Why, you'd be home in a jiffy with them dollars after the war." His eyes glittered with lust.

Lorena felt a deep disgust that was new to her. Before she disliked the sergeant, now she loathed him.

She reached for her journal.

He pulled it just out of her grasp. "Uh, uh," he said, displaying a twisted, evil grin.

She stared down at him a rage building inside her. "I have nothin' to trade."

The Sergeant stood up and his eyes moved lewdly from her red hair to her hips. "Oh, yes you have, dearie!"

Lorena took a step back, the touch of

belligerence in his voice making her afraid.

The sergeant took a step toward Lorena. She noticed he had put his rifle butt down on the floor and his ammunition belt on the back of the aisle seat. Her eyes fixed on the bayonet in its scabbard, swaying with the rhythm of the train.

The sergeant looked unsteady rocking counter to the sway of the train as if he were drunk. His eyes were bright with desire.

Lorena recovered and her eyes flashed with anger. "I have nothin' to trade," She repeated.

The sergeant's smile faded. "Suit yerself, dearie." He put her journal on the seat, reached back, for his rifle and ammo belt and stepped into the aisle.

Lorena breathed a visible sigh of relief, and her first rage lowered to a silent ferocity.

As the sergeant passed Lorena he turned sideways.

She leaned back against the seat to let his large bulk through.

When he reached the point opposite her, he pushed forward and his belly touched her middle. Lorena sucked her stomach in and she leaned away trying not to smell his body odor and alcoholic breath. He bent his face so close to her she could see the small gray hairs of his three-day beard and the depravity in his eyes.

She tried to slide into the seat but he pinned her in place with his large bulk.

"Sure you won't change yer mind?" he said, his leer coming back.

Lorena pushed him away with both hands and scooted sideways. "I'd rather die first."

With surprising speed, the sergeant dropped his rifle and lunged at Lorena. The rifle hit the floor, the ammo belt landed on the seat, and like a snake, slithered to the ground.

The sergeant grabbed Lorena's shoulders and pulled her down to the floor. In a split second he was on top of her and with a clumsy move lifted her dress.

Without thinking, Lorena fought back. She screamed, scratched his face and drew blood.

The pain she inflicted seemed to excite the sergeant further, and he reached down and groped her. She tightened her legs together.

The sergeant laughed at her efforts. He held her left hand down with his right and with his other hand he squeezed her breast.

Frantic, Lorena gouged at his eyes with her free hand, hoping to hurt him enough to free herself.

He let go of her breast, easily pushed her hand away and held it down.

She bucked and squirmed desperate to get out from under him.

Still laughing at her struggling, he let her arm go, reached down and ripped her pantaloons away, exposing her.

Mortified she screamed again and thrashed about, but because of his steel grip a feeling of helpless coursed through her.

"Go ahead and scream, dearie, no one'll hear ya this far back in the train."

Pinning her with his bulk, he reached down and unbuttoned his pants. He raised himself slightly and moved his hips toward her with his swollen member exposed. When he touched her stomach, hysteria gave her strength unknown before, and she violently thrust her hands out and pushed him away.

Suddenly the sergeant reached back and lashed out, striking Lorena across the face.

Stunned, Lorena's lips turned white, like a person who's been shot, and she stopped moving.

"That's better, dearie. Now just lay still and enjoy this. You're an old hand at it, ain't ya? I heard ya say ya got a couple a kids." He laughed again, moved on top and prepared to penetrate her.

Lorena lay immobile and coldly calculated her chances. There were none. Shutting her eyes tightly and gritting her teeth, she prepared for the inevitable.

She laid her hands down to brace herself. Her left fist opened and her flat palm touched the frayed rug, her right hand did the same but struck metal. *The ammunition belt!*

The belt had fallen near where she lay. With a feverish hope she frantically ran her fingers along the evenly spaced conical ammunition until she found the bayonet. With a desperate move she pulled at it. The entire belt moved with the bayonet until it caught in the foot of the seat. The blade then slid out of the scabbard.

Lorena's trembling hand held it at the side of the Sergeant.

Staring into Lorena's angry red face, the sergeant laughed at her as he began to violate her.

With a hate she had never felt before, Lorena reached back as far as she could and with a scream plunged the razor sharp blade into the soldier's side.

For a moment the sergeant's face went blank, and then he shrieked. Again and again, with the strength of black Irish rage, Lorena plunged the knife into his bulk until, frantic to escape the bloody blade, he rolled away from her.

Lorena staggered up and stood over the wounded sergeant, shaking with fury. She held the bayonet in her trembling hand, dripping his blood on his stomach, her foot, and the floor of the rocking train.

The sergeant looked up at her, his terrified eyes pleading. "Help me," he croaked.

With her heart pounding in her chest, she went to her knees. For a minute she stared at him. Then she lifted the bayonet with both hands and cried out, "You goddamned Yankee bastard, I'll help you, I'll help you go straight to Hell!" Lorena plunged the bayonet down into his neck and blood spurted on her face and chest.

The sergeant tried to speak through the blood welling up in his throat, but he could only bubble.

For a moment he stared at Lorena, then the frightened light in his eyes went out.

She stayed in that kneeling position staring at the dead man for a full minute.

Suddenly she realized the enormity of what she had done and hated herself. A black depression rolled over her and tears of frustration and rage came down bloody cheeks and spilled onto her soiled dress.

After a few moments she pushed the guilt away, and with a great weariness she wiped at the blood on her face with her sleeve, smearing it. Slowly she got up.

Lorena felt weak and sat down on the seat closest to her. For a long while she sat next to the body, staring at the sergeant's corpse. She hated looking at him but was too spent to move.

Deep in the recesses of her mind something was nagging at her. Finally it surfaced and she sat bolt upright. "God, the Corporal. He'll be back here any minute."

Lorena scrambled to the door of the rail car and looked through the window into the next car. Several soldiers were at the far end of the car smoking and playing cards. She could see the corporal leaning over and watching another trooper studying his cards. She quickly went back to the barred window and looked out at the landscape rushing past. Her face was drenched with sweat and her breath came in short, sharp gasps. The railcar appeared to be moving at a fearful clip. She shook her head. *The train is going too fast for me to jump.*

She tried to calm herself and think. *We're in a hilly region. Sooner or later the train will hit a curve and we'll have to slow down. Then I can jump off. I just hope the curve gets here before the Corporal.*

Lorena started to bite her nails and tasted blood. She stopped and looked at her shaking hands. Her eyes went wide with horror. *Oh, God, It's his blood.* She spit, and wiped her lips with the back of her hand. She spit again, and wiped her hands on her dress.

Maybe I can dump his body off the train and claim he never came back. No, no good, how would I explain the blood on the floor and on my dress. Lorena fell to her knees to pray. Before she started, her prayers were answered. The train whistle shattered her thoughts and the train began to slow.

Lorena went to the back door. It was secured with a rusty lock. Frantic, Lorena searched the car for something to use to break the lock. *The rifle.* She ran back to where the Sergeant had dropped it.

To reach the rifle Lorena had to step over him.

His eyes were open and staring at her, accusing.
No matter where she went, they seemed to follow
her. Feeling nauseous, she gathered her skirt and
stepped over the body and saw her journal on the
floor where it had fallen during the struggle.
Lorena picked it up, wiped the bloody cover with
the hem of her dress, and stuck it in her pocket.

Grabbing the rifle, she moved quickly back
over the body and ran back to the sliding door.
She raised the weapon and thrust it down to
break the lock. She missed completely. She lifted
it again, concentrating as hard as she could, and
this time felt the sweet feel of contact. The old
lock fell to the bare wood floor with a clatter.

Now only a large, rusted metal bolt separated her
from freedom. The train whistle screamed again
loudly, and the train car leaned sickeningly as it
moved around a sharp curve throwing Lorena
against a seat. She grimaced when she heard the
screech of metal on metal as the wheels ground
against the track.

When the train straightened, she let go of the
seat and went to the door again.

Lorena pulled at the handle of the bolt to
unlatch it. The bolt was rusted shut. It wouldn't
budge. Lorena cringed. *God help me, it won't be
long before the Corporal comes back.*

She reached down and picked up the rifle
again. The stock was cracked but it was still in
one piece. Lorena smashed the butt of the rifle

against the bolt and the stock broke into two pieces. She tried it again with the remaining barrel. It still wouldn't yield.

Distraught, Lorena inserted the barrel under the handle and levered the rifle against the unyielding part. It wouldn't move. A frantic Lorena applied all her strength until beads of sweat mixed with tears ran down her cheeks. *Damn, it just won't give.*

Frantically she kept after it. Lorena's muscles trembled with the effort but it wouldn't slide and she began to feel defeated. She was ready to give up when, with a last effort, she heard a small screech and felt a slight movement.

Just then, over the whistle indicating the train was speeding up, there came the distant voice of the corporal singing;

"Old Dan Tucker was a fine old man—

Panic mixed with Irish courage surged up in her. With renewed strength she put the rifle against the handle and pulled with all her might. Lorena's muscles ached with the strain and sweat poured down her face, her chest, and her back. *I don't have enough time! He'll be here in a moment. Oh, God! Keep pulling, Lorena.*

Finally the rust grated against the metal and the handle gave again. Slowly, grudgingly it moved a bit more and finally the bolt started a rusty slide. Lorena gave a final enormous effort and the bolt scraped free.

Laughing hysterically, Lorena pulled the door back and it slid open. She felt a blast of cool air and stared at the green blur of trees. The train had straightened and was rapidly picking up speed.

She looked down and saw the dark brown ground hurtling past. Small rocks and boulders lined the tracks. Lorena felt dizzy. She had to hold on to keep from falling. *Oh, God, I can't jump now, the train is going too fast.*

She heard the corporal's voice just outside the rail car door.

—*Washed his face with a frying pan, combed his hair with a wagon wheel, died with a toothache in his heel*—

The door to the car opened. "Hey, Sarge, chow's on. You ready to be relieved?" His eyes locked on the body and the blood.

"Oh my God, what the hell!" His jaw went slack and he looked up and saw Lorena perched at the door ready to jump. "Hey, you—"

Without another thought, Lorena leaped into the unknown. The ground came hurtling up and smashed into her. For a moment she felt nothing. Then she felt an exquisite pain and the world turned black.

Lorena

They'll be looking for me—

Chapter 9

When Lorena woke she felt numb all over. She shook her hands and feet and they came alive with pins and needles. *Thank God the train is gone. But the Corporal will probably get it stopped just up the line somewhere. I've got to get going.* She checked her limbs and moved her hands and feet. *Good, nothing broken.* She tried to get up, felt a sharp pain from her hip into her leg and fell back down again.

I have to get up. They'll be looking for me—

First getting on her hands and knees, she forced herself past the pain and stood up. She looked up at the sky, and putting the sun on her left, started moving, first limping, then running through her pain like a mad woman, heading south toward home.

****

*From the private journal of Lorena
Boykins Oakwood*

August 31, 1864

*This has been the most terrible day of my
life. I've killed a man.*

*Never in my wildest nightmares did I
think I could have done a murder, but I
have. What is more horrible is that I
would do it again.*

*The sun is down and I am sitting in a
cornfield, only God knows where I am.
My dress is torn and I am bloodstained
and filthy. To add to my situation, flies
are buzzing around me because of the
dead man's blood that splashed on me.
They are not ordinary houseflies, but
large green and blue pests, and they are
relentless. My arm hurts from brushing
them off.*

*I have tried to sleep but I can't. To pass
the time I am writing this by a moon so*

bright it's almost like daylight. It comforts me to keep my journal.

It was hot in the day and now, at twilight, it's cold. Even though I am far from the train I believe the Yankees will try to find me, so I stay off the roads. The fields are stifling hot, and my mouth and nose get clogged with dust. All I can see in every direction are rows and rows of corn. They are interminable.

I have not seen any people and the only companion I have is an occasional scarecrow. They are cold company.

Because he forced me to leave my children and my home, I have grown to hate General Sherman with a passion I never knew I had. By now I hope our lads have driven him out of Atlanta, and that he is lying in a Georgia field somewhere, rotting. My one goal now is to get back to my home and family, and I will do so with the help of God or, if need be, the Devil.

Chapter 10

Lorena woke with a start, blinking hard against the bright sun. She sat up and groaned with distress. *God, I hurt all over; I hope I can walk.*

She got up slowly and took a few steps. *I'm limping but at least I can move. Maybe I can find a stream and wash up a bit.* Gritting her teeth, Lorena made sure the sun was on her left and started limping south.

Even through her pain, Lorena remembered the smelly, stifling train and exulted in her newly won freedom. As she made her way through the endless cornfields she prayed for her return to Georgia. *God, help me to get back to my family, I miss them so.*

She was brought sharply back to reality when she heard the metallic grind of train brakes in the distance. *Oh, God, don't tell me I've been going in circles and heading back toward the same train tracks.* Ignoring the pain in her hip, Lorena whirled away from the sound, and began to run, trampling the corn. Every few steps she turned expecting to see blue coats, or worse, hear the barking of dogs.

Lorena half ran, half walked until she got so exhausted, she had to stop. Breathing hard she flopped unceremoniously down on the rich black dirt. For a long while she cocked her head and listened while she caught her breath. She heard nothing but her own breathing. When she felt somewhat recovered she got up, squinted up at the afternoon sun, making furrowed lines around her eyes, put the sun on her right and, ignoring the pain, walked on through the rows of corn. A few times she thought she heard dogs yapping a long way off. Stopping to listen carefully, Lorena's eyes swept around the fertile fields. She heard nothing but crickets and the brushing of corn stalks.

After Lorena felt she was safe she looked closely at the fields around her. She marveled at the dark, rich black soil and how large the great, cultivated fields were.

Wondering where she was, Lorena tried to calculate the distance she had traveled since jumping from the train, but arithmetic was not her best subject and she soon gave it up.

Walking steadily, Lorena sang and hummed,

then later began to whistle to keep her courage
up. Finally tired to exhaustion, she concentrated
on just putting one foot in front of the other.
Fearing surprise she stopped every so often to
listen. She heard nothing but she never felt quite
sure she had lost her pursuers.

The corn was up to her chest and pushing
through it made the going slow. She longed for a
path.

The hurt from the jump had eased everywhere
except Lorena's right hip. When she stepped
down with her right foot, a sharp pain radiated
down from her hip to her knee adding to her
misery.

Darkness of the second day came quickly, and
with it, a thousand phantoms.

With every step she took she saw the face of
the sergeant pleading with her. "Damn Yankee
rapist," she muttered, "he should have left me
alone."

With the night came the cold, and the pace of
her pushing through the corn slowed to a crawl.

Thankfully the moon was bright again so
Lorena could see around her.

Tiring, she began to wish for a place to lie
down. *Not in this field. God knows what animal
would find me out here.*

She kept on walking, head down, so exhausted
she began to doze while she took one step after
another. Suddenly she bumped into something

solid and was jarred awake. Losing her balance, she sat down hard and the pain in her hip flared.

"Ohhhhhhh!" she gasped, pressing her hand against her hip. When the pain subsided, Lorena reached out to touch the impediment. It was made of wood. *A fence! Civilization!* Ignoring the pain she scrambled to her feet. "Oh, God, let there be a barn nearby."

Lorena quickly went over the three rail fence scratching her legs in the process, then fell face down on the other side scraping her hands. She sat up and looked about her. *It's a road, it's rutted and dusty, but a road.* She got up and wiped her hands on the bosom of her bloody dress. Her stomach growled with hunger. *Oh my, I must be a sight. I can't worry about that now. I have to get some sleep, and something to eat. If there's a farmhouse maybe I can even get a bath and some clean clothes.* "Hah! One measly dirt road, and I think I'm back on Peachtree Street." She laughed aloud. "Maybe I can order a steak at Chastain's."

Lorena walked along the lane, her face caressed by the sweet breeze of the night. She breathed deeply and looked up at the star-studded sky. *Oh, dear God, I only hope I'm still going toward Atlanta and home. In any event I'm grateful just to be out of those choking fields.*

Out of nowhere came a series of barks and Lorena jumped. It was followed by the appearance of a small, snarling, black and white dog. A frightened Lorena bolted away from him and ran down the road with renewed energy. After chasing her for fifty feet the dog stopped and stood on the road, his legs braced, his whole body shaking as he barked at Lorena.

Her heart flipped in dismay when she heard a deep, masculine voice in the distance.

"What is it, boy, you see somethin'?"

Lorena kept running after the dog broke off the chase. Off to her right a large building loomed near the road. *A barn.* She quickly scaled another fence, this time she didn't fall or scratch her legs. With every step she took she expected another animal to jump out at her. She was relieved to get to the barn unmolested. Her body trembling with impatience, Lorena scrambled about looking for the entrance.

Next to the large barn doors she spotted a small entrance door, and went to it. Lorena quickly turned the handle and pulled the door toward her. Opening it quickly, she slid inside.

Standing absolutely still, her heart pounding furiously, Lorena strained her eyes forcing them to get accustomed to the dark. She wrinkled her nose at the familiar animal odors in the air. After a few moments she could hear gentle stirring and grunting of several of the beasts. She waited quietly until they settled down.

Desperate for sleep she ignored her fright and looked for a place to lie down. She took a few steps forward and struck her shin. "Damn!" she exclaimed. The animals stirred again and she heard a horse whinny softly.

A wild thought raced through her brain. *I could take that horse and be on my way in a jiffy.* She shook her head. *No, I haven't fallen to the level of a common thief yet.*

After holding her hands down as if it would help quiet the animals, she reached down to feel what she had bumped into. She felt cool water. Joyfully she fell to her knees and scooped up the liquid with both hands. She stopped when she felt so bloated she couldn't drink another mouthful. Then, ignoring the animal odor in the water, she splashed her face and neck with the cold liquid.

After wiping her face with the hem of her dress, Lorena got to her feet and, her eyes now adjusted to the dark, looked about her for some familiar shape. Nursing the pain in her hip and now her shin, she limped forward, feeling her way as she went. Then she found it, a pile of hay. Careful not to step on a pitchfork she thought might be nearby, Lorena sat down.

The thought that she might have lost her journal in the fall from the fence flashed across her mind and she swiftly felt her pocket. The familiar feel of the small book and her pencil made her smile.

For a few minutes she sat quietly, staring into the darkness, numb from her two-day ordeal. The animal noises returned to gentle breathing and soft snorting. Lorena's own breathing was still shallow with fear. For a while she was afraid to lie down. Suddenly the day caught up with her and she began to cry. Fearing she would make too much noise, she put her hands over her mouth and sobbed. After a few minutes she lay down and in an instant she was in a deep sleep.

Chapter 11

𝕹octurnal demons pursued Lorena in the form of blue-coated devils with gray beards.

Awakening with a start, Lorena shook her head to get rid of the cobwebs. Then she stretched and opened her eyes. She stopped in mid yawn and recoiled in fright. Someone was there, looking down at her.

Recovering her wits, Lorena breathed a sigh of relief. It was a young girl that looked no more than ten years old.

The girl was thin with a face full of freckles and two tightly wound pigtails touching her shoulders. Her hair was almost as red as Lorena's, reminding her of her own Sarah.

The girl rocked back and forth without speaking, staring at Lorena.

Acutely aware of how she looked, Lorena was surprised the girl had not run out the door screaming about the witch that was in the barn.

Smiling as pleasantly as she could, Lorena said, "Good morning." She slowly reached down and in a futile gesture, smoothed her dress, then brushed at her hair. "I was walking down the road and got real tired. I didn't think anyone would mind if I slept in your barn."

"I *do* mind," a masculine voice growled. "What are you doing on my land?"

At the same moment Lorena heard the man, she jumped up at the snarl of a dog and the forbidding click of a shotgun. Her heart pounding, she whirled towards the sound.

A hulking, round faced man, burned brown by countless hours of toil in the sun confronted her. He took off his hat and wiped his sweaty brow with the back of his hairy forearm. His wide brimmed farmer's hat had made an indented band of white skin around his forehead above which was a thatch of graying hair mixed with its original brown. His eyes were so pale blue some would think him blind. He was dressed in a plaid shirt and overalls, and he had the Winchester pointed right at Lorena's middle. The Shepherd dog beside him strained at his leash, bared his teeth and barked viciously. The small black and white dog Lorena had encountered the day before stood on the other side of the farmer yelping and whining, adding to the din. Between barks a low, ominous growl came from deep in the Shepard's throat.

Lorena was frightened and could only make voiceless gestures.

The man put his hand on the big dog's rump and pushed him down to a sitting position. "Rex, you stay put." He turned to the smaller dog. "You too, boy, *quiet!*"

He spoke to the girl without taking his eyes off Lorena. "Daughter, come over here, next to me." He snapped his fingers, indicating with a motion of his head for the girl to come to him.

For a moment the girl seemed undecided, then she ran quickly to his side.

The Shepherd began to bark again and the man slapped the side of the farm dog's head. "*Stop it,* you mangy mutt." The dog ignored the order and continued his barking. With an abrupt movement the man poked the dog's side with the barrel of the gun, and the dog yelped. The man let go of the leash and the dog slunk out the door, his tail between his legs. The spotted dog followed him with fearful sidelong glances at his master.

The man turned back to Lorena. "Lady, you'd best start talking." Holding his shotgun with one hand, the man nervously brushed back his hair and put his hat back on. The spotted dog came back and sat whimpering at the door.

Finally Lorena found her voice. "I was going... visiting up North. I was in a rail car with another person. He— " Lorena stopped.

"Go on."

Lorena nodded toward the child indicating she didn't want to continue.

The farmer's eyes dropped down to the torn and bloody bodice of Lorena's dress, and he turned to the girl. "You'd best go on in the house now, Josie. Tell your Ma to come here quick. Tell her we got *company*."

The girl stopped rocking, gave Lorena a fleeting, embarrassed smile, then turned and scampered out of the barn.

"Lady, you finish your story and it better be good or I'll drag you right on down to the Sheriff's office."

Lorena absently brushed at a piece of hair that had straggled over her eye and tried to speak, but fear rose up and froze her throat.

The man yelled again so loudly it startled her. "You better damn well talk right now, Lady."

Lorena looked down and began to cry softly. The man gave an impatient move with his gun but let her weep.

Finally she sobbed a few times, wiped her tears with the back of her hand and looked up at the man, praying he would believe her. She found her voice and continued with a half-true story.

"On the train, this person just up and attacked me. No reason, no provocation. He just attacked me. He ripped my dress," she colored slightly, "tore my, uh, under— uh, other clothing and—" She sobbed again, vividly remembering what

116

happened. Lorena looked up to continue and noticed, with relief, the man had lowered his gun.

Just then the barn door opened and a woman bustled in with the child right behind her.

The woman went right to Lorena, kneeled down, reached her hand out and took Lorena's. She looked Lorena over, let her hand go and brushed Lorena's wind-blown hair back. "Oh my God, you poor thing. Josie told me…. She turned her head and glared at her husband. "Robert, put that damned gun away. Can't you see this woman is half frightened to death?"

"Dammit, woman, you don't even know who she—

The woman stood up and faced the man, both fists on her ample hips. "I don't need to know anything," she said with a touch of exasperation, "this is a helpless, frightened creature, who has clearly seen better days. Now you go do something sensible. Go make a fire and fill the tub with hot water." She turned to her daughter. "Josie, fetch me a cotton dress from my closet." She pursed her lips in thought. "The light blue one'll do."

The girl nodded her head and ran out the door. The woman yelled after her. "And bring a set of my underwear too."

Lorena was wide-eyed with surprise at how this woman had spoken to her husband. She had heard that Yankee women were outspoken but had never witnessed it. Deep down she was pleased.

Lorena looked her benefactor over carefully. The woman was dressed in a light colored, homespun cotton dress, with a matching sunbonnet stuffed in her dress pocket. She had on a pair of general store reading glasses that pinched the end of her nose. Her black hair, streaked with gray, was tied in a tight bun at the back of her head, a comb holding it in place. The woman had an open, honest, peasant's face, full of compassion. Lorena took hope.

After Josie left, Robert ambled after her scratching his head. He had his gun over his shoulder and was muttering under his breath. "Women!"

The woman knelt down again, put both her hands on Lorena's shoulders, and looked at her face and dress. "My God, what's happened to you?" She shook her head. "Never mind, we'll put it all right again." She turned her head to the barn door and shouted, "What's keeping you two?"

The woman's friendliness enveloped Lorena and a great weariness descended on her. She leaned her head against the stout woman's shoulder and cried.

"You poor dear," the woman said pulling Lorena close and patting her head, "Don't you mind Robert, he's really a good man. We'll set you right again, just as right as rain."

Instinctively, Lorena put both her arms around the woman and held on to her tightly as she tried to let go of all that had happened the last three days.

After a few minutes of impatient waiting the woman helped Lorena up, and arm in arm the two women walked to the house, Lorena limping noticeably on her injured hip. As Lorena hobbled toward the farmhouse they leaned against each other for support, like two ancient crones.

****

When Lorena got to the farmhouse she sat in the kitchen staring into space, slack jawed. She came alive when she was given a plate of hot food which, forgetting her manners, she ate ravenously.

While Lorena devoured the plate of meat and vegetables, the woman put a large pot of water on the wood-burning stove while her husband dragged in a large metal tub. When the water got hot Josie and the woman poured the contents into the tub.

"Robert, make yourself scarce."

His face coloring, the farmer beat a quick retreat, his daughter right behind him.

Following the warm bath, the scrubbing presided over by her new friend, Lorena was given a cotton gown, walked up the stairs and put in a soft, downy bed. In the middle of thanking the woman, Lorena fell into a deep, dreamless sleep.

When she awoke, birds were singing, and the sun was just coming up over the horizon.

Lorena got up, felt lightheaded and quickly sat back down on the bed. After a few moments she got up again, this time more carefully. She stood still for a few moments, holding on to the brass bedstead until the dizziness stopped. When she tried to take a few steps she felt dull pains in her back and hip. Ignoring the pain and holding on to the wall, she slowly dressed, putting on the dress she found at the foot of the bed. When she finished she made her way out of the room to the staircase.

She heard low voices from down the darkened staircase, and cautiously held on to the banister as she went down the steps. After a few steps the pain began to lessen. When she got to the bottom she walked toward the voices. Even though they spoke softly, Lorena recognized the voices of the mother and daughter. Opening the kitchen door, Lorena smiled self-consciously. In the air was the mouth-watering odor of sizzling bacon that stimulated her appetite.

Mother and daughter were sitting at the kitchen table. The squeak of the door made the mother turn abruptly. When she saw Lorena she smiled back and pivoted in her chair to face her. "Well, good morning, you certainly look a lot better."

"I almost feel like a woman again. How can I ever thank you?"

"Tosh. Can't claim to be a Christian and, when trouble comes, not show it. Glad to be of help."

The woman turned to her daughter. "Josie, show the lady to the privy." She turned back to Lorena with a smile. "I think she'll need it about now.

Lorena nodded, blushed slightly and followed the girl outside.

When they got back, Lorena sat down at the kitchen table opposite the woman.

With a nod of her mother's head, the daughter obediently left the room. "Don't stray too far, Josie, there's work to do this morning."

The woman cocked her head slightly and smiled broadly at Lorena. "By the way, I'm Myrtle, Myrtle Olsen. The big ox that held the gun on you is my husband Robert."

Lorena smiled back and bowed her head slightly. "My name is Lorena Oakwood."

Lorena looked over at the stove. The woman followed her gaze.

She turned back to Lorena. "You hungry? Of course you are. Here, let me fix you something." The woman fixed two plates and sat down at the table opposite Lorena. While the two women were eating Lorena noticed that Myrtle cut her ham into perfect squares. Lorena wondered.

After two eggs, two slices of bread, bacon and ham, Lorena sat back and let out a deep sigh.

Myrtle reached out and took Lorena's hand. Her face had a puzzled look. "You strike me as a woman of means. That dress you had on was expensive. I know I never had anything like it. Probably never will." She looked away, as if regretting what she had to say. "It was in such bad shape I had to burn it." She looked back again eagerly. "I don't understand what's happened to you. You're like someone who fell from the moon, right here, in the middle of nowhere, you stumble onto our farm, exhausted and hungry." Myrtle smiled and looked at Lorena eagerly, like a child waiting for a Christmas story. "How about telling me what happened?"

Lorena half smiled but her eyes stayed guarded. "Like I told your husband, a man attacked me, and I jumped off the train and ran."

Myrtle looked at Lorena's slim body. "You beat off a grown man? Nobody on the train offered to help you?" Myrtle's eyes narrowed.

Lorena's eyes got cloudy and moist. "We were alone in the car— He was an animal, a beast. All I could think of was getting away."

"God damn all men," Myrtle muttered under her breath. She looked at Lorena and shook her head slowly. "Sometimes mine's not any better."

The distrust disappeared and she looked at Lorena with compassion. "Well you don't have to worry now. We'll point you up north to where you were going."

"No, not north, I want to go south, to Atlanta."

Myrtle stood up suddenly and banged the table. "I knew it, you're a southerner!" Her eyes became suspicious slits again, and her brow furrowed knitting her eyebrows almost together. "You're not a spy, are you?"

Lorena laughed. "No, I couldn't spy if I tried."

Myrtle's face relaxed as she sat down and joined Lorena's laughter.

Lorena stopped and turned serious. "No, I just want to go home. Perhaps if you could loan me enough money—?"

"Money? Hah! We're just poor dirt farmers. I ain't seen a greenback for morn' a year. We live mostly on credit, until the crops are in. Then we pray we get a decent price for them." She shook her head sadly. "Most of the time we go deeper in debt at the end of the year. We can give you a meal and a place to stay, but after that... She shrugged her shoulders.

Lorena smiled and shook her head slowly. "Well then, if you'll point me toward Atlanta I'll be on my way."

"You'd best get another night of sleep. You'll feel a heap better with some more rest. Tomorrow we'll take you to our preacher. He might be able to help you some." Myrtle tapped her ample stomach and laughed. "For sure we'll send you off with a full belly."

They both laughed together and Lorena got up, went around the table and hugged the woman as hard as she could.

Chapter 12

From the private journal of Lorena Boykins Oakwood

September 3rd 1864

Well, these Yankees have kidnapped me, browbeat me, almost raped me, and turned me into a murderess. Now they have me running like a common criminal. I think I will go to the front with General Lee and take up a gun against them when I get back That is, if I get back.

After the most disastrous day of my life, I did meet up with a very kind woman named, Myrtle Olsen. Good thing she showed up. Her husband, Robert, was ready to shoot me or turn me over to the law. I wouldn't be surprised if these Northerners would want to hang me for killing that wicked soldier, even though the murder happened through no fault of my own!

They, the family, are taking me to town today to see their preacher. Maybe he can loan me enough money to buy a train ticket home. Home, home is so close, and yet, so far away.

These people keep no slaves on their farm. It was so strange to see them do all the menial work themselves. But they seem not to mind it so much.

I even helped them some myself. Yesterday I milked a cow. I guess Old Bessie didn't want any of her flies to land on me, so she kept flicking her tail against my face. When I told her in no uncertain terms to stop it, she turned her head and mooed at me. It appears Yankee arrogance extends even to their livestock.

There's many a slip twixt the cup and the lip!

Chapter 13

The wagon bounced over the rutted road throwing the occupants right and left. Both horses plodded over the uneven ground, heads down and eyes sad, as if they were looking forlornly into a dismal future. Robert held the reins, occasionally urging the horses on with a slap on their rumps and clucking sounds he made with his tongue.

"Are we there yet, Papa?"

Robert laughed. "Not yet, Josie."

Lorena and Josie sat in the back of the buckboard holding on to prevent them sliding into the sides, while Myrtle sat up on the front seat next to her husband.

Myrtle half-turned. "Hush, Josie," she said, "we'll be there soon enough. You all right, Lorena?"

Lorena was holding on to the side of the wagon

with both hands. "Yes, Myrtle, I'm fine, just fine."

Myrtle looked over the side of the wagon at the ground and said wistfully, "I'm just sorry we couldn't do more for you."

Robert turned his head and spit a stream of brown tobacco juice over the side of the wagon but said nothing.

"Lorena smiled gratefully at Myrtle. "You've done more than most. I'm grateful to you both."

Myrtle glanced at Robert and lapsed into silence.

Lorena felt a bit melancholy because she and Myrtle could not continue their budding friendship. *Maybe after the war I can invite them to Atlanta,* she thought. *I think the South will need friends up here.*

Lorena stared back down the road, concerned about what she would do next. A plan had formulated in her mind during the night. *If I can get enough money, I will take a train to Washington, and once in the city I know so well, I would make my way to the Navy Yard Bridge. Getting that far, I could then slip across the bridge into Maryland and make my way further south. From there it would be easy find my way to friends I know in Abington, Virginia. I have several relatives just over the border in North Carolina and I'm sure if I could get there they would help me get to Atlanta.*

But as Alexander Dumas said, 'There's many a

slip 'twixt the cup and the lip!' The Yankees will be looking for me for sure. And I still have to get enough money to at least get to Washington. If the preacher can't give it to me I'll have to get it somehow, but where? How? I'll have to think of something—

"How much longer, Papa?"

"Soon, Josie, soon."

"Sit still, Child," Myrtle said as she leaned back and slapped Josie.

Lorena winced. *I've never struck my children although, Lord knows, sometimes I've wanted to.*

Robert leaned back without taking his eyes off the road. "We'll be coming to the town of Rock Island soon, Lorena. It's a river town and there are some rough characters there, but if you stay away from the Mississippi River and the two legged wharf rats that hang around there you'll be all right."

Lorena nodded. She had been quiet during the trip, contemplating her future.

Lorena was shocked by what she saw in the mirror when she washed her face that morning. She was suddenly and permanently old. Her angular features were much thinner after her ordeal. Her green eyes now held a sadness that hid a smoldering anger not there before, and her formerly smooth brow had permanent furrows. The bright red hair she used to be so proud of had long strands of gray. It was now curled conservatively in a bun and mostly hidden by the bonnet Myrtle had given her. Her formerly creamy white face was sunburned to a pale pink.

She was also given a blue cotton dress that reached the floor, brushed the tops of her riding boots, and swept the ground as she walked. Myrtle's underpants were sizes too big, and hung loosely on Lorena's frame. Periodically Lorena had to pull them up and tighten the drawstrings.

"Oh, good, I see some houses," Josie cried, "we're almost there."

A peculiar smell greeted Lorena at the first contact with the town of Rock Island. After a few moments she realized it was unburied garbage. She shook her head ruefully, realizing this town was a duplicate of thousands of immigrant towns. She remembered their Baptist preacher orating one Sunday, about the heathen immigrants and their unplanned hovels cropping up all around the country, even in Atlanta. She remembered that before the war there was talk among the men of closing the borders to foreigners to stop them from coming to America, especially the Irish papists. New York, Chicago and other Northern cities were already reeling from large immigrant onslaughts.

Lorena remembered reading in the Atlanta Monthly Intelligencer, that the North was using immigrants as soldiers. *They must not be very good soldiers. Stonewall Jackson made the*

*Dutchmen scatter at Chancellorsville, and the
Atlanta newspaper said the same men also ran at
Gettysburg. But John Oakwood told her General
Cleburne's Southern Irishmen were fine soldiers,
and some of the Yankee Irish were good fighters
too, especially the Fighting 69th.*

They soon came abreast of the first house.
Lorena stared at the ramshackle, windowless
collection of wood as they passed by. She thought
of her own palatial home in Atlanta, with its easy
living among soft summer nights. The thought of
it brought back the parties with her family and
guests, the women gossiping, and the men
bragging about their latest hunt. In her minds
eye she could see John Oakwood and his cronies,
leaning against the white Greek columns,
drinking juleps and smoking long, sweet-smelling
cigars. A forlorn feeling of longing for her home
and family filled her and her eyes moistened.

Lorena was wakened from her revelry by a
small black dog darting among the legs of the
uncaring horses, barking incessantly. The two
horses plodded on with only a cursory glance at
the annoying cur.

A baby, sitting next to the front door, half
covered with the splashing of mud, began to cry.
A young mother, looking like a child herself,
appeared at the doorway in a faded, creased
cotton dress. She looked at Lorena sullenly. The
hovel reminded Lorena of the desolate shacks the

Negro field hands lived in on Grandfather Oakwood's plantation. Only here the slaves were white.

Josie waved but the woman ignored her, and the crying child. With a look of distaste she turned and disappeared back into the shack.

"They live like our Negro slaves." Lorena muttered aloud.

"Yes," Robert tossed back without turning, "but they're free to leave whenever they want."

Lorena reddened and did not answer. For a while there was a pointed silence.

As the horses plodded down the road, Lorena could see other shacks that were little more than hastily erected shelters. Every hut seemed to have an emaciated dog and a squalling baby, each of them vying to out clamor the others. Above the putrid smell of garbage was the odor of cooking. Lorena fought nausea.

Robert moved the horses past the squalid area at a brisk pace. Lorena's eyes went back to the first shack and stayed fixed on it. As they moved away from the place she turned her head slowly staring at the crying baby until the shack was out of sight.

Gradually the houses improved, along with more palatable odors. Lorena took in a long, sweet breath.

The flat Illinois land ended when they came to a long decline and started down. Lorena could see a broad expanse of water ahead of them. The lengthy sloping hill went all the way down to the water's edge.

Robert pointed over the horses at the river. "That there's the Mississippi River." His finger made a small arc. "That new wooden bridge over there goes to the arsenal that's just been built. It seems Harper's Ferry was too easy for the Rebels to take so they moved all the guns up here." He pointed to a long flat structure. "That's the Rock Island arsenal and foundry."

Lorena stared at the pristine buildings on the island. *Our foundry is so puny compared to that. Everything here is bigger. What were our leaders thinking—*

Robert interrupted her thoughts. "Right next to the arsenal is the prison camp." He shook his head. "Lots of sickness there. I guess it's overcrowded." Robert pointed to a place in back of the barracks. "I brought some produce to the prison a while back and walked by the new graveyard. There are a whole lot of graves there for such a new place."

So that's the prison camp the General wanted to send me to. She shuddered. *I better be careful. I might end up there yet.* When they reached the bottom of the decline they moved on level ground toward the bridge.

When they got to the new structure, Robert clucked his tongue and urged the horse onto the wooden bridge. "Use to be it took an hour to take a ferry over this river. With this new bridge we can get across in a jiffy. We'll be over the river and onto the other side before you know it." The horse's hooves made a clattering sound as they stepped on the bridge and started toward the distant end. After half mile the bridge split; the smaller part forked down to the prison camp.

Looking down from her vantage point, Lorena could see the Confederate prisoners. Even from a distance she could see their uniforms were worn-out. Most of the prisoners sat outside the barracks looking hot and listless. She shuddered to think she might have been the only woman among those desperate and lonely men.

She tore her eyes away and looked at the river. It appeared cold, dark and foreboding. Small islets of sand poked through the black water. Lorena wondered what kind of fish could live in that malevolent place. She shook her head and looked up river. Her eyes brightened. A great steamboat was coming right toward them. "Look, Josie!"

The boat's great paddlewheel churned up water, propelling it forward, white steam rose from its single stack and it began whistling furiously to announce its presence. Along the banks people gathered to see the gambling ship and wave at the people on board. Gay handkerchiefs fluttered bravely back at them from two decks. Lorena could easily make out the large letters along its side, *Pride of St. Louis*.

Going in the opposite direction a barge, its deck loaded with coal passed alongside the paddlewheel. Lorena watched with interest as the captain guided the barge safely through the numerous sand bars. At the front of the barge, to avoid grounding on a sand bar, a lone sailor measured the depth of the river. The water carried his voice clearly to Lorena, as he yelled to his captain, "Mark one... Mark twain."

Reaching the end of the bridge, Robert stopped the horses and turned to Lorena. "This is the town of Davenport." Then he pointed a finger at a group of tumbledown buildings along the waterfront. "And that is Bucktown! It's a good place to stay away from."

Lorena looked at the deserted streets and old buildings. "It doesn't look like much," she said.

Myrtle spoke in hushed tones as if intimidated. "It's quiet now, but at night it's an evil and dangerous place. Men drink and gamble all night." She reached back and put her hands over Josie's ears. "There are women in this place who sell their bodies— Her face reddened and she couldn't continue.

Robert clucked his tongue and the horse started moving again. "I wouldn't come down here at night," he said, a touch of fear in his voice, "for anything."

****

Robert urged the horses up a long hill. When they got to the top the animals slowed breathing heavily. Robert guided the beasts along the main street, until they reached a small white building, and stopped.

"We're here," Robert exclaimed turning half way around, "this is our church."

The chapel was small, but so pristine white, it almost hurt the eyes. Lorena had seen many Baptist churches just like this one on the outskirts of Atlanta. It had a grass yard wrested from the muddy soil, and flocks of multicolored wild flowers that were planted all the way around the edge of the building.

Lorena looked up at the tall steeple with a bell and a cupola at the top. If a man stood in the cupola and looked north, he would see flat cornfields stretching as far as the eye could see. Looking south he would see the long, steep slope going down to the Mississippi River.

A platform lay just beneath the bell. Lorena imagined that every Sunday some favored boy would stick cotton in his ears, climb onto the platform, and happily ring the bell to gather the faithful. A flower-filled graveyard could be seen behind the church.

Lorena wondered where the great bell had come from and how the churchmen had lifted it up to the cupola.

Looking back down the street Lorena could see the wide dirt road that served as the main street of the town. Beyond that a long decline down to the river, the waterfront, and Bucktown.

Turning the other way, Lorena saw several wooden structures. One building had farm implements outside signifying a hardware store. A sign hanging from the second floor of that building had a sign with the picture of a large tooth, indicating a dentist's office. Next to the hardware shop was an undertaker's shop with a lawyer's office on top. A few stores on the opposite side of the street rounded out the commercial district.

A large wooden walkway and overhead, to shelter shoppers from rain and mud, fronted all the stores.

Robert wrapped the reins around the brake.

"Lady," he said abruptly, "the missus and I talked it over and we think you ought to speak to the Reverend and get some help from him." He nodded his head, as he spoke, adding emphasis to his words.

"Now you have to understand, he ain't no sissy preacher," Robert said emphatically. "He works in the fields same as the rest of us." The farmer pointed to the church. "But as you can see, he loves the Lord and he built this here house of worship, with our help of course. I don't see his horse so he ain't in the church just now but he'll be here right smart."

The farmer stepped off the wagon and gave his hand to Lorena. She got down off the wagon, dusted off her dress and turned to Myrtle, realizing this was goodbye.

"Myrtle, I want to thank you for all you've done. I swear I will repay you when I get home."

Moving her stout body gracefully, Myrtle stepped down off the wagon seat and the two women went to each other and hugged fiercely. "No need to thank us, Lorena," Myrtle said as she stepped back, "it was our pleasure."

"Can we go to the store? I want some candy."

"Hush, Josie"

Robert got back up in the seat and Myrtle stepped up and sat down beside him. He unwrapped the reins and looked down at Lorena. "Now you go on into the church and wait there. The preacher'll be along any time now. He comes here every day after his work."

Smiling as if he were glad to be relieved of a burden, Robert made that familiar clucking sound with his tongue, snapped the reins on the horses' back and the buckboard pulled away.

Lorena watched Myrtle turn to Robert and, her face turning red, angrily tell him something.

Josie waved goodbye, her pigtails bobbing furiously.

Lorena sadly waved back and watched them until they reached the General Store.

Myrtle, still red-faced and talking heatedly,

got out of the wagon and stormed inside.

Lorena laughed when she saw Robert heave a great sigh of relief.

Feeling an unexplained sadness in leaving them, she shook her head, turned to the church and went in the front door. *I must write them when I get home. I am so grateful to Myrtle.* Somewhere, deep down inside her, she knew when she got home things would change and the social gap would be too great.

The inside of the church was plain and cool. It was a simple building made of pine wood, with hard bench seats, oak floors and a rough-hewn altar from which to preach the gospel. Paneled windows, facing west, caught the afternoon sun and lit up the chapel.

Lorena sat down on a bench and prepared to wait. She touched the plain pinewood seat. *As smooth as glass. These people must truly love God to make such a fine place of worship. I hope there's no North or South inside this building.*

Lorena felt safe in the church and for the first time in many days relaxed completely.

The sun moved westward and shadows grew long, and Lorena felt a wave of fatigue come over her. She lay down on the bench and, as hard as it was, she soon fell asleep.

****

Lorena awoke with someone looming over her. Her heart pounding she bolted up and tried to scoot away but was stopped by the back of the bench. She slid back down and cowered.

"Don't be frightened little lady, you're in the house of the Lord. He and I will protect you."

The man spoke to her with the calmness of a relative and Lorena felt relieved. She took the hand extended to her and sat up, blinking and shaking her head to clear her mind. Two candles flickered nearby and it took a moment for her eyes to adjust to the meager light. Shadows, like predatory beasts on the walls made by the shimmering candlelight kept her on edge.

He was still in the shadows and Lorena wished he would step into the light so she could see him.

Chapter 14

"I'm John Pomeroy, the pastor of this church, and I welcome you in the name of Christ."

Lorena smiled at her new benefactor forgetting the shadows.

The pastor stepped into the light and Lorena flinched. He had a patch over one eye and the other side of his face was scarred badly. He was a large man, heavily muscled, with a deep, melodious baritone voice that reminded Lorena of the Negroes who sang, coming home from the cotton fields at sundown. He was well over six feet tall and had the pungent odor of a man who worked with his hands. Overlaying that was the sweet aroma of the tobacco in the pipe he contentedly puffed. His countenance was almost round, his face bearded, his manner friendly. But, strangely, his eyes held no sparkle and little joy. The scars on his face puckered just above his cheek marring the serenity of his face.

"Pastor, I am so glad to meet you. I was on a train that had an, er, accident and I, er, was thrown clear and I wandered for days...."

The pastor got a quizzical look on his face and his good eye blinked.

Lorena realized she was still half asleep and running off at the mouth. She stopped for a moment and tried to gather her wits.

"I wandered about until I reached this farmhouse and the people there, the Olsens, took me in and brought me here." She smiled weakly. "They're members of your church."

The pastor's face looked critical. "Yes, I know the Olsens." He started to turn then stopped and eyed Lorena suspiciously. "Why didn't you stay with the train?"

Lorena's stomach tightened into a ball. "I guess I blanked out when I was thrown from the...." Lorena's voice trailed off.

"Hmm." The pastor tapped his pipe on his boot and the lit embers fell to the wood, sparking, then dying out. He turned and walked to the window. It was then that Lorena noticed his severe limp.

He stared into the darkness for a few moments then he whirled and spoke in an accusatory tone. "Your accent, it's not from here. Where did you come from? What's your name?" There was winter in his voice.

All right, Lorena think fast. Lorena swallowed hard and clenched her fists. "Why, my name is Lorena Oakwood, and I'm from southern Indiana."

The pastor took a step forward and cocked his head like a fierce bird. "What town?"

"Ah, er—" Lorena's felt her face get warm.

"I thought so. Who are you? What are you doing here?"

Caught in her lie, Lorena decided to confess at least some of the truth. She started with the attack by the sergeant, and finished with her daring escape. She pointedly left out the incident with General Sherman, and the killing of the sergeant.

When she finished the pastor remained silent. He filled his pipe and struck a match against his rough pants. It flared up as he put it to his pipe and Lorena was dismayed to see the light show a granite-like face, hard and unforgiving. Against the light she could see that under the scars on his face his one cheekbone was concave, as if pushed in by a giant thumb.

He took a few puffs to get the pipe going. "You're from the South, aren't you?" he said with a studied calm that underscored intense anger.

Lorena looked down and shook her head slowly.

"Look at me!" the pastor roared.

Lorena's head snapped up.

"You see *this*?" He pulled off the eye patch and Lorena looked through an eyeless hole into his skull. She shuddered.

"And this," he said heatedly. He pointed to the misshapen scar blazing across his sunken cheek. "I got this at the Hornet's Nest at Shiloh. And this," he tapped his bad leg, "when I was stupid enough to come back to the army after losing my eye. One of your Georgia Rebels put a minié ball in me, at Antietam, and shattered my thigh while I was crossing a bridge with General Burnside. Some general he was," the pastor said heatedly, "a private coulda led us better." He pounded his thigh. "I almost lost the damn leg. It hurts so much sometimes, I wish they *had* cut it off."

The pastor threw the eye patch angrily to the floor and moved closer to Lorena.

She stared at his damaged face and shrunk back.

"You want me to help you?" His voice was sharp and menacing. "The only help you'll get from me, Rebel, is to help throw you out of my church. And if you're a spy, why, I'll gladly help string you up."

He stood up to his full height and pointed at the door, his beard trembling with righteousness and his eyes blazing with hate.

To Lorena, her own eyes wide with fright, he looked like an angry prophet from the Old Testament.

"Now, get out of my church. Get out and stay out. And the Devil take you with him." He grabbed her by the shoulders and with the strength of his fury, lifted her off the seat, turned her, and propelled her toward the door.

Lorena stumbled to the front of the church, threw open the door and fled down the front steps. On the last step she tripped and went sprawling face down. Her hands scraped on the small stones that made up the walk, and drew blood, but she was too terrified to notice.

She quickly got up and ran along Main Street, her boots pounding in the dirt.

Lorena heard the door of the church slam shut. It was as if the resounding noise of the closing door was the final separation from the last of her respectability.

****

Reaching the top of the decline, Lorena slowed down and looked fearfully behind her. Nothing. She stopped and took a deep breath. The preacher was not on the street. She looked around her. The stores were shuttered, the shopkeepers gone. She was alone.

Lorena stopped and her eyes moistened. She fought the tears and forced herself to take stock of her situation. It looked bleak.

She wiped her hands on her dress and walked

slowly down the long hill toward the shoreline.

When Lorena got to the river, she found it dark and lonely. For a few moments, she thought of going back to the Olsen's farm but gave it up when she contemplated walking all that distance in the dark.

Lorena stepped out on the nearest wharf and walked to the end. She put her elbows on the railing, and stared down at the water.
The river looked black and forbidding. She fought the urge to leap over the railing and end her misery.

At that time of night all the buildings were shuttered and dark. A few feet away she spied a barrel. She walked to it, sat down and stared over the Mississippi River to the blinking lights on the distant shore.

Lorena soon became aware of the sounds of the river. Water slapped against the sides of boats and a light wind made their mooring lines creak. Across the water, above the quiet splashes from the boats, came the distant sporadic clamor of people laughing and shouting. Even though they were strangers, Lorena longed to be with them... with someone... with anyone....

Depression threatened to overcome her and she fought it off.

Lorena got up put her hands on the railing and looked up and down the river. To her left it was dark and forbidding. She swiveled her head the other way. Even though she saw lights and heard noise, the place looked equally ominous, it was Bucktown.

It sure looks different at night.

Bucktown was alive now, with all its lanterns blazing. Lorena could see men wandering about, going in and out of several different buildings. She heard pistol shots and wondered.

Despite the excitement, Lorena yawned. "I've got to get a place to sleep," she muttered. She left the wharf and began to walk along the river away from Bucktown. Her path took her along a cobbled street past darkened warehouses.

I'll find a place to sleep tonight, and then decide what to do in the morning. She looked back at the lights. Even with the warnings the activity looked inviting. Chiding herself she looked right and left for any place of refuge. Finally she saw a building with a sign hanging only by one hinge. Squinting her eyes she made out the faded word, LIVERY, made barely visible from the lights of Bucktown.

Lorena slipped in the side door of the barn-like building. It was dark in the cavernous structure, and she stood still for a time until her eyes became accustomed to the dim light. Although she couldn't see anything, she could hear several horses nickering. When she finally could see, she noticed a pile of straw for the horses. She strode to it, and wearily sat down. She sat there for a few moments then, after passing her hand through her hair she laid down on her side.

After a few moments she turned on her back and tried to get comfortable. Suddenly the night and all the troubles of the day crowded in on her. Lorena sat up and stared dumbly into the darkness, trying to solve her dilemma until her head nodded and she laid down again. Soon she was fast asleep, with fear and disillusionment for bedmates.

Men seek nothing in Bucktown but sweet pleasure

Chapter 15

Lorena woke with a start and sat up abruptly, a cry of fear stifled in her throat. She peered into the dim light coming in between the slats of the barn walls, trying to discern fearful shapes that looked ready to pounce on her. After a few moments she heard only the soft breathing and quiet neighing of the horses in their stalls. She lay back down again and tried to go back to sleep.

Suddenly the two front barn doors swung open, daylight poured in, and the shadow of a giant filled the doorway. Lorena bolted upright, her heart pounding in her chest.

The giant took a step forward out of the light and Lorena saw him shrink to normal size. She breathed a sigh of relief.

Then he saw her. "What are you doin' in here, Lady? This is jes fer horses'." He pointed the way he had just come from without looking. "The hotel's that way."

Lorena could see him clearly now. He was

young with sandy hair and a freckled face that appeared to hold no guile. He had on Union Army pants held up by blue suspenders. His plaid work shirt was old but clean, and he wore a large Mexican straw hat. Lorena laughed to herself despite her predicament. *That hat would not only block the sun, but all the stars too.*

She looked down demurely and said contritely, "I had no place to stay last night. I didn't hurt anything." Lorena looked up at him and laughed aloud. "I didn't take a horse. You can count them."

The boy's face was serious. "Yes'm, I'm sure you didn't, but Mr. Hickey, the owner of this here livery, he's also the owner of the hotel, bath house an' a restaurant. An' you jes done beat him out of a dollar." He smiled a youthful, twisted smile. "An believe me he wouldn't take kindly to that." Then he smiled broadly. "Yes'm, and not many folks beat that man for anything, much less a dollar. I know!"

Lorena stood up and brushed off her dress. "Is there any place I can go to, uh, you know—"

The boy looked puzzled, then his face lit up. "Oh yes'm. Jes go on around the back. Nobody'll be around here this early."

Lorena started toward the back door.

"They'll be some water there to splash on yer face too."

Lorena slipped out the back door, found some bushes and squatted. The air was cold and she trembled. When she finished she looked for the water the boy had mentioned. The only thing she saw was a horse trough. Bending over, she recoiled when she saw bugs and debris floating on top. She reached down with both hands, pushed the bugs aside, and splashed the tainted water on her face and neck.

Thirst winning out she brushed along the top of the water with the back of both hands, shut her eyes, then dipped them down, drew the water to her mouth and drank. Lorena quickly spit out the putrid water.

Standing erect she took the bottom of her dress and wiped her face.

Sensing someone watching, Lorena opened her eyes. The boy was standing at the door, staring at her raised dress. His jaw was slack, his mouth open and his tongue out. To Lorena he looked like a puzzled, friendly hound dog.

Lorena dropped the garment quickly.

She smiled to herself. *A week ago I would have been shocked.* "How about giving a lady some privacy, Boy."

The lad colored crimson. "Oh, yes, ma'am. I'm sorry." He turned away quickly, "I gotta feed the horses," he said and disappeared back into the barn.

Lorena laughed aloud, smoothed her dress and walked back into the livery. She watched the stable boy put an oat bag on a horse, and move his hand gently along its withers. The horse whinnied as Lorena approached. She went to the opposite side of the horse and put her hand on the horse's neck and patted him. Her stomach growled with hunger.

"This filly reminds me of my own mare," she said almost to herself. A sudden feeling of home and family filled her and she choked back a sob. Lorena smiled weakly and moved around the front of the horse. She gently rubbed the horse's velvet nose then looked directly into the stable boy's eyes, hoping to make him understand.

"I'm a long way from where I live. I have no money and no one will loan me any. I guess I will have to work somewhere to get enough to get me back home."

The boy turned away and quickly went to the next stall. Lorena followed him.

"I ain't got no money," he said, avoiding her eyes.

Lorena looked at him earnestly. "I don't want anything from you. Just tell me where I might go—"

"The Preacher might help."

Lorena shook her head ruefully. "I tried there."

"What about the Sheriff?"

Lorena's face reddened, and she looked away.

"Oh!" the boy exclaimed, "I reckon I understand."

He reached for another oat bag, filled it from a large sack, and put it on the second horse.

"Things been hard here on the river lately, Ma'am, what with the war and all. The soldiers tell me they ain't been paid fer months. I don't think there's many jobs with the merchants." He thought for a moment, lifting his eyes up to the top of the barn. "It's mighty busy in Bucktown though. Why don't you try something there?"

Lorena felt warmth creep up from her neck.

The boy's face got red. "I didn't mean you had to... He turned away and picked up a shovel. "I have to get to work."

Lorena thought it was time to leave before someone else came. "I want to thank you for... for everything. My name is Lorena."

"I'm Jess," the boy said, waving at her without turning back, and started to shovel manure.

The smell became overpowering and Lorena was glad to step out into the daylight. She was surprised to see how close the livery was to Bucktown. In the dark it seemed much further away.

Lorena walked past various warehouse buildings into Bucktown. The place seemed less intimidating by daylight. It was still early and the streets were deserted. She stopped, picked errant pieces of straw from her dress, brushed the dust off and ran her hands down in a smoothing motion. She primped her hair then started walking down the street.

"Hey, Lady, you got a quarter?"

Lorena jumped with fright. She looked down and saw a man lying in a doorway. He was a colorless man with dull blue eyes and a leathery face. He had a long scar that traveled from his right ear, over his cheek, to the tip of his jaw.

She started walking again and the drunk grabbed at her and loosely gripped her ankle.

She pulled her leg away in disgust and quickly distanced herself from him.

He half sat up. "Don't go, Lady."

Lorena half walked, half ran back out of Bucktown. *I haven't sunk so low that I would resort to work in that kind of place.* She began the long walk up the slope to the merchant shops at the top of the hill.

When Lorena reached the crest of the hill, the sun was already up and moving across the sky. She felt moisture on her brow and dabbed the perspiration with the back of her hand. She could see that a few merchants were already at their shops, doing their morning chores. Lorena studied the signs indicating the establishment inside. A scissor for the barber, a tooth for the dentist and a large weathered eye for the oculist. *No training for that*, she thought.

Lorena braced herself and started toward the closest store. A large sign over the door announced, Sam's Grocery. *There's a possibility.*

A bald man with a thick fringe of gray hair at the base of his skull, long arms and an ample belly was sweeping the wooden walk. He stopped, leaned on his broom and seemed to appraise Lorena favorably as she approached.

He looks a lot like Mr. Buchanan. Lorena took heart

"Good morning." The man leaned the broom against the building. "You're out mighty early, uh, Ma'am."

"Good morning, sir." Lorena smiled and felt ashes in her mouth. She had not brushed her teeth for several days. *I hope I look better than I feel.*

"Sir, I hate to interrupt your work, but I need employment. Just for a short while," Lorena was quick to add.

"Hmm." The man looked her up and down, enjoying what he saw. "Maybe there's something we can do."

Lorena felt a surge of relief in her chest and smiled. Suddenly her eye caught a movement at the front door.

The door flew open. A woman stormed out and confronted the merchant. She was one of those matrons who did the work of the world. She was short, thickset and heavily muscled. She had graying hair tied in a knot at the back, and a square face, red with anger.

She grabbed the man by the arm and pulled him close to her. "You'll put her in the store over my dead, cold body, you bastard." She yanked the man back toward the entrance.

He stumbled back and stopped at the open door. "Now, sweetheart, be reasonable. You know we need some help. Winter's coming and the farmers and river rats will be coming in for supplies—

"I'll do the extra work," she shouted as she yanked him again and turned him to face the door. With a grunt she pushed him into the store, and slammed the door shut. Then she whirled and faced Lorena.

Lorena was standing open-mouthed in the dusty street.

The woman stepped off the walkway and stood, hands on her hips, staring at her supposed adversary. The door opened again and this time a small child, no more than two years old, came out. The chunky little girl went to the edge of the walk, got down on her knees and struggled off the walk into the street.

Lorena watched her with an aching heart, remembering her own daughter's first halting steps.

When the child got down she waddled straight to her mother and hid behind her skirt. She held on to the woman's fat leg with one hand, while she sucked her thumb with the other.

The matron continued to glare, then raised her fist and shook it at Lorena. "That good-for-nothing is *my* husband and this is *my* store. You stay away from both." Then she turned on her

heel, grabbed the child by the arm, stepped up on
the walk and pulled her inside the store. The door
slammed shut with a resounding bang ending all
conversation.

Lorena stood where she was, dumbfounded.
She could hear the woman shouting obscenities at
her husband through the closed door. The man
was yelling back, while the child was crying
loudly, adding to the symphony of chaos.

Lorena stood there for a few moments longer,
then shook her head and walked away, their
angry voices trailing her.

She wandered down the street until she came
to the last store on the left. She looked in the
window and saw movement. A newly painted sign
in the window said *Ready-made outfits for ladies
and gents.* Over the door were the words, *General
Store,* in big bright letters.

Maybe I'll have better luck here. Lorena opened
the door and heard the familiar tinkle of a bell
announcing a customer.

The inside of the store was gray and dark, and
pungent with a thousand familiar odors.
Overriding all the others was the distinct smell of
leather. Next to the door, stacked in two rows,
from floor to ceiling, were new leather saddles.
Facing Lorena was a long wooden counter heaped
up with work pants and plaid shirts. Two large
jars of hard candies flanked the clothing. Behind
the counter, on the left, were iron skillets and

kettles. Next to them were bolts of cloth, ready to be sewn into dresses of all kinds and shapes. On the right was a mannequin with no face, dressed in a flowered cotton frock.

Shotguns and hunting rifles hung on pegs surrounding three large pictures on the wall. In the center hung a large portrait of President Lincoln. Flanking his image were similar pictures of Generals Grant and Sherman.

Lorena stared at Sherman's likeness and felt the juices in her stomach curdle into a hate so poisonous she felt compelled to lash out. Only her need to keep things peaceful stopped her from destroying the picture. She forced herself to turn away.

She walked to the counter. In front of her, at the center of the counter, was a long glass case housing a row of handguns. They looked very much like the guns made at The Atlanta Foundry. A picture directly in back, on the wall, showed a man in buckskins twirling two Colt pistols. At the bottom of the picture the words stood out in bold print.

> **The new Colt six shot, 45-caliber.**
> **Called The Widow Maker,**
> **It will tame the Earth.**

Lorena tore her eyes away from the guns and wandered down the aisle. She walked along the shelves where there were cans of peas, tomatoes, and corn. Her mouth watered.

Sacks of dried beans and coffee were stacked on the floor ten high. The smell of the coffee tantalized Lorena.

Piled next to the sacks were all the other supplies necessary for a long mid-west winter. A thick layer of dust covered the shelves and cobwebs hung from the ceiling.

Farm implements such as hoes, rakes and harnesses for the livestock were hung neatly on wall pegs around the store. Lorena took it all in.

As she walked toward the counter the doorbell tinkled. Lorena's stomach tightened when two soldiers, dressed in the gray uniforms of prison camp guards, entered and started browsing among the goods. Lorena quickly turned her back to them, moved to the mannequin and busied herself studying and touching the dress.

Lorena was suddenly startled by a man's voice. "Can I help you boys?"

Lorena looked back at the men then quickly turned away.

"Yes," one of the soldiers said, "here's a list of goods we need at the prison. The Colonel has already signed for it."

Lorena heard the rustling of paper and a pause, and then the shopkeeper spoke again.

"I'll have it out to the quartermaster by noon."

The soldiers half saluted and browsed for a few

more minutes. "I guess we better get back," one of
them finally said.

The other stretched and yawned. He stopped
in mid-yawn when he spotted Lorena. "Well,
looky here."

He took a step toward her.

Lorena's heart pounded and she shrunk back.

The shopkeeper quickly moved from behind
the counter to her side. He turned to the soldiers,
his voice firm. "I'll have the goods out to you by
noon."

The soldier stopped and a look of annoyance
crossed his face.

His companion, reading the determination on
the storekeeper's face said, "Hey, Sarge, we better
get on back." He said it with the surly patience
and indifference of a subordinate.

"Sure, Corporal," the sergeant said, not taking
his eyes off Lorena.

"Well, let's go then." The corporal was holding
the front door open, an impatient look coming
over his face.

"I'm coming." The sergeant turned, slowly
moved to the door and muttered something to the
corporal.

Lorena could hear their laughter from outside
as the door closed. She turned to the shopkeeper
and gave him a grateful, "Thank you."

"Yes, Ma'am, some of them soldier-boys are
pretty rough. May I help you?" The shopkeeper

addressed her still holding the military supply list in his hand.

The man was heavily jowled, with a round, pockmarked face, a large stomach and burly chest. A leather apron barely covered his girth. Thinning brown hair, graying at the temples gave him a fatherly look. There was an aura of prosperity about him.

Lorena smiled and prayed inwardly. "I hope so. My name is Lorena Oakwood. I ran into a little bad luck and I need a job to make some money so I can get home—"

The man held up his hand, stopping her. "So you're the woman. Yes, the preacher came around and told all the shopkeepers about you."

Her hope vanished.

"I can do most anything," she said pleading. "Inventory, bookkeeping. I can measure, sweep," Lorena pointed to the rifles on the wall. "I know about guns—"

The man smiled, shook his head and shrugged his shoulders. "I'm sorry ma'am, but you understand...." He pursed his lips and shook his head. "His congregation, well, most of them are my customers. One word from him and— He shrugged his shoulders again.

"Yes, of course, the preacher." Lorena dropped her head and turned to leave.

"I'm sorry to tell you this, but there's not much work in town. You might get something in the

Tenderloin down by the river. The preacher has no say over there."

"Tenderloin?"

The man laughed. "Yes, the Tenderloin. Also known as Bucktown. It's called the Tenderloin by some because the tenderloin is the sweetest part of the T-bone steak, and because men seek nothing in Bucktown but sweet pleasure." He smiled indulgently. "You know, the sweetest cut of life is the *Tenderloin*.

Lorena walked to the door, opened it and stared down at the river. The shopkeeper followed.

"There'll be something there for you, I'm sure."

Lorena turned back to him to say something tart and was surprised to see that he was looking at her with compassion.

"Thank you. I'll think about it." Lorena nodded goodbye and walked out the door blinking at the morning sun.

For a while she stared up the street at the church. Then she turned and stared down the long hill to the river and Bucktown. Her mind raced looking for a way out of her dilemma. Her heart sunk. *There's no way out.* For a time she looked undecided, then with a resolute set of her shoulders, she took a step down the hill. She stopped, hesitated for a moment, and glanced at the wedding ring on her hand. With a decisive move she slipped off the ring, tied it securely in her lace hanky, and put it in the dress pocket alongside her journal. Then she set her jaw and started down the steep decline making little tottering steps. When she got to the bottom she strode purposefully toward the Tenderloin.

A touch of arrogance, and devilment

Chapter 16

𝕿he overwhelming smell of sweaty men, stale women and rich tobacco greeted Lorena as she pushed open the door and hesitantly stepped into the saloon.

Lorena had waited by the river all day. During the morning a hot, sticky miasma drifted off the Mississippi bringing with it the pungent odor of fish and men's garbage. She spent the afternoon thinking of her home and children, trying to ignore the pangs of hunger.

When dusk finally arrived, Bucktown came alive. It was an eclectic group of people that populated Bucktown. Unshaven river men, soldiers and farm hands populated the streets along with men and women dressed in finery. Many of the more unsavory men were already in a drunken revelry and fights broke out easily. Lorena heard gunfire in the distance. The occasional woman she saw seemed to be of the lowest class and was always in the company of a man of the same caliber.

Lorena hung back in the shadows, away from the unpleasant looking people.

Walking aimlessly down the street she spied a two-story building with many people going in and out. She stared at the building as if it would, at any moment, burst into flame. Steeling herself she crossed the street, hesitated for a moment, then opened the door. Loud piano music, shouting and raucous laughter from inside assaulted her ears.

Lorena stepped into the saloon, stopped and almost gagged at the strong odor of perfume and whisky. She recovered and looked about in wonder. She heard about these places but had never had the opportunity or courage to go into one. However Lorena had a reluctant curiosity about risqué places common to all women of her class. After all she had read Balzac.

Inside she found herself in a large room with sawdust covered wooden floors, scuffed by thousands of work boots. The darkness of the saloon contrasted with the brightness of the enormous mirror that covered the entire back wall of the room. The silvered glass reflected the rest of the saloon, making it look larger than it was. Stacked in neat pyramids on a counter in front of the mirror were multicolored bottles of whiskey. Atop the bar were two barrels. A burly bartender, drenched with sweat, was busily pouring beer from the kegs into glass mugs. A few harried women were carrying the mugs of beer and glasses of whisky to the gamblers and loafers.

Hanging from the ceiling in front of the mirror, swaying slightly from the tumult in the saloon was a life-size oil painting of a redheaded, reclining nude. She was stretched back, openly displaying her charms. Lorena touched her own red hair, felt her face get warm, and quickly turned her eyes away from the picture.

A thick layer of blue tobacco smoke hung like a formless blanket between the open first and second floors of the building. Four men stood at the bar drinking beer and whiskey chasers.

Four women were with them. The women were dressed as bright as butterflies, their low cut gowns revealing powdered shoulders. A gash of red lipstick smeared across their mouths, with red rouge painted on their cheeks. Lorena thought she detected pain in their eyes.

The women's heads darted back and forth from Lorena to the men, as if she were new, unwelcome competition. Two of the women, their faces blank and sagging with age and fatigue, leaned back with elbows heavy on the bar, awaiting what they knew the night would bring. The other two were young and still had some spirit. They tossed their heads and engaged the men in playful banter.

Without thinking Lorena pinched her cheeks and bit her lips to make them look redder.

Brass spittoons sat at the foot of the bar at either end. The large brown stains around them proving the poor aim of the patrons.

Lorena marveled at the great assortment of men filling the room. Some of them were soldiers from Camp McClellan and the Rock Island Arsenal. They wore the traditional blue. The guards from the prison camp were dressed in distinctive gray uniforms. The other soldiers derisively called them graybacks. They had a look about them that was not pleasant.

Farmers in overalls and river men mixed in an uneasy truce that could, at any moment, turn volatile. Some of the patrons talked and joked with the brightly dressed ladies circulating around the room, teasing and enticing the men into drinking beer, playing cards and going upstairs with them for other pleasurable pursuits.

Loud, raucous laughter drew Lorena's attention to the center of the room. One of the girls was laughing loudly at something a soldier was telling her. Lorena's eyes moved to the table next to the laughing woman. It was then that she saw him.

Three men sat at a round table, cards in hand,

eyeing each other with suspicion. Bills and coins lay in disarrayed piles in front of each man. Two of them were dressed in work clothes, another in a wrinkled gray uniform. The fourth man was quite different.

When Lorena's eyes fell on him, her heart quickened and her breath caught in her throat. He stood out clearly in the chaos around him, like a stallion among mules. She was surprised that she could feel any emotion other than the fear and helplessness she had recently acquired.

The gambler had a lean, intense face with an aquiline nose. His jaw was firm and jutted forward a tiny bit, as if in defiance of authority. He had a thin, black mustache that went the entire length of the upper lip. The clothes he wore looked expensive. They consisted of a formal black cutaway jacket, and Confederate gray striped pants. He was booted to the knee in black leather, with his pant legs tucked inside the boots like a cavalry officer. His immaculate white shirt was complimented by a large gray, and black striped cravat, with a diamond stickpin in the center. Smoke from the slender, black Mexican cheroot in his hand, curled around his head like an unholy halo. The black wide brimmed Stetson that he wore tipped rakishly to one side. He was, Lorena thought, the handsomest man she had ever seen.

Her breath came back but her pulse was still raised, and she had difficulty taking her eyes off him. Lorena noted he had a touch of arrogance, and devilment in his face. To her surprise, it excited her.

When their eyes met he immediately stood up and smiled, took off his hat, put it over his heart and bowed slightly. His eyes never left her face.

Reluctantly she nodded back, her heart still racing.

He put his hat back on, touched the brim, smiled again and sat back down. But his dark, alert eyes continued to watch Lorena intently, even while he played his cards.

Almost against her will Lorena forced herself to look away but for some reason, inexplicably to her, she still felt drawn to him. After a moment she glanced back at him. This time she noticed he was thin and tall, and had the pale complexion of a man who avoided the sun. Yet he had a vigor and alertness about him that displayed at least an acquaintance with the outdoors. She forced her self to look away again.

He's certainly a handsome devil, she thought, her mind delving into places she knew it shouldn't go.

Lorena looked around for the owner then stole another glance at he gambler, and again her breath caught. Sitting back, waiting for the cards to be dealt, he looked at her with a daring expression on his face, his black eyes sparkling with life. His mouth was smiling, but his lips retained a touch of the cynical. He dealt the cards keeping the small cigarillo delicately balanced in his left hand.

Lorena felt her face get warm again as she felt the men at the bar cycing her. She turned away from them and looked around the room for the owner. Seeing no one in authority she took a deep breath and started walking toward the bartender. As she approached the bar, the men there leered, and nodded to each other. Other men from all over the room stopped their drinking and games and stared at her. The noise in the saloon dropped appreciably.

The gambler took it all in and frowned, his eyebrows knitting almost together under a furrowed brow. The sounds of the saloon rose and fell until Lorena reached mid-way to the bar. Then the entire place went quiet, all eyes on the handsome, farm-dressed, red-haired woman.

Lorena avoided their looks by keeping her head down, and did not see the burly bartender step out from behind the bar to confront her. The men laughed when she bumped into him. Flustered, she excused herself and stepped back. The noise in the saloon came up appreciably.

The bartender looked her over eyeing her plain cotton dress. "You sure you're in the right place, lady?" He was a big man, double chinned and heavily muscled, with the pitted red face of a persistent drinker.

Lorena colored a deeper red. "Y-yes," she stammered, "I, er, want a job." *Good God, I sound like an idiot. Get a hold of yourself, Lorena.*

The bartender laughed. Despite his powerful build, his voice was high and grating, like chalk on a blackboard.

He reached out, grabbed Lorena's dress by the skirt and held it out with two fingers. The saloon went quiet again, as if by signal. Even the piano player stopped his pounding.

Lorena felt her whole body get warm. Beads of perspiration popped out on her forehead.

"You want to be one of my girls, in this dress? You look more like a schoolmarm to me."

He laughed loudly and was joined by the men nearby. The men around the room started to play and talk again.

Two men at the gambler's table started snickering. They stopped when the pale man stood up, a dangerous glint in his eyes.

Lorena snatched her dress back. "I don't want to be one of your *girls*. I just need to make enough money to get home."

"And where might that be, little lady? You sound like a Rebel to me."

Lorena froze.

The voice was steady and ominous. "You might be a little more courteous to such a lovely lady as this."

Lorena began to breathe again. It was the gambler. He had moved to the back of the bartender as stealthily as a shadow.

The gambler stepped between them, putting his back to the bartender and facing Lorena with a child-like, ingratiating half smile. "Excuse my friend's bad manners, Miss." He took off his hat, swept it across his chest, and gave Lorena a cavalier bow. "May I introduce myself, I am Preston Lord, Late of the Confederate Army, and the great State of Mississippi." He kept the cheroot in his mouth while he talked, to keep his hands free, and the cigar wagged up and down with his words.

Preston then turned, glared and tapped his finger on the bartender's chest. "An' this is the owner of this here establishment. He has a very big chest in order to house the biggest heart on the Mississippi River. An' just to show you how big his heart is, he was just about to offer you employment." He smiled at the bartender, his black eyes glinting venomously again. "Weren't you?"

The bartender glanced down at the slow, deliberate movement of Preston's hand under his coat. Men stopped talking and stared at the unfolding drama.

"Who? Me?" Small beads of sweat popped out on the bartender's brow. "Oh, ah, yes," he said, absently brushing back his thinning hair, "we could use someone to mop and sweep up the sawdust, every noon and night." He looked around the saloon. "And wash the glasses—

Preston's hand tightened on the handle and he lifted his derringer an inch out of its holster. His eyes squinted from the smoke coming up from the cigar. "Now we don't want to tire the lady too much, do we?"

The bartender's eyes darted back to Preston's hand. "No, I guess she won't have to mop." He turned to Lorena. "You can start today. Fifty cents a day."

Preston's face hardened and the bartender blanched. "No? What the hell, make it a dollar."

Preston nodded, his features still hard.

"An... an... and your meals," the bartender stuttered, and looked entreatingly at Preston. By now the silence in the saloon was again complete, with all eyes on the gambler, the lady and the bartender.

Preston smiled and relaxed his face.

The bartender breathed a sigh of relief and quickly retreated back to the bar. A buzzing started in the saloon and the men began to laugh and drink again.

"You can start on the glasses back here," the bartender said over his shoulder as he moved quickly behind the relative safety of the counter.

"Hey, Preston," came a shout from the table, "you gonna play or fool with the lady?" There were loud guffaws from the others.

Preston turned his head toward them, hesitated, took the cheroot from his mouth and grinned. "Hold your horses," he yelled back good-naturedly, "I'll be there in a minute." He turned back to Lorena, his eyes placid and his manner soft. "Don't pay them any mind, Miss. They are as harsh as the land they work on, but they mean well." He nodded his head toward a group of soldiers in gray uniforms. "I'd stay away from the graybacks though. They're mean as snakes, an' aptly named after the close resemblance they have to the lice we had to pick off our bodies in the field."

Lorena grimaced, remembering how close she came to being a prisoner.

"You go on and do what the barkeep asks," Preston said. He pointed a finger around the saloon. "These men drink hard and get quarrelsome but I'll be here to make sure no one gets rough with you."

Lorena immediately felt close to the stranger. His accent was familiar and comfortable, like someone from home. "I don't know what to say. How can I ever thank you?" Her eyes moistened.

Preston colored. "Now, now, we'll have none of that. But, I would like to know your name."

"Lorena, Lorena Oakwood."

"Dammit, Lord, you coming?"

Preston bowed slightly. "Duty calls, and I must

go. But I will be watching over you." The gambler took Lorena's hand, turned it over and kissed it gently.

There was more laughter from the men at the table.

Lorena's face got red, and her heart fluttered, but she managed a small smile.

Preston went back to the table, sat down, picked up his cigar and blew a cloud of smoke into the air. He clamped the cheroot in his teeth, smiled at his three compatriots and shuffled the deck. He looked back at Lorena and said, "My deal, gentlemen."

As he dealt the cards, he began to cough. Lorena cringed as she saw Preston drop the deck, get up from the table, and cough his way out the front door to the fresh air outside.

Lorena followed him.

The large white handkerchief he put over his mouth could not block the distress on his ashen face. Lorena held the door open looking helplessly at Preston, bent over, his body racking with each cough. She could not help but notice that with each cough the handkerchief turned more scarlet.

Chapter 17

𝔉or Lorena, the time moved slowly. Amid the chaos in the saloon she noticed that many times during the evening one of the women would take a man by the hand and go up the stairs to one of the rooms on the second floor. She felt embarrassed for the women.

At first the men saw something special in Lorena and respected her. After the whisky took effect they relaxed their standards and some of them reached out to touch her as she wiped the tables and collected the glasses. She would cringe and push their hands away, but as time passed some of the drunks became more brazen.

Preston watched Lorena while he played his cards. When the men began to get the better of her, suddenly and quietly he was among them. Whispering something into an offending man's ear, the man would suddenly sober. He then immediately apologized to Lorena or simply turned away. Soon she found she was almost free of harassment.

Lorena smiled often at Preston, and each time he would nod and touch the brim of his hat in response.

I appreciate his help, but I have to learn to rely on myself more. He won't always be around.

Lorena was wiping a table when an officer in a blue uniform sat down hard opposite her. She looked up right into his eyes, saw terrible pain and took a step back, shaken.

"You!" He barked at her. "Get me a drink." His body weaved drunkenly.

"It ain't my fault," he muttered to no one in particular, "It's Stanton. He wants to starve those people, not me."

"Huh?" Lorena said, then recovered. "Yes, sir, I'll get one of the girls to help you right away," and she left quickly.

After she got one of the waitresses to tend to the drunken officer, Lorena watched him raise the glass of whisky to his lips and put it down empty. He did that three more times in the span of two minutes. Lorena watched his eyes. They were burning as if he had a high fever, and were shadowed as if in persistent pain.

Lorena waited until Preston got up to go outside for a breath of fresh air and she joined him.

Even outside Bucktown was uneasy. Sounds

from many throats noisily filled the air and an occasional burst of gunfire punctuated the night.

A thin grayback, with a face made sallow by drink and the meager light from the saloon walked by, opened the door and staggered into the tavern. Following him into the saloon was a scruffy looking girl half his age. "Wait, sojer," she slurred, "I want a drink too."

Lorena's eyes were fixed on the girl following the soldier into the saloon. When the door closed Lorena exclaimed indignantly, "Why she's barely more than a child! Where are the authorities that can stop this sort of thing?"

Preston laughed. "Authorities? In Bucktown? Hah! Some poor souls *think* they're in charge around here. But you have to know by now that the Devil runs things in Bucktown."

"I can see that," Lorena said, an edge in her voice.

Preston smiled. "How is your first night goin'?" he asked politely. Then he saw the troubled look on Lorena's face. "What's wrong," he asked abruptly, is someone botherin' you?"

"No, no one's bothering me, but... if it's true that the eyes of a man are the window to his soul, then I have just seen a tormented soul at the bottom pit of Hell."

Preston eyed his cigar. "Oh, which soul is that?" he asked, indifferently.

Lorena opened the door and pointed to the

officer she had just left. "The terrible look in that man's eyes frightened me."

Preston followed her finger and nodded his head knowingly. "That's Colonel Andrew Johnson, same name as the Yankee Vice President. He's the Commandant of the prisoner of War camp in Rock Island and, I think, a decent chap."

Lorena watched the colonel drain another glass of whisky. "If he's a decent man then why does he look like that?"

"Maybe 'cause he's been given an impossible task."

Lorena shrugged her shoulders. "Why does he drink so heavily?"

Preston took a big drag on his cigar and pulled it down into his scarred lungs, then expelled the smoke into the dark. "Ever hear of Andersonville?"

Lorena shook her head and said, "No."

"It's a prison camp near Americus, deep in the heart of Georgia. The few men who have escaped from there tell a tale of abuse and starvation beyond description. They say hundreds, maybe thousands, are dyin' there monthly." The anger inside Preston crept into his face. "I saw some of the prisoners who came back from there. They were gaunt, lank skeletons that defy description. Their flesh had yellowed and their joints were swollen by exposure. Bluish lips and feverish eyes deep set and blackened with hunger. And worst of all, that fleetin', piteous, scared smile. No man who has ever witnessed one of those men will ever forget him." Preston stared into space for a few moments.

"I was told that most of the men that got out were in such poor condition from slow starvation, they soon died, swiftly and silently, unable to combat the blood poison and eventually the lung disease that attacked their ravaged bodies."

"Starvation? It can't be! Lorena exclaimed. "I've been to Americus. I know the people who live there. There are farms and food aplenty. The Georgians are a hospitable people. They wouldn't let a dog starve, much less a man, even if that man is a Yankee."

Preston's face turned dark and he scowled, his brows almost meeting. "The soldiers who have come back say the Commandant at Andersonville is a Swiss named Wirtz, not a southerner. They also say he's a beast. He has a wounded arm that won't heal and leaves him in great pain. Because of that, to get even I suppose, he crowds thousands of soldiers together in a space made for hundreds, and give so little food to the men that, when it's thrown to them, they fight for it like caged animals. Of course the food is taken by the strong. The weak and timid are left to die. I've also been told that the guards have a demarcation line near the wall called the deadline. If you step over it the guards shoot to kill. No questions asked, no reasons given." Preston's face turned hard. "I've heard that many men have stepped over the deadline just to get out of their misery."

Preston shook his head sadly. "Some day the South will pay dearly for Andersonville."

"My God! I can't believe it," Lorena gasped. "But what's that to do with Colonel Johnson?"

Preston grimaced. "The Yankee Secretary of War, Stanton, in his infinite wisdom, has put the Southern prisoners on a starvation diet right here in Rock Island. Of course that's retaliation for the despicable conditions at Andersonville. The colonel has to enforce it, and it's killin' him. As I said, he's a decent man."

A head popped out the door and said, "Hey, Lord, you coming back?"

Preston nodded, turned to Lorena and bowed slightly.

Lorena watched Preston's back as he opened the door then she followed him into the saloon, shaking her head in disbelief at what she had just heard. As she passed the drunken colonel Johnson, she saw him staring at the bottom of his empty glass. Lorena felt great compassion for the man.

As the evening wore on many of the men got roaring drunk and began touching Lorena again. Even Preston was not able to completely stop their pawing of her. Later in the evening she was totally exhausted by the work, and the brazen feeling of her body by the more aggressive men.

At the height of the ribaldry, the bartender called to her from behind the bar. She came to him and he slapped a glass full of whiskey on a metal tray spilling a third of it. "Bring this drink over to that soldier boy there," he said smiling crudely, "the other girls are busy."

As she turned to deliver the drink he laughed in that high pitched grating sound, "And get a quarter from him."

Lorena took the tray and looked for the soldier. One of the men in a gray uniform stood up and waved at her.

As she approached the table, she was immediately repulsed. The man had a large thatch of unruly brown hair and a straggly beard to match. His hair reminded Lorena of the sergeant on the train. His uniform jacket was stained and dirty, his nose was hooked, and his eyes were beady and too close together.

Thank God I didn't get put in his prison.

When she put the drink down on the table, she could smell the unwashed bodies of the men at the table. The hooked nosed man sat down, leaned forward and stared at Lorena.

She backed up a step. "That'll be a quarter, Mister.

He dropped two quarters on the table and smiled with brown stained teeth. "They's lots more where that came from Missy." He looked at the other graybacks at the table and they all laughed.

Lorena squared herself with her hands on her hips as if ready to do battle. The men at the table stopped laughing and Lorena bent over and reached for the coin.

Hooknose grabbed her hand and said, "Why don't you set with us a spell?" His eyes were locked on her like a steely-eyed cat with a slow swishy tail.

Lorena tried to jerk her hand back but the soldier held on to it tightly. She looked into his eyes and saw the look of the sergeant on the train. Her heart began to race. She glanced at Preston but he was looking away, involved in an arm-waving argument with one of the other gamblers.

Her fear gave her strength. "I'm not one of the house girls," she said as she broke free and turned away.

But another laughing grayback grabbed her, and propelled her back toward Hook Nose. He caught her around the waist, and pulled her close to him. She leaned back and tried to break free again but this time he held her securely. He was so near she could smell the whiskey on his breath. He smiled and she saw rotted teeth and smelled a fetid breath. She struggled to get away.

"House girl or no," he said, "makes no never

mind to me. C'mon, little lady, let's me n' you make a little lovin'"

A flash of anger came over Lorena, and she felt the fury of a thousand years of Irish fighters come over her. It was the same rage coursing through her that drove her ancestors to war and murder. She stopped struggling, raised her leg and drove it down on the toes of his foot with her boot.

Hook Nose screamed, released her and grabbed for his injured foot. Enraged, the grayback snarled at Lorena and lunged up at her.

Lorena took a step back, brought the tray over her head and then swung it at the foul man with all her strength striking him full in the face. On the way down, he hit the table, breaking three of its legs as he fell to the floor, unconscious. At first soldiers at the table were stunned and moved back. Then they recovered and began laughing at their fallen mate.

Lorena looked down at the unconscious man, held her skirt up and daintily stepped over him. Then she reached down, picked the two quarters off the floor, put both fists on her hips and spat on him. Holding her head up, she walked back to the bar to an increasing crescendo of applause.

His mates picked him up and carried him out the front door, while at his table, Preston leaned back, tipped his hat back further on his head and laughed until tears rolled down his cheeks.

Lorena

****

At three o'clock in the morning the last of the drunkards was thrown in jail by the sheriff's deputy. The bartender came from behind the bar and yelled, "Everyone out! Closing time!"

Slowly, reluctantly, the beer hall began to empty.

Two men walked over to the bartender and began speaking to him in low whispers. In a few moments the whispers got louder until all concerned were arguing loudly.

"A twenty dollar gold piece just to stay the night?" said one.

"We don't want to buy the girls, just use 'em fer a while," said the other.

"Take it or leave it, Gents." The bartender turned away.

They looked at each other, sullenly paid the price and were taken upstairs by two of the amused women.

In a few minutes, while Lorena swept the hall upstairs, she heard deep snoring. She smiled imagining the men sleeping peacefully with the women dutifully at their sides. Lorena's tolerance level had been raised considerably.

Within a half hour, the last of the customers and girls staggered out the door. Only the bartender, Lorena, and Preston remained.

When she finished sweeping, Lorena

approached the bartender. "Mister," she said hesitantly looking up at the second floor, "where can I sleep?"

"Sleep?" he said, perplexed. "You can't sleep here. The whores got all the rooms. Ain't you got no place to stay?"

"Of course she does." Preston held out his arm for Lorena to take. "An' I'll make sure she gets there."

"Wait." The bartender stepped from behind the bar looking sheepish. He absently brushed back the remnants of his slicked back hair, and handed Lorena a silver dollar. "Miss, you did a good job tonight. I'm really glad to have you."

"Thank you, sir," Lorena said, carefully putting the coin in her pocket, "I'll be back tomorrow."

"Be here by three o'clock," the bartender said, raising his voice to Lorena and Preston as they walked out the door into the night.

The evening was cool and the breeze refreshed Lorena's damp skin. She wanted to protest his taking her to wherever it was, but was too tired to object, and just stumbled along beside him half asleep, desperately trying to keep up with his long stride. Finally her modesty overtook her exhaustion.

"Listen, Mr. Lord, I'm not like those women at the saloon. I appreciate what you've done, but—"

Preston stopped. The moon's reflection twinkled in his eyes as he looked at Lorena gravely and bowed slightly. "Ma'am, you're obviously a lady in strained circumstances, but I assure you that you are as safe with me as you would be with your own mother. An' please, call me Preston."

A relieved Lorena, wanting to believe him, breathed a great sigh and continued walking.

They walked up the long hill, past the stores, turned down a dirt road and stopped at a sprawling wooden home at the end of the street. They went around the building and Preston stopped at a side door. He opened it and held it for Lorena. She tensed and hesitated.

Preston smiled reassuringly. "I rent this room from the widow Morgan. You will take my bed tonight."

Lorena's brow furrowed with concern. "But where will you sleep?"

He pointed to an open door at the rear of the room. "Have no concern, dear lady," he said in his rich baritone voice, "I have a favorite couch in yon livin' room that will welcome me, as it does sometimes when I am gone for a while, and Mrs. Morgan rents my bed."

Lorena entered the room and Preston followed.

"But Mrs. Morgan—" Lorena protested.

Preston interrupted. "She is away, visitin' her daughter and her gold-seeking son-in-law in California." Preston laughed. "He hasn't found any gold yet, but it does keep him out of the army."

He bent over, struck a match and lit a candle.

Then he took her hand, held it for a moment and squeezed it gently.

"An' now I pray you will make yourself at home, and I bid you goodnight." He brushed his lips on the back of her hand and, like an elusive shadow, slipped through the door and was gone.

Lorena looked around the room and almost wept with joy and relief. It was clean and neat, and the large bed looked wonderfully comfortable.

Thank you God. I have a decent place to sleep and a man to protect me.

Lorena leaned against the door and absently latched it. She blew out the candle and when her eyes adjusted to the dark, saw the outline of the bed in the moonlight coming through the window and went to it. Without removing her clothes or the cover, she fell on the bed and slipped into a nightmarish, General Sherman filled sleep.

Many times during the night, she woke to the sound of Preston coughing somewhere in the dark.

The last bright flame of a beautiful old life

Chapter 18

$\mathfrak{L}$orena soon hardened to her new life. She learned to avoid the playful touches of the loafers and soldiers, and Preston was always there to stop the more aggressive river men.

One night, a few days after she began, Lorena finished her chores, said goodnight, and stepped through the outside door.

Preston leaned against the edge of a building across the street rubbing the two-day old stubble on his chin. When he saw her, he quickly stood straight, bowed with a nod of his head and touched his fingers to the brim of his hat.

As always, the moment Lorena saw him her breath came hard, her heart fluttered, and she forgot how tired she was.

A warm breeze coming down the main street rustled the trees as they bent gently under the draft.

Preston crossed the street offered his arm, and

Lorena slipped her arm in his. In sweet communion they silently began the long walk home.

During their walk up the long hill each night, the harsh world fell away and Lorena felt as if she and Preston were the only people alive. She walked slowly, stretching out their time together, pretending they were back in the midst of the slow charm of a time gone by. *Our moments together seem like the last bright flame of the beautiful old life that is ending.*

Feeling Preston's arm against her breast, evoked emotions never felt before. She tried to push the feelings away.

Lorena thought back on her marriage. She married young, as was the custom, and soon found her husband was not a warm man. The few times they had been intimate he was perfunctory and, when his lust was satisfied, immediately left for his own room leaving his bewildered young wife in tears.

In Washington, and later Richmond, the men in high places she dealt with were close to Lorena, but only on an intellectual level. Never had she, from any man, felt the kind of warmth Preston gave her. Lorena's womanhood came alive.

Ever since I met him all my senses are awake. I touch an object and feel its smoothness or every bump that makes it rough. I can hear even a butterfly's wings, while I taste the sweetness in life's wine. I can smell the forest and its flowers, even inside my room. And the sunsets, ah the sunsets. Each time the sun goes down I now see God's miracle one more time.

Lorena relished the new thoughts and feelings.

Her heart was full, but Lorena wouldn't speak of these things because her feelings were confusing her, and confused thoughts could not shape themselves into words.

Oh, Preston, what have I been doing with my wasteful life, cavorting among silly and futile people. From the day I married John he showed no emotion, so I buried my love. But now Preston has discovered me, and he mines that rich vein of feelings that has long been buried inside me. Perhaps when he has mined it all I shall be free.

The silence between them was eloquent, but she had to speak if only to quiet her heart.

She turned her head to look at him, the clean lines of his profile visible in the dark by the moon's reflection. "Preston, do you think the South will ever right itself again?"

Preston gave her a smile of infinite patience. "If you mean by that, will the South ever be as it was before the war?" He compressed his lips and shook his head slowly. "No, the War Between the States is, as the Bard said, 'a tale told by idiots, full of sound and fury, signifyin' nothin'.' The South we knew, of charm, and culture, and quiet hearts, is dead.

"I fit really well in that South before, but like most of our people I will not be able to live easily in the new South. Many of our people will be have difficulty fendin' for themselves without slaves to do their menial chores. Men and women who before lived for ridin' an' shootin', an' balls an' beaus, will be forced to go into commerce for which they are ill suited.

"Slavery is dead also. Good thing too. White people live in constant fear of their slaves. That peculiar institution was like holding a rabid wolf by the ears.

"You know that only one in a hundred of the poor farmers that make up the troops of the Rebel army even owned a slave. They didn't have a personal stake in the war an' they couldn't get any gain in a victory.

"The only people that substantially benefited from holdin' Africans in bondage were the large plantation owners. Since the price for cotton was so high, they wouldn't listen to the agricultural colleges and rotate crops to replenish the soil. So, the only way to keep the profits coming was to buy more land, keep replantin' cotton, and purchase more slaves, who, by the way, got no wages, and who begat baby slaves who also grew up to work the cotton fields."

Lorena nodded, trying to understand. She thought of Ravetta and her children and a small shudder went through her.

"Our only hope is that the firebrands who started this foolish war will die off quickly and let the moderates, like Secretary of War Breckinridge, take over. President Davis is too much of a fanatic."

"But we have such brave men and fine generals—"

Preston laughed. "Yes, and we have thoughtless young men, blackened by the sun, so thin with hunger that their facial bones look like they will break through the skin, who are totally reckless with their lives. An' they are led by generals who think only of *the cause,* and their *own* glory. Meanwhile a barrel of flour in Richmond is one hundred Confederate dollars, an' sugar is three dollars a pound. You know the Yankees have foundries by the dozen an' unlimited manpower, and as Napoleon said, 'Victory goes to those with the largest Battalions.'"

Pictures of the horrid day at the hospital and Mr. Buchanan flashed through Lorena's mind.

"But we have cotton," she argued.

"Yes, we do." He pointed down to the river. "An' the cotton lays on the decks of Southern ships, an' on the wharfs in New Orleans, going nowhere. The English were our best customers, but when the war began they stored up on cotton. They are masters at blockade and knew what the North would do. An' when they need more cotton, they forsook the South and turned to Egypt.

"Instead of us makin' our own things from cotton, we depend on others to manufacture dresses and other clothing. Now that England won't buy our precious bales, they stay on the Southern wharves rottin' unless one of our patriotic plantation owners can secretly sell it to some Yankee trader."

"But we have mines," Lorena protested, "and iron to make guns. I know. I used to be a secretary at a gun factory."

Preston laughed softly. "Yes, we have mines, and lots of iron ore in Georgia and Alabama, but the men who work the mines are conscripted into the Rebel army. The Confederate government asked for slaves to work the mines, but the plantation owners won't give them up. So we don't make much cannon and we manufacture few guns. Therefore we have to get our weapons from England an' France. That means sending them what cotton we can get out of our only free port in South Carolina in payment. But the Yankees are smart. They let the cotton go out, but they intercept the guns comin' back in from our European trade port in Bermuda.

"The Confederate government banked on the hope that England would intervene and act as a mediator in the Civil War. But before the war her seamen were given twenty dollars for every slave they freed, no questions asked. When Lincoln outlawed slavery with the Emancipation Proclamation, the English *had* to side with the North."

"I see," Lorena said sadly. "Then it's really all over."

Preston's hands balled into fists and his eyes narrowed. "All over but the killin'. Generals Lee, and Breckinridge, Secretary Stephens, and even that toady, Hunter, *want* to end the war. But President Davis, with Judah Benjamin whisperin' in his ear like Iago to Othello, keeps the armies fightin', hopin' for a miracle. And so we lose thousands more brave souls each week. When the war is finally over the Yankees will have killed off most of our farmers. Who, in God's name, do our leaders think will feed us then?"

He shook his head and grimaced. "Poor General Lee. His intellect tells him his army is beaten. But his mind is at odds with his heart, which cannot countenance defeat. He has pulled rabbits out of his hat so often we think he can do it again and again. I guess he thinks so too.

"Time will soften our feelin's and experience will show the folly of our misguided comrades who fought against their own best interests. When I realized all of this, it was then that I thought it best that we be defeated."

Lorena could think of nothing more to say and she and Preston walked up the rest of the hill in silence.

When they reached the door to Preston's part of the house, he opened it and Lorena stepped inside. He followed her in and stood by the door to the living room while Lorena lit a candle. Flickering shadows danced around them on the wall. She walked to Preston and put her hand in his. "Thank you for waiting for me. It makes me feel safe being with you." Lorena could not hide her feelings. Her heart was in her eyes.

Preston turned her hand over and brushed his lips against the back of it. He raised his head up, his black eyes sparkling pools of light and intelligence.

He hesitated for a moment then said, "Goodnight, dear Lorena—"

Impetuously, she interrupted. "Won't you stay for some tea?"

For a moment there was indecision on his face, then he smiled. "Of course."

In a few minutes the fireplace was blazing and Lorena put on a pot of water to boil.

Lorena stood by the fire musing. *I wonder what draws me to him. There's an air about him, a certain strength, and kindness, and intimacy....*

While the tea was brewing they began to talk. They lost track of time as they spoke on many things, some previously forbidden to Lorena by other men.

"You amaze me, Lorena. I can't believe the depth of your knowledge."

Lorena smiled inwardly remembering the countless joyful hours in grandfather's library, absorbing the knowledge of the sages. *And Balzac.*

Preston smiled and took her hand in his. Lorena blushed and looked down. *For the first time in my life a man is listening to me, really listening. And I don't have to live up to someone else's expectations. I can be myself. I realize now I never spoke to John Oakwood, not really. I didn't live with him. We lived around each other. John and his entire family always looking for the image, never the reality.*

Finally, daylight crept through the windows. Shards of light appeared on the walls. Preston stood up, pulled back the curtain and blinked at the bright sunshine. "I guess the night has passed." He turned to Lorena and smiled his boyish smile. "Maybe we better get a few hours of sleep."

She laughed. "It's almost time to go to work again."

Preston bid her goodnight and slipped into the other room.

Lorena felt let down after he left. Each moment with Preston seemed more exciting than the last. Each day she looked forward to seeing him, talking to him, touching him.

Lorena, you're acting like a schoolgirl. Remember, you're a married woman with two children. But I fear myself when I am near him. It's like I am half a person away, but when he's with me he makes me whole. Dare I admit that for the first time in my life I'm in love?

****

Every night Lorena put her dollar in a jar and placed it under the bed. Soon she would have enough to get back home to Atlanta.

Atlanta. It seems like another world, another lifetime. I am past anguish about my children? I wonder if John is all right? I know I should telegraph and tell them I'm alive? But where would I send it. God knows where John is, or what's happened to Ravetta. She cringed when she thought about her children being forced to live on the street with Ravetta.

Maybe if I could find out where General Hood's headquarters are. But something held her back. There was something about her liberty away from John. For the first time in her life, she felt free. Her father sheltered and smothered her as a girl, then handed her off to John Oakwood. He suffocated her even more. Preston was liberating.

Ah Preston! There's something about him, something different I feel from him. He gives me something I've never experienced before.

Before the morning light came, Lorena fell asleep dreaming about sitting with Preston on a desert Island near tables laden with forbidden fruits.

War is cruelty and you cannot refine it
-—Sherman

Chapter 19

From the private journal of Lorena Boykins Oakwood

October 1st, 1864

In the midst of all my misfortune it seems that God smiles upon me. I have met a most wonderful, kind, and literate man. He reminds me of my father in looks, but there the resemblance ends.

In the case of my husband, I know no more about the inner thoughts of John Oakwood's mind and heart than the day I married him. With Preston, I am

frank and free, and in just a few short
weeks I know so much about him.

He opens his mind to me and shares his
heart with abandon. Every day I look
forward to being with him. He assuages
my loneliness, and protects me from the
trials of life.

I fear I have very mixed emotions about
him. I am a matron, and should be
ashamed of myself for having these
feelings. But, the truth be known, when I
am with him, for the first time in my life
I feel truly alive. There is no cure for
what I feel. And worse, there is no relief.

Alas, poor, dear Preston is ill with the
soldier's cough. But even that frailty
seems make him more vulnerable, and
therefore more desirable.

I must stop this foolishness and
remember that I am a married woman
with children. Still....

****

Twilight came and with it a quieting of the earth. There was a great pause that comes to all things at dusk. For a few moments, before it dropped over the horizon, the sun hesitated in the sky, as if to look over the good work it had done that day and bid the earth goodnight.

As the large red orb slipped down through the pink cirrus clouds out of sight, a breeze came up, and the tops of the pines bowed as if in deference to the wind. Night crept over the land making the earth darker and the autumn colored leaves at the foot of trees, for a moment, seem brighter. The air carried a hint of the scent of winter, and birds, black against the darkening clouds, glided home on the cool landward draft off the Mississippi River.

In the disappearing light, Lorena and Preston made their accustomed way down the dusty street towards the cottage from a picnic in a park near the river. He walked easily beside her; a folded newspaper tucked under his free arm.

Lorena now felt easy at her work, and even had moments when she thought of things other than survival. As the day turned into night, she felt more alive than she had been for a long while, but she also felt a strange sadness from Preston.

"What a wonderful day for a picnic. I'm so glad we spent the day together. I haven't been on an outing since, I can't remember when."

Preston smiled fleetingly. "Yes, I had to nudge the bartender a bit but he soon saw the light."

They both laughed.

Lorena stole a glance at Preston. His eyes always ready to twinkle were shadowed. His tongue usually so eloquent and jovial was silent. He seemed remote and responded slowly to any inquiry.

"Is something wrong, Preston?"

He looked at her with a mixture of concern and surprise on his face. "No, dear Lady, why do you ask?"

"No reason." She turned to him. "You seem sad."

Preston stiffened and Lorena thought it best not to dig any deeper, but her heart picked up his sorrow and held it. She had grown so fond of the tall, handsome Mississippian she could feel his moods. *Maybe he's worried about his health.*

"Lorena," Preston said softly, "I saw somethin' in the newspaper I think you ought to see." He handed Lorena the folded paper. It's several weeks old.

The inkling that something was wrong now turned into full-blown fear. Her heart sunk and her hands trembled as she took the daily. Lorena slowly opened the paper and looked at the headline. Her blood ran cold. The bold print screamed up at her.

3 cents daily

The New York Herald
November 27, 1864. Atlanta, Georgia

Sherman takes Atlanta

FORCES EVERYONE TO LEAVE.
General Sherman speaks out on the war.

By David Conyngham

DIRECT FROM THE BATTLEFIELD, THE LATEST WORD FROM GENERAL SHERMAN:

"War is cruelty and you cannot refine it, and those who brought war into our country deserve all of the curses and maledictions a people can pour out... You might as well appeal against a thunderstorm as against these terrible hardships of war...

"I have made all civilians leave Atlanta and have burned all buildings that, in my opinion, contribute to the continuing the war...."

Lorena felt faint. She closed her eyes and began to sway.

Preston was suddenly by her side and grasped her elbow.

She patted his arm. "It's all right, let me finish. She looked down at the paper and continued to read:

> "... The hardships are inevitable, and the only way
> the people of Atlanta can hope to once more live in
> peace and quiet at home is to stop the war, which can
> alone be done by admitting that it began in error and
> is perpetuated in pride."

Lorena found herself sobbing uncontrollably in
Preston's arms. "Oh Preston, what will happen to
me, to us, to my family? My children may be
wandering the countryside, homeless."

Preston's face was dark with anger. "Those
damnable Yankees. This article makes me want
to take up arms against them again."

When Lorena finally stopped crying she stared
into space, her heart and mind in a jumble of
thoughts and feelings.

"Preston, I have to get back to Atlanta, and
soon."

"We'll figure a way, Lorena."

A great sadness enveloped them both as they
continued toward the cottage. Suddenly a
shooting star blazed across the sky and
disappeared. Almost in a whisper, Preston said,
"Look up there." He pointed to the sky and
Lorena followed his finger above the setting sun
to a bright light in the heavens.

"That's the North Star. It's a beacon for all the
navigators on the ocean because it never varies
its position." He looked at her and smiled softly.
"It would be good if you chose that star too. It's

always been my guide. An' when I die I pray I will go there for all eternity." He took her hand and kissed it. "I know I haven't much longer on this earth—"

"Preston—"

He held up the palm of one hand and she stopped in mid-sentence.

"And when that day comes that you leave this veil of tears, I would like you to join me there. We'll be two stars in the same constellation, forever." Preston's face took on a melancholy look and his eyes glistened.

He took both her hands in his and faced her. "Dearest Lorena, I know, after all, you must leave me and go back to Atlanta."

Lorena felt her face get warm and her heart opened to him like the petals of a flower. At that moment she was his, and Lorena knew she would give herself to him fully, without reservation.

There was a long silence as they both regained their composure. In a few moments they began to walk again. To dispel the sadness, Lorena began to hum.

That's a pretty melody," Preston said, "I don't think I've ever heard it before."

Lorena laughed. "It's a song about me. It's called *Lorena*. She began to sing in a soft, breathy voice:

The years creep slowly by, Lorena,
  The snow is on the grass again;

Three Came Home

The sun's low in the sky, Lorena;
* And frost gleams where flowers have been*
But the heart throbs on as warmly now
* As when the summer days were nigh;*

A hundred months have passed, Lorena
* Since last I held thy hand in mine*
And felt your pulse beat fast, Lorena
* Though mine beats faster than thine,*
A hundred months— 'twas flowery May,
* When up the hilly slope we climb,*
To watch the dying of the day
* And hear the distant church bells chime.*
We loved each other then, Lorena
* More than we ever dared tell.*

After the song was done they both fell deeply in their own thoughts. Finally Preston spoke. "That's was just beautiful, Lorena. Thank you.

Again there was silence. Suddenly Preston stopped and took Lorena by the shoulders and looked into her eyes visible by the moonlight.

"Lorena, I can tell you are a woman of quality, but—" Preston searched for the right words. "How did you get here? Why were you penniless? Are you runnin' away from somethin'? Who are you, Lorena Oakwood? Lorena, I care deeply about you. Please tell me what brought you here."

Lorena looked at the ground to gather her thoughts. She felt close to Preston and it was easy for her to talk to him but, although she didn't want to hurt him, she had to tell the truth.

"I am the wife of General John Oakwood, of Hood's Army of Tennessee. I have two children—"

She saw Preston start and pain come into his eyes.

—a girl and a boy." She moved away and stared into the darkness, her eyes glistening.

Preston moved to her side.

"I was leaving my work at the Atlanta Foundry Works, during the battle of Atlanta, when I had a most unfortunate incident. I ran into General Sherman in a foul mood. When he found out I worked for the Confederate cause, in the foundry, he got very angry and put me on a train heading north to Canada. I was not allowed to take any extra clothing, and no money. And I was to make my way back without assistance."

Preston clenched his fists. "What?" He thought for a few moments and then muttered under his breath, "The bastard."

"While we were going north in the prison train another general came aboard and countermanded General Sherman's order. He instructed my guard to bring me here to the Rock Island prison camp, to serve the Confederate prisoners.

"My God!" Preston exclaimed.

"It gets worse. On our way to the prison, the guard on the train attacked me. I was fortunate to get the best of him and, with a little luck,

killed him with his own bayonet." Beads of
perspiration popped out on Lorena's forehead and
she began to shake, reliving the experience in her
mind.

Preston clenched his fists and stared at
Lorena. There was a new respect in his eyes.

She dabbed at her brow with a handkerchief,
and nodded her head sadly. "It's all true, every
word of it."

He shook his head slowly, gently took her hand,
and they began to walk again.

"I jumped off the train and ran as far and as fast
as I could. A farmer and his wife took me in and
eventually brought me here. You know the rest.

"The bastard," Preston repeated. He stopped, let
go of her hand and turned to her, his eyes flashing
with anger. "An' I thought I was through hatin'
Yankees."

"I don't want to hate anyone, Preston, I just
want to get back home."

Preston raised his head. "And you shall, dear
Lorena, you shall." He took her arm in his own and
patted her hand reassuringly.

When they reached the front of the house Lorena
walked up the three stairs to the porch. "And now I want
to hear all about you, Preston. Let's sit down here."

Lorena sat down on the top step. Preston sat
down one step beneath her, leaned back on one
elbow and crossed his legs.

After a few moments he leaned forward, put

his arms around his knees and rocked a few times.

Lorena smoothed her dress and put her hands in her lap. She listened to the crickets' sing their night song while she waited for Preston to speak.

"Well you know my name, but not all of it. My full title is, Preston, Beauregard, Harrison, Lord. You know I am from Mississippi, but more accurately, Pascagoula. I'm a Southerner, born and bred, but I have a Yankee curiosity." He laughed. "At least that's what they tell me.

"My father had a ranch on the Pascagoula River, near the Gulf of Mexico, where we raised fine, blooded Arabian horses. I used to take them to New Orleans, and usually fetched a good price for them. After sellin' them I had a pocket full of money, so, before I went back home I always took a big bite of the city life, card playin' and, well, you know—"

Preston stopped rocking, stretched his arms back behind him and leaned on them. "Daddy didn't approve, but I loved the life I lived, horse racin' and gamblin' and such." His face reddened slightly. "I guess I was makin' a good job of bein' a bad guy. Anyway, when I got of age, I left the sandy beaches of the Gulf of Mexico, and went to the University of Mississippi for a few years, but life was too turbulent, and I was too lusty and willful to stay in a classroom." He laughed. "They almost kicked me out twice."

He shook his head ruefully and stared at the sky, watching the constellation Sirius chase Orion on its eternal quest, while he gathered his thoughts. Finally he spoke again.

"I was twenty years old when the war came. Me, an' all the boys at the University got war fever. My daddy could have got me out of the fight 'cause we were supplying horses for the Confederacy, an' we had mor'n twenty slaves, but could I sit ignobly by while others fought my battles for me? I thought not. So I joined up. In fact my entire class enlisted at the same time. The Confederate Army kept us together and named us the *Mississippi Rifles*. Each of us was practically born in the saddle an' thought we were heading for the cavalry. But the cavalry was full up so we became infantry. Still, not a one of us imagined we were in danger. We thought of splendor an' heroes, of trumpets an' glory. We thought of waving flags an' bloodless cavalry charges. We were fools.

"We missed the battle of Manassas an' were only afraid Generals Beauregard and Johnson would whip all the Yankees afore we could get a piece of the war." He laughed ruefully. "In fact we actually envied the men returning with crutches and empty sleeves." He shook his head slowly. "Later I found out that the war was like carrying around your own death certificate. Only the date was missin'.

"Me an' the other boys were put in with other Mississippi boys, the 20th Mississippi, Colonel Barkesdale's regiment. Because of my experience with horses, I was made head of cavalry in the regiment. Our job was to be the eyes and ears of the regiment. But we managed to get a few licks on the Union cavalry.

"With ol' Snow Top, Colonel Barkesdale, leadin' us, our infantry won the first few battles easily. My horsemen had the alertness and vigor of a people that spent our boyhood years in the saddle, while the Yanks were mostly city boys, so we rode circles around them early on." He shook his head. "But after Antietam, they seemed to get the hang of it and we began to face lots better horsemen."

Preston rubbed his shoulder absently. "Antietam! That was the place I was wounded the first time. I took a ball in my shoulder." He smiled ruefully. "That's where I learned about the gratin' sound when a ball hits bone and the thud when it strikes a softer part of the body."

Preston got thoughtful. "You know, we instruct men to do bloody work, never thinking that which we teach will return to plague the teacher."

He shook his head and returned to his narrative. "I was treated by the army doctors for a while but, unfortunately, I was left with a stiff arm. I couldn't load and shoot real well, so they sent me home to get better. While they was nursin' me at home, the Mississippi Confederate cavalry came to the ranch and confiscated all our horses, payin' Daddy with worthless Confederate script. That left us destitute. I got a rifle and tried to stop 'em but Daddy said to let 'em take the horses. 'It's better than lettin' the Yankees have 'em.'"

Preston put his hands back on his knees and began to rock again. He looked at Lorena and she smiled encouragingly.

"While I was healin' up I got a chance to ride around to our neighbors. Most of the farmers had gone into the army. But many, if not all, of the cotton planters were home, as well as their sons. It seems the planters got a law past that made every white man who had twenty slaves would be exempt from military duty less'n he had a mind to fight. The planters all had more than enough slaves for them an' their sons to be exempt. As the boys in my company used to say, 'It's a planter's war and a poor man's fight.'

Laughing sardonically, Preston said to Lorena, "I bet they's lots of young sprigs in Atlanta what got soft, safe jobs with the government an' is definitely not in the fightin'."

Lorena smiled sadly and nodded her head in the affirmative.

"Later, when Daddy went to work for the State Militia an' my shoulder healed up, I got restless and went to Tennessee to join up with Nathan

Bedford Forrest's cavalry." He shook his head. "When I got there it was April; it rained all the time. Forrest took us to a damned swamp, for our bivouac, to keep us away from the Yankee cavalry. Half the company was dead of sickness afore we got out of there. Preston clenched his fist, tapped his chest and said, his hidden anger showing through his eyes, "I got the cough at that place, I still ain't got rid of."

He shook his head and grimaced. "After a few months in the saddle the cough got me so bad, I had to go to a hospital in Richmond. I was there for so long they thought I was a shirker. When I got well enough so I could at least ride, Forrest was away in Tennessee, so I joined up with Jeb Stuart.

"It was a different army with Stuart. With Forrest it was all business. With Stuart there was fightin', but along with the fightin' there was fun and parties. Stuart had a banjo picker by the name of Sweeney who could pluck all day and dance all night. An' we did. Women and girls came from all over to Stuart's fancy balls. I don't know how he managed it, but his wife never said a thing about all them ladies fawnin' over him.

"General Lee treated Stuart like a prodigal son so he got away with a lot. But it all stopped when General Lee called us up for a march North. Lee reorganized the army into three corps, with Longstreet, Ewell, and Hill, each in charge of an army corps. He gave Ewell Jackson's ol' corps. That gave Ewell, with a size seven shoe, the job of filling the shoes of Jackson who wore a size fifteen."

Lorena touched Preston's hand and he patted hers absently.

"Anyway we staged outside Richmond, marched up through Maryland, where we were supposed to pick up volunteers, all the way to Pennsylvania. To General Lee's chagrin, only a few Maryland boys joined up.

"When we got to Pennsylvania, one of our Generals, named Heth, a relative of Lee's, heard there were shoes in a warehouse at a place called, Gettysburg. Since half of his troops were barefoot he headed there."

Lorena nodded her head knowingly.

"In the meantime Stuart stayed with Lee all the way through Maryland. As I said, Lee was expecting the Marylanders to volunteer for his army, but no one came. I think it broke Lee's heart but we got very few soldiers from Maryland.

"Stuart scouted for General Lee's Army of Northern Virginia all the way to Pennsylvania. Then Beauty, that was General Stuart's nick name, took us away from Lee's army. We went to skirmishin' and foragin' and rode completely around the Yankee army. We fought a few battles, captured lots of Bluebellies, and more'n a hundred and twenty five wagons with supplies. We had a grand time.

But, in the meantime General Lee stumbled into Gettysburg with no cavalry to guard his flanks or keep track of the new Yankee General, Meade."

Lorena saw Preston's face turn hard.

"When we finally got to Gettysburg, the battle had already started. The trouble was we were exhausted and had no fight in us when we got there. On top of that General Lee was so mad I saw him raise his arm and almost strike Stuart. No one had ever seen Lee lose his composure like that before. As I said before, it seems that when we rode around the Yankee army we left General Lee blind an' deaf. Without his cavalry he had no eyes nor ears to tell him where Meade's army was." Preston smiled wanly, and shook his head.

"Lee forgave him though an' immediately put Stuart to work guardin' the army's flanks. That was when they needed foot soldiers so bad Stuart dismounted me, along with a bunch of other men, and I wound up in Hood's corps, under Longstreet."

At the mention of Hood's name, Lorena felt her stomach tighten.

"As I said, we missed the first two days. On the third day we were placed in the line in front of a place called Devil's Den." Preston's voice lowered. "It was aptly named, after the owner who lived there."

Lorena noticed Preston's face had turned cold. There was a note of bitterness in his voice.

"Before we got there a great battle had been fought an' there was a dead man for every boulder in that damned place." Preston paused and was silent for a few moments.

"After that battle half the place was ours an', I was told, fairly won. I thought the rest would be easy, but was I wrong. That night I slept on my rifle in the den, and when I woke the Sergeant gave me new orders. I was to report to the Virginians under Pickett. I hated to leave those mortal men, with whom I had forged an immortal bond, but orders are orders.

" A few companies of us boys marched over to Pickett and we staged under some trees. Then we were told we were going to charge the Yankee line an' end the war. I almost gagged when I got a look at the ground we were supposed to charge over. At first, when they told us we were to take the high ground charging over a mile straight ahead, I thought they were jokin'. Yankee guns bristled at the top of that hill and it looked like a well nigh impossible job to me." He shook his head. "'Course I ain't no commander and I thought our generals knew what they were doin'.'"

"While we were waitin', the Yankees spotted us and let us have a taste of what they had in store for us. For a half hour they gave us the worst bombardment I ever saw. The shells tore through the trees and landed among us. It blew some of the boys to Kingdom Come right in front of me." Preston's eyes darkened with the memory.

"After a while, Lee ordered General Longstreet's artillery chief, Colonel Porter Alexander, to start his own bombin'. The noise was deafenin'. I thought for a while the earth would split open an' we'd all fall in. Union soldiers that live here in Illinois, an' were at Gettysburg, told me Porter fired too high and got only the cooks and teamsters in the rear. Later I heard he almost got General Meade with one of his shots."

"Too bad he didn't," Lorena said with feigned solemnity, and they both laughed.

"When Alexander stopped firin', General Picket cantered his horse along the line shouting, 'Up, men and to your posts. Don't forget today that you are from Old Virginia'. Inspired, we got into formation and started up that long hill with General Pickett just in back of us."

Lorena noticed Preston's voice dropped into a monotone, and he looked as if his mind was far away. "We were supposed to get to the top and break the Yankee line."

He smiled wanly and came back to the present. "God it was tough goin'. As I said, it was at least a mile an' uphill all the way. After fifty yards or so, I got to a head high fence with my squad and we started to climb over. When we got to the top, we were sittin' ducks for them. They picked us off...."

Preston got dreamy eyed and stopped speaking. For a long while he just stared into space. Then he smiled and shook his head.

"I was in battles before, but nuthin' like that one. Bullets were flyin' and people were fallin'. It was like, well, if you stuck your hat out you could catch a hatful of bullets. I ain't never seen anythin' like it, before nor since. I finally got over the fence and got to runnin' behind an officer. Later I was told his name was Armistead and that he was one of the best officers in the army.

He was so close to me I could see his fringe of gray close-cropped hair. Kind of old to be runnin' with us, I thought."

Preston shook his head. "Then he turned and I saw the flush of victory on his face. I remember it like it happened only an hour ago. He had his hat on the point of his sword holdin' it up to guide the men. While he was runnin' the point of his sword cut a hole through his hat and it slid halfway down. He was yellin' like a banshee over his shoulder, 'Over the hill is home, boys. Over that stone fence is your wife and family. Come on boys give them the cold steel.'

"He was racin' for a knee high stone wall at our front with me right behind him. We both reached the wall at the same time. I gave the Rebel Yell an' scrambled over the wall with several other men who made it. The Yankee front line buckled an' then gave way. They began to run. I thought we had 'em, but then I saw a large green Irish Flag being waved by a madman leading other Yanks runnin' up to take their place. Damn, now it seemed like the whole Yankee army was in front of us. I found out later we outnumbered them, but it didn't seem like it at the time. I guess the big difference was, they had cannons and began usin' 'em like shotguns on us, sprayin' canister right in our faces. The slaughter was awful. Canister makes men melt away."

Preston stopped speaking, absently put his hand in Lorena's and squeezed it. She did not pull away. A tear trickled down her face.

After a few moments, Preston began speaking again. "Armistead got to the first cannon before I did, put his hand on the barrel like he owned it and turned around to urge the men on. 'Soldier,' he shouted to me, 'we can't stay here, we have to get past that clump of trees—'Suddenly he staggered and fell to his knees. I saw a stain on his uniform where he'd been shot. I ran to him and tried to help him up. When I lifted him he shrieked and I quickly laid him back down. Then he groaned and asked me to carefully help him sit up."

Preston stopped and looked at Lorena his face full of pain.

"When he sat up, he reached into his breast

pocket an' pulled out a small black book. I looked into his eyes and they were at peace. 'If they capture you, give this to General Hancock—

"He was interrupted by *my* scream. I felt a white-hot streak of excruciating pain in my thigh an' I guess I must have passed out. Next thing I knew, a big fat Yankee doc was wantin' to take my leg off. I guess I yelled so much they let me be." Preston shook his head. "In the Yank hospital the docs tried to save me but I kept sinking.

"Death drew near to me an' in ghastly silence we stared into each other's eyes for several weeks. Then in one solitary instant death blinked an' gave up. Slowly I returned to life."

For a brief moment, Preston looked up at Sirius chasing Orion and then looked down and studied his shoes. "When I healed up enough they took me to this Rock Island prison camp. Between my cough an' my leg they figgered I was unfit even for prison duty so they gave me a parole and here I am, workin' along the Mississippi River, still tryin', but not too hard, to gamble my way back home, to Pascagoula."

They both laughed.

Preston's eyes got distant again. "We lost a lot of good men that day. In the prison camp the boys that were captured along with me tol' me that after the battle you could walk on the dead bodies from one end of the Gettysburg field to the other without steppin' on the ground. You know,

Lorena, citizens at home can never know one hundreth part of the misery brought on by this terrible rebellion."

Lorena could see, even by moonlight, Preston's deep-set eyes were full of sadness.

"After Gettysburg I knew I'd had enough. Wakin' up in serious pain every mornin' will do that to a man. It was that moment, I suppose, that the Army an' I parted company. A few day later the Yanks paroled me an' let me go 'cause of my wound. I knew the Confederacy was hard up for men an' would put me back in the army if I went home. But I'd had enough of killin' so I didn't go back South.

As Preston spoke excitedly he slipped more and more, back into the slurring brogue of a born Mississippian.

"I knowed a little about cards from my wild days, so I got on a Mississippi River boat an' started gamblin' fer a livin'."

He laughed. "One day the durn boat clobbered somethin' on the river and sank right opposite Bucktown." He laughed. "I figgered it was a sign, so here I am." He smiled that ingratiating half smile of his. "The folks up here didn't mind that I'm a Reb an' likewise. Sometimes I win a few hands and sometimes I don't." His voice lowered. "But at least I don't do no more killin'." He smiled and touched his gun. "Leastways I hadn't yet."

He turned full toward Lorena. "If all them

firebrands of secession coulda come up here and see what these Yankees have in manpower and factories along the Mississippi, just in Iowa and Illinois, they'd a never started this damned war." He paused. "We in the South are an agricultural society, but the Yanks have more agriculture than we ever dreamed about, an' so much more. They have lots of heavy industry. Foundries, shipyards, gold mines, silver mines, an' scads of land an' people. More people than we ever thought of. Even if it's true, that every Southerner is worth three Yankees, they have twenty men to our one. Even if they can't equal us, they'll just wear us down." He laughed a little too loudly, as if the truth he spoke was too absurd for his listener to comprehend.

"We got cotton an' slaves, but we can't sell the cotton. An' the slaves? Well the slaves have no loyalty to us. Except for a few, they desert the plantations as soon as the Yankees come, an' they follow the Union Army blindly. I understand they're even makin' soldiers of them." He was thoughtful for a moment. "You know, they'll probably make good soldiers at that."

Lorena's heart skipped a beat when she thought about Ravetta and her children.

"The Confederate Congress just passed a law allowing our Negroes to become soldiers too," Lorena said in a low voice.

"Is that so? I guess it had to come sometime

given the disparity in our numbers." Preston got up, dusted off the seat of his pants, and held his hand out to Lorena. "I talk too much. It's been a long day, let's get you inside."

Neither one spoke they made their way to the side entrance. When they reached the door Lorena turned and faced the gambler. *He is the complete and perfect model of a young Southerner, cultivated, courtly, brave to a fault, and living by his own personal code.*

Lorena put both of her hands in his. "I don't know how I will ever be able to thank you, Preston Beauregard Harrison Lord, for all you have done for me."

"Oh, dear lady I wish I could do more. I wish I could—"

Preston stopped, took her hand and brushed his lips on the palm.

Without thinking, Lorena, her chest heaving, her heart racing wildly, moved close to him, pressing her lips on his, and holding him tightly.

With surprising ease he lifted her up and, cradling her in his arms, opened the door. Lorena buried her face in his chest, her arms wound around his neck. He gently laid her on the bed and silently sat down beside her. The reflected light of the moon coming through the window lit up the room

Preston looked down at her, his dark brown eyes burning brightly. "Lorena, I've known a few women, but I believe I am in love for the last time."

"Oh, my dearest, and I'm in love for the first."

Lorena's heart was beating so hard she was breathless. Her pounding pulse was making whooshing sounds in her ears. With trembling hands she reached up for Preston and pulled him down to her. An emotional current that swiftly changed to desire swept through her like a hot summer wind. She looked deeply into Preston's eyes and thought they were the color of dark October leaves as seen at the bottom of a bubbling brook.

He took her in his arms and, in the same motion, gracefully lay down beside her. This time their kiss was not so forceful, but was long and passionate. Lorena felt herself like petals on a flower, opening up for a bee to taste the honey.

In a few moments she was unclothed. With another lingering kiss, she felt a warmth creep over her abdomen, and moisture trickle between her thighs. He kissed her hair and both her eyes, and then her lips again. Slowly and carefully she moved him on top of her and he gently penetrated.

Lorena groaned feeling a thousand different sensations. Her mind reeled back and she realized it had never been like this with John Oakwood. She thought of a dozen ways to admonish herself to stop, but with every thought she pulled Preston closer and raised her hips even higher. The feeling was electric, like two bare wires touching. She had never felt any of this before. Her heart was filled with love for this kind and gentle man, and the lust she felt before only in secret dreams overcame her reason.

In a few moments the electricity began to come in waves from her loins to her chest and she grabbed Preston's hands and put them on her swelling breasts. Then she held his hips and pulled him closer with each thrust of her own body. Soon the waves began to course entirely through her body and she began to shake and moan. She felt Preston begin to tremble and heard him gasp. Lorena pulled him to her and had to bury her mouth in his chest to muffle her screams as she exploded.

After it was over, they both calmed and lay silently next to each other.

Lorena was amazed at her behavior, but glad she had experienced whatever had happened. She covered her nakedness with a blanket and looked at Preston sheepishly. There was such love in his deep black eyes that she would willingly, and gladly, given herself to him again. Instead he sat up abruptly and began to put on his clothes.

Lorena wished she had the courage to tell him to stay with her, but she didn't. *John did this too. Are all men like this?*

When he finished dressing he bent over, kissed her warmly and stood up. His mouth worked as he tried to say something but couldn't. In a moment he was gone.

Lorena watched the door to the living room close and snuggled against her pillow. She stayed naked, with a vain hope that Preston might come back. With a smile that stayed on her face the entire night, she drifted off to sleep thinking, *Whatever the end of this is to be, the future is no longer in our hands.*

At dawn Lorena woke, lazily stretched, yawned and reached out for Preston. Then she remembered he was gone. She opened her eyes and sat up. She compressed her lips into a thin line and shook her head ruefully.

What's wrong with me? Why did he leave? I need him near me. Oh, Preston, I've loved you all my life, but up to now it was only the shadow of the promise of you.

She thought of her husband, and her children, and something black and guilty came over her. She deliberately pushed the vision of her family away, got up and opened the door to Preston's room.

Lorena

I don't want to live without you

Chapter 20

𝔚hen Lorena got to the saloon late that afternoon, the sun was dipping in the west and threw her shadow long on the entrance door. She pushed the door open and stepped in.

The usual blue/gray smoke filled the room, the bulk of it drifting slowly to the second floor. Lorena absently wrinkled her nose at the now familiar mixture of smells. Alongside the odor of raw whiskey was the strong scent of perfume, overridden by the fragrance of men's sweaty bodies.

There were two solitary drinkers at the bar surrounded by three brightly colored girls. Two of the card tables were busy, with Preston in his usual place, his poker face betrayed only by his shining eyes, watching the faces of his three adversaries carefully. His only movement was a slow raise of his thin, black Mexican cigarillo from the table to his lips and back again.

When he saw Lorena, he got halfway out of his seat and touched the brim of his black Stetson.

Lorena saw a different look in his eyes that warmed her. She acknowledged his greeting with a brief nod and a loving smile.

Preston tipped his head in a cavalier gesture and sat down.

With a wave to the bartender, she got her broom and began to sweep the debris already littering the floor.

As she finished the first half of the floor, she heard a familiar sound. When she turned toward Preston, he was already on his feet, bent over coughing into a white silk handkerchief. His cigarillo lay on the table where it had fallen from his hand. The three men playing with him stopped the game and stared at him.

Lorena forced herself not to look at him and turned back to sweeping, trusting that his coughing would soon stop as it had before. But this time it persisted, and soon Preston was back in his chair, bent over double, coughing up a bloody mixture.

Finally Lorena could not stand it any more and ran to him. When she touched his arm he leaned back in his chair and looked up at her. His eyes were bright, and his face ashen. Two distinct, round red spots colored his cheeks, as if one of the whores had painted him with her rouge.

Preston gripped Lorena's arm weakly. "It's all right, my dear," he said between spasms, "just give me a minute."

Lorena's spirit sank at his appearance. His face was chalk white and his brow was covered with sweat. He was trembling uncontrollably. She took her own handkerchief and patted his forehead, then kneeled and put his head on her chest. "Preston, you need a doctor."

He looked up and smiled so sweetly it almost broke her heart.

"No, my dear Lorena, if I die now, I die happy in the arms of the woman I love." He smiled weakly. "Besides, the sawbones in town is a worse drunk than these men," he said, vaguely waving at the other men at the table. "I don't think he could help me. The army doctors said—"

Suddenly he sat up straight and began another fit of coughing. Soon his handkerchief was stained with bright red blood.

When he finally stopped coughing his Stetson lay upside down on the floor, and he was unconscious in Lorena's arms; his breathing rapid and uneven, and coming in shallow wheezing gasps.

Lorena looked imploringly at the card player closest to her. "Help me lift him and get him to a bed."

The man stood up knocking over his chair and stared at the gambler. There was an unreasoning fear in his eyes. "Not me, ma'am. That stuff might be catching." Chairs scraped and fell over as the other two men also beat a quick retreat.

Lorena looked toward the bar for the bartender. She saw him at his usual place staring at them, absently wiping a whiskey glass.

He looked at Preston, a bit of fear showing on his face.

She begged him with her eyes.

He responded by shaking his head and turning his back to her.

Lorena looked all around and raised her voice. "Is there anyone here who'll help me?" As if they were a herd of animals in fear everyone in the saloon pulled away. The piano stopped playing, and several girls ran up the stairs and disappeared into the rooms.

Lorena gritted her teeth and tried to lift Preston. She struggled with his gangly body that seemed to have gained weight.

"I'll help you, Ma'am." Jess appeared from nowhere.

"Thank God you're here, Jess. Get him under his arms, I'll get his legs."

Jess lifted him easily while Lorena grabbed his ankles. "Where to, Ma'am?"

Again Lorena looked at the bartender. Again he turned away.

"Home, I guess," she said dejectedly.

Lorena and the stable boy carried the

unconscious Preston out of the saloon door through the dusty streets of Bucktown and started up the long hill. Jess walked backward both hands under Preston's armpits. Lorena, looking ahead, had his feet between the ankles and the calfs.

Over Jess' shoulder Lorena could see the top of the Main Street hill. It looked a long way off. She saw the church steeple in the distance. In her minds eye she heard the preacher. "And the Devil take you with him."

She wondered. *Am I being punished for adultery?* She looked down at Preston. *Dear God, don't punish him for my transgressions. I love him so.* Guilt, riding on the pain from carrying Preston, coursed through her body. Though Preston was a slight man, he was dead weight when unconscious, and the burden began to tell on Lorena. Soon the pain in her injured leg made her limp noticeably. The muscles in her good leg began to tremble with each step, and her arms began to ache. Soon her back pained so severely she feared dropping him. Steeling herself against the pain, she set her jaw and kept on trudging and stumbling up the hill.

Jess was young and strong but soon even his muscles began to tremble. Driblets of sweat appeared on his brow.

After an eternity they reached the top of the hill, went past the stores and turned down the dirt road. Finally they reached Preston's doorway. Jess held on to him with one hand and with the other opened the door. Lorena struggled in and they laid Preston on the bed. For a while Lorena stayed at the foot of the bed trembling and breathing hard. Sweat ran down her face and neck and her dress stuck to her body.

Jess had his red handkerchief out dabbing his forehead.

When Lorena's breathing finally returned to normal she took the blanket at the foot of the bed and gently covered Preston.

Dear God, he looks so frail and weak.

She turned to the livery boy. "I want to thank you—

"It's all right Ma'am." Jess looked down at Preston and frowned. "I seed many a soldier in the same condition. I know what it's like to be sick like that." He took off his hat, held it in his hands, and shook his head slowly and knowingly. "Never seed many of 'em come back from that there condition." He looked at Lorena hopefully. "But keep up yer spirit Ma'am, some of 'em survived." He put his hat back on. "Is there anything else I can do?"

Lorena shook her head no, and sat down on the edge of the bed and took Preston's cold hand in hers. She felt completely spent.

Jess walked to the door, put his hand on the latch then turned around. "The doctors used to put cold towels on the brows of the sick boys, Ma'am."

Lorena nodded to him. "Thank you, I'll do that right away."

"Good luck Ma'am." He quietly opened the door, started to turn, stopped, shrugged his shoulders, shook his head slowly and left.

Through the closed door Lorena heard him singing sadly:

A frog went a'courtin' and he did say,
ring somebody with a cambo.
On his back was a whiskey jug,
ring somebody with a cambo.
Caminiro caminero, caminiro caro,
strata boba latta bobba ring some,
ring somebody with a cambo....

Lorena listened absently until Jess's song faded in the distance, then wearily turned her attention back to Preston. She put cold towels on his brow, then sat on the bed took his hand and stood vigil as the sunlight dimmed into darkness. When it became completely dark, she got up and struck a match to light a candle. She put it down on the table next to the bed. She put her hand to his brow. It was hot. Lorena freshened the towels and sat down next to him again. The candle flickered, throwing ghostly shadows on the wall.

Putting a hand to his brow again, Lorena felt a

sickening wave of depression, and burst into tears.

When she stopped she got down on her knees, turned her face upward and clasped her hands together. "Dear God, Preston's a good man. I know he hasn't always been an angel, but who has? I know I've sinned, and whatever I've made him do please forgive him and, if you can, me too. I adore him so. And we both love you." She bowed her head, sobbed and continued to pray silently.

With the fading of the sun came the cold. Preston began to shiver and Lorena took the towels off his brow and got him another blanket from the couch in the living room. He continued to shake and Lorena despaired. She looked around the room desperately. There was nothing else. *I guess I'll have to keep him warm.*

Without hesitation she slipped into bed with Preston and pulled the covers over them. She held his thin body next to hers, warming him. In a few moments he stopped shivering and his body relaxed.

Lorena lay on her side, her arms wrapped tightly around her lover. His breathing was shallow and noisy. It sounded to her like his breath was going over liquid in his lungs. *No matter what he says, drunkard or not, in the morning I'm going to get the doctor to look at him.*

Preston's fever and her own warmth warded

off the evening cold, and in a few minutes the exhausted Lorena fell into a restless sleep.

The burning candle was a nub when she woke. The flame on the small wick danced bravely against the darkness but lost the battle as it snuffed out. Lorena got up and lit another candle.

Lorena came to Preston looked lovingly down at him, this time without any guilt. She leaned over him and put the candle on a small table next to the bed.

His eyes were open, looking at the ceiling.

"I see you're awake," she said, as she sat down on the bed and shook her head. "You gave me quite a scare." She smiled then frowned.

He didn't answer.

Her brow furrowed.

"Preston? Preston?" Lorena shook him lightly. His head lolled away from her.

She brought the back of her fist to her mouth. "Oh, God! Noooooo." Lorena stood up and fell back a step as though physically battered by the flood of pain that thundered through her heart.

She went back to him and threw the cover off Preston, felt for his pulse, dropped his hand, then ran to the other side of the bed. Preston stared at the wall, sightless.

Not wanting to believe what had happened, Lorena went to her knees and touched his cool face with her hand.

"Preston, don't die on me. I don't want to live without you."

Realizing the worst, Lorena's eyes rolled up and she gave a keening wail like a stricken squaw. After a few moments she stopped and laid her head on Preston's cold hand. Her eyes moistened with love, and she stayed that way until daybreak.

Chapter 21

From the journal of Lorena Boykins Oakwood

January 10th, 1865

The winter of life must be terribly cold for those who have never loved.

I can't believe Preston is gone. I never loved him so much as in that instant death took him. I must leave this place as everywhere I look, everywhere I go, he is there, reminding me of what might have been.

My heart hurts so that sometimes I wish we had never met. Yet I would not trade one small moment of our time together for all the rest of my life.

237

Preston, somehow you stirred my soul and raised it from slumber, and even though you are gone, I still feel fully alive.

For a while I hid from the thought that you were the only man I ever wanted. But, God help me, it's true.

It's perverse. The more love I gave, the more I got.

Life must be awfully sad for those who have no memories.

I kiss a million goodbyes to you, dear Preston. You are the lucky one; you rest in peace while I must go on, alone.

On cold, lonely nights I will look up at the heavens and find the unchanging North Star. I know you will be waiting there for me, and when my life is through, if God grants, I will come to you.

Lorena

For the first time in my life I knew love

Chapter 22

𝕿he funeral was brief and simple. Among the few that attended with Lorena were, the preacher, Jess, the piano player, and several of the girls from the beer hall. Two of Preston's gambling regulars, bleary eyed and unshaven, showed up after the bible reading.

Lorena kneeled dry eyed next to the pine box, dressed in a frilly black dress and veil, borrowed from one of the girls. Several of the women dabbed their eyes, while the men stood around, hats off, looking uncomfortable.

Preston left no money that anyone could find, and was buried in Boot Hill in a pauper's grave. A few of the men he gambled with anted up and paid for a simple pine casket. Lorena gave all the money she had saved for the headstone.

The preacher reluctantly gave the eulogy, praying that God would forgive Preston's gambling and living in sin. He looked directly at Lorena when he said 'fornication' and she turned crimson under her veil.

After the prayer the preacher left, limping away in a hurry, trying to avoid talking to the others. The gamblers filed past Lorena and expressed their condolences, followed by the women.

As the ladies went past the open grave, each one touched Lorena's arm. She looked up at the women and thought, *These women, they look different, almost dignified. Their faces clean of rouge, and they all dressed in unaccustomed black. Preston would have approved. He loved honesty.*

"I'm so sorry," the first girl said earnestly, but never making eye contact. She was pale, and her voice quavered when she muttered her condolences.

Tears streamed down the face of the second. "I thought Preston was the finest…." She could say no more. She squeezed Lorena's hand and rushed away.

The third was dry eyed and stony faced. She touched Lorena's hand and almost spoke, but changed her mind and also left hurriedly.

In a few minutes everyone was gone except Jess and the gravedigger.

Jess, hat in hand, a mournful look on his face, held his hand down to Lorena. "Time to go, Ma'am," he said softly.

Lorena turned to him, her eyes swollen with grief and smiled a sad half-smile. "You go on, Jess, I want to be with him just a little while longer."

"Yes'm." Jess pulled his hand back and ambled down the hill softly singing his mournful song. *"A frog went a courtin' and he did say...."*

His song faded away into nothingness and Lorena was left alone with Preston and her thoughts. *Only death could have ended such a love.*

The gravedigger sat down at a respectful distance, leaned his back against a tree, put his shovel on his lap and picked his teeth with a dirty fingernail.

Lorena stood up. The cool wind blew her smooth scarlet hair about her shoulders, and made the mourning dress flap against her legs.

Lorena picked up a handful of earth and leaned over the freshly dug ground. She let the dark soil filter through her fingers and drop on the pine casket. *This will be a lonely place for such a loving man.*

"Preston," she murmured, "don't worry, you'll always be with me, just behind my eyes. You will always be in my heart, and you will forever have a part of me with you."

Lorena shook her head. *For the first time in my life I knew love, and now it's been taken from me.* Her eyes clouded over and a sticky cloak of depression came over her. She felt physically sick at the thought of Preston lying in the cheap pine box underneath the earth. She sat very still letting the grief pass through her mind and body and come to rest heavily in her heart. *For the rest of my life I will have to live in a world in which there is no Preston.*

Dear, dear Preston, leaving you is the cruelest cross I will ever bear. How can I go back to the cold arms of John Oakwood after loving you? But the longing for her children intruded on her thoughts, and she knew that somehow she had to get started soon, for Atlanta.

Preston called him Blaze

Chapter 23

Lorena walked away from the grave, sat down on the cold ground and put her back up against the rough bark of an old, spreading oak tree. She felt a sprinkle and looked up. The sky was a dismal gray with large thunderclouds roiling about the horizon. Droplets of cold rain fell to the earth, trickled off tree leaves and touched her face. *Even God sheds tears for dear Preston.*

She watched the gravedigger go to work dropping soil over the casket, felt a little sick, and dropped deeper into her black mood. *What will I do? Preston protected me. Now I'll be alone at the saloon and, after paying for the headstone, I don't have any money left. What can I do—* She felt helpless, like a pinned butterfly on a collector's board. She closed her eyes. To remember Preston, his rich, thick black hair, his spare, muscular body, his loving face and his piercing brown eyes, was a comfort to her.

"Ma'am?"

The voice, though soft, startled Lorena. She looked up quickly.

Jess had his back to whatever light there was throwing his face in darkness. "Sorry, Ma'am, I didn't mean to frighten you."

She put her hand on her chest and breathed again. "Oh, it's you, Jess. I thought everyone had gone."

Jess stood quietly, head down, as if he were ashamed, the brim of his hat partially blocking his face. Behind him, attached to a tether in his hand, was a horse as black as midnight all over, except for a white streak across his nose. The stallion was pawing at the ground and snorting softly.

Lorena marveled. Even to someone who knew nothing about horses, this was a magnificent animal. The horse stood proud and tall, with a barrel chest and enormous vitality showing in his coal black eyes.

To Lorena he looked tireless, and the way he behaved at this, their first meeting, indicated he had the disposition of a valiant dog.

"Yes, Ma'am, but I had to come back to give you something."

Lorena stood up and faced the lad. "Yes," she said with a small, sad smile, "what is it?"

"Mister Preston said if anythin' ever happened to him, I was to give you his prize horse." He held the tether toward Lorena. "He didn't ride it much, but I exercised him some and took real good care of him at the livery. He's seventeen hands high and as handsome as any horse I ever seen. Mr. Preston called him, Blaze."

Lorena's heart swelled. This horse is... mine?

Jess held out his hand and opened it.

Lorena stared down at a small Colt pistol. "This is yours too," Jess said, "and be careful with it, it's loaded." He put it in the horse's saddlebag, and turned back to Lorena.

"He said he wished he could leave you some money too, but things were kinda bad lately. But he gave me this to give to you— in case something ever happened to him— which it did." Jess opened his other hand displaying a large diamond.

Lorena reached out and took the stone out of Jess' hand. She recognized it as the stickpin Preston wore in his cravat. Her eyes widened and she looked at it as if she were contemplating an unknown specie of fish.

Lorena slowly closed her fist around the diamond. Her voice trembled. "How much do you think I could get for this?"

"Oh, at least twenty or thirty dollars, Ma'am. It's a real treasure."

She looked at the horse and then at the boy. *That pistol for protection, the horse to ride, and the money I'll get for the diamond. It will be enough. Thank you, Preston, oh, thank you.* She put the stone back in the boy's hand. "If you would be so kind as to sell it for me, I think I will be on my way home."

"Home, Ma'am?"

"Yes, Jess, home! Where the sun always shines and it never rains. Home!"

The boy's usually dour face broke into a smile. "Yes'm."

Lorena took Jess's hand, her thanks showing in her eyes.

The boy took off his hat and looked down at the ground. "The times that bred as fine a man as Mr. Preston are as gone as he is. I'm sure sorry he's dead, Ma'am."

Lorena closed her eyes and two tears made their way down her cheeks. She slowly shook her head. "Preston didn't die, Jess, I did."

Lorena

The mountain looked formidable

Chapter 24

Under scudding gray clouds the mountains looked purple. As Lorena approached the foothills, the purple turned to dirt brown, and then the going got rough. The crude map the livery boy had drawn for her was a straight line to Georgia. Jess didn't bother to show the elevations.

Lorena stopped at a sluggish green river to let the horse drink. She slid down off the saddle, ground reined the horse, and reluctantly filled her canteen. Putting her hand over her eyes, she squinted up at the top of the mountain. It looked forbidding. She looked at the mountains to her right and left. They went on endlessly in both directions. "No use trying to go around these mountains, Blaze, we'll cross them right here."

Blaze, feeling a slack rein, bent his head down to crop the grass. "Poor baby," Lorena said kindly, "I'll feed you and then we'll cross."

Lorena filled the feedbag with oats and put it on Blaze. Then she took off her Stetson and shook her head. Her red locks tumbled down over her shoulders. She patted Blaze then absently ran her fingers through her hair. It felt coarse and dirty.

Three days on the trail. I didn't realize how much of a city girl I've become. Not only do my feet ache from walking, but my butt burns like fire from this saddle. When I get to Atlanta, I don't think I'll ever get on a horse again.

She patted her pocket. *These two ten dollar gold pieces Jess traded for the diamond worries me as much as being alone. That money would be a prize for a bandit.* A small jolt of fear went through her as she remembered the sergeant on the train. *And I would be too.*

Lorena reached into the saddle bag and felt for Preston's pistol. She caressed the cold barrel and felt reassured.

Lorena sat down on a fallen log, rolled up her hair and held it as she put her hat back on. Only a peek of the red showed as she tucked some errant strands under the brim. After a few more minutes of rest she got up, took the feedbag off the horse and let him take another drink.

Taking a deep breath, she grabbed the pommel

of the saddle, looked up at the steep climb and gave a long sigh. She put her left foot in the stirrup, swung her other leg over the saddle and mounted. With a dig of her heels, she urged Blaze toward the mountain.

As she loped along toward the base of the mountain, the horse's hooves beat out Preston's name on the hard ground; *Preston Lord—Preston Lord—*

I have to forget him, Lorena thought, *he's part of my past I'd best leave dead.* But she could not. *Preston Lord—Preston Lord—* He stayed with Lorena until she reached the rock strewn ground at the foot of the mountain. Lorena stopped and looked up the path made by Indians in years past. The path and the mountain looked formidable.

Her resolve firm, Lorena dug her heels in Blaze's ribs and the horse bolted up the path.

Later that afternoon as Blaze and Lorena climbed the mountain she could feel what warmth there was ebbing away. The higher they went the harder it was to breathe. A brisk wind kicked up and intensified the cold. She looked down at the tree line then up to the summit. *In the summer this crossing would be pleasant.*

When the sun dipped behind the mountain, the temperature plummeted precipitously. As the blood-red sun sank over the horizon, heavy clouds filled the sky and covered the sunset. After that, darkness came quickly. When the full blackness of night came the cold turned intense. Lorena looked at the blackened sky and thought, *It'll snow before morning.*

Lorena stopped the horse, reached back into the saddlebag and took out Preston's wool jacket. The coat had his smell about it and she almost cried. After a few moments she buttoned it and started back up the trail. The wind whipping down off the mountain had icy fingers that found small chinks in her fleece armor and chilled her. Soon she was beating her arms against her body to keep warm. Blaze's skin flinched at the cold.

I'm so damned cold it feels like the wind is going right through me.

As they climbed higher Lorena's breath came in short gasps. The wind whipped about her whispering; *Go back, get off my mountain.* Lorena thought she might be delirious from being up so high. She knew she was when she found herself shaking her fist at the top of the mountain and yelling, "You won't beat me. The Yankees couldn't and you won't either."

The mountain path was strewn with rocks and boulders, making Blaze's way difficult. Lorena's hip began to hurt with every step the horse made. Breathing began to become more and more difficult. Her head began to swim.

Lorena stopped the horse leaned forward and patted his neck. She got down and stood still for a moment to gain her composure. In a few minutes the dizziness stopped. Lorena made her way to a spout-stream coming down off the mountain, cupped her hands, catching the cascading water, and drank the cold liquid. Blaze dipped his head and slaked his thirst from a pool formed by the stream of water making a depression in the rock floor.

Wiping her hands on the jacket, Lorena turned to the horse, the wind whipped her face. "This damn wind has the temperament of an unchained demon." She patted the horse's neck. "We better camp soon, Blaze, it's getting too dark to travel. Too damn cold too."

Lorena walked the horse forward until she reached a flat spot. She dismounted and looked around for wood to make a fire. She found a rotting tree that had tried to grow between two large boulders and snapped off some of its dead branches. Using a rock for leverage, she stepped down hard and broke the branches into smaller pieces. She made a ring of stones and piled some of the wood in the center. Lorena then took the rest of the wood and stored it at the foot of one of the boulders.

Soon a blazing fire lit the campsite. Lorena spilled the brackish water from her canteen and replaced it with the fresh water from the stream. She filled the coffee pot with water, brought it to a boil, and threw in ground up coffee beans. While the coffee boiled she reached into the saddlebag, felt her gun, pushed it aside, and pulled out a piece of jerky. The dried beef was cold and stiff but chewing it patiently allowed her to finally swallow it. When she thought the coffee was done, she poured the black fluid into a tin cup. It was hot and she had to blow on the liquid a few times before drinking. Warmth and energy spread through her veins as the raw caffeine hit her blood stream. She drank two cups and was finally warm enough to relax.

While Lorena sat at the fire, Blaze came up behind her and nuzzled her ear. Lorena turned to him and fondled his sensitive nostrils. She got up, watered him from her hand, and put an oat bag on him. When he was finished she ground reined the horse then spread out her blanket roll and lay down next to the larger of the two boulders hoping it would block the wind.

Lorena tried to sleep but the wind picked up and whistled down the mountain making her restless. She sat up and looked up at the sky. The clouds had blown away and the moon was full and bright. After a few minutes new clouds drifted across the face of the moon, making shadows play and dance on the mountain. Lorena lay down again but still couldn't sleep. The horse didn't rest either. He whinnied and nervously pawed at the ground. *I guess the wind is making Blaze jittery too.*

Lorena sat bolt upright. "What's that?" she said aloud. She tipped her head to one side and listened intently. Just above the wind the sound was repeated, high pitched and mournful. Lorena shuddered. *It sounds like some kind of animal on the prowl.*

For a long while Lorena sat still and tense, her back pushed tightly against the boulder. Finally her frozen brain started to work and she dashed to Blaze and opened the saddlebag to get the pistol. Eyes wide and ears alert she made her way back to the boulder, pressed her back against it, and slid down to a seated position. She tried to quiet her pounding heart but couldn't. With a trembling hand she cocked the hammer. Another howl, this time much closer. Lorena froze and stared wide-eyed into the blackness around her. A sense of dread engulfed her.

Blaze dragged the rock he was tied to and whinnied loudly. He reared up and pawed the air then came down alert and trembling.

Another howl. This time several answering voices began to a long wavering cry back, until the entire mountain seemed to be echoing their baying. Lorena's adrenaline surged, and her heart pounded in her chest. *Wolves!*

As suddenly as it started, the howling stopped. Thick clouds passed over the moon and an ominous darkness closed in around the camp.

She sat stiffly, all her senses fully alert. The air currents stiffened, and the whistling of the wind got louder.

Flickering shadows made Lorena look at the

fire. She watched with dismay as the fire started to dwindle. Individual flames leaped up as the charred wood collapsed; the fire was losing its battle to stay alive.

Reluctantly Lorena put the gun in her jacket pocket, got up and carefully made her way to the woodpile. It was dark where she stored the wood and she looked intently at the shadows before she reached down and quickly filled her arms. She knew she was vulnerable, so she speedily made her way back and threw half the wood on the fire.

"That was dumb," she said aloud, "I smothered the fire." She took a step toward the saddlebag where the matches were, when she noticed a small flame licking up through the new wood. With a sigh of relief she moved to Blaze, untied him and led him closer to her place at the boulder.

Satisfied she could do no more, Lorena leaned back down against the boulder and again slid down to a sitting position. She wrapped the horse's reins around her left wrist, reached into her jacket pocket, took the gun out and gripped it in her other hand. Nervously she threw her blanket over her legs.

The warmth of the fire made her drowsy and she spent the next half hour fighting off sleep.

She was nodding in a state of stupor when the reins jerked her wrist. Her head snapped up and she was instantly wide-awake.

The horse neighed and pranced nervously on the hard ground making sparks where his iron shoes struck the rock. The wind had eased off and a light snow was beginning to fall. Ignoring the cold, Lorena threw off the blanket, stood up and looked about, her eyes darting back and forth, adjusting to the dark. She could see nothing in the blackness except pristine snowflakes drifting to the earth. She gripped her pistol tightly making her knuckles white.

After a few minutes, the horse quieted. Lorena breathed a sigh of relief, sat back down and tried to relax but couldn't. Giving up the idea of any more sleep she got up and moved closer to the embers of the fire. There was still coffee in the pot and she poured herself a cup. Her hand was shaking so badly she spilled half of the black liquid.

Lorena took a sip and spit it out. It was too strong to drink. She put some more wood on the fire, sat down by the flames and put the pistol in her lap. A dismal thought came to her. *What if I don't have enough wood to last the night?*

Blaze nervously began to neigh again, this time making a discordant clop, clop, as he pranced about. Lorena searched the dark, her heart thumping. The metal cup dropped from her hand making a clanking sound as it fell to the rocky ground.

Suddenly they were there, two lightening fast,

gray colored wolves appearing out of the night. Lorena froze for a moment then stood up slowly hoping not to spook the predators.

Ignoring her, the wolves went to work. One wolf slunk to the rear of Blaze while the other faced him, head low and snarling. As if on a pre-arranged signal, they sprang at Blaze together.

With a quickness born of fright, Lorena vaulted back and screamed. The gun flew off her lap and dropped to the ground.

With a mighty backward kick Blaze sent the female wolf behind him flying with a broken back. Her whimpering stopped with a quick death. The other wolf scored by biting the horse in his vulnerable foreleg. With a cry of rage the horse flung him off leaving a deep wound, made ragged by the wolf's razor sharp teeth.

Terror stricken, Lorena backed toward the fire. Forcing her brain to work, she looked for the pistol.

The stricken wolf, crazed by the horse's blood in his mouth, but deathly afraid of the wounded stallion, shook off his fall and turned toward the weaker prey.

Lorena searched desperately in the dark for the gun.

Oh, God, there it is. It was a few feet from her, the cold, blue barrel glinting dully in the firelight.

His head low to the ground, the wolf was all snarling teeth and yellow eyes. He began to stalk Lorena.

Desperately trying not to bolt, Lorena inched toward the gun. The wolf followed her every movement. Finally she reached the pistol and began to bend for it slowly, carefully, expecting at any moment a flesh tearing, life ending charge.

Suddenly, with an astonishing agility and a blood-curdling cry of hunger, the wolf lunged at Lorena.

She dropped to her knees, snatched the gun off the ground and pulled the trigger twice. The mountain exploded with two resounding echoes. She missed both times but the loud report of the gun was enough to make the wolf veer away.

Lorena got up and stumbled toward the boulder in terror. For a split second she turned her head and in her mind could see the wolf coming out of the darkness after her. She imagined his teeth tearing at her and the horror of it made her scramble wildly to the boulder.

When she got there she looked for the horse and her heart sunk. *Gone.* Lorena put her back against the boulder and looked into the dark for the wolf. *Nothing.* Her heart was pounding in her chest, and the blood thumping through her body made whooshing sounds in her ears. She was trembling all over and her hands shook uncontrollably. *Oh my children, my poor children,* a voice in her head said over and over.

While she was praying, like a fleeting gray shadow the wolf reappeared.

Lorena's stomach balled up in a black knot. *Oh, God, he's back.*

The wolf stepped into the light of the dying fire, stopped and stared at Lorena. He slinked forward a step and stopped again, his head so low it barely cleared the ground; his yellow, unblinking eyes fixed on her. Saliva, mixed with the horse's blood, dripped from his jaws.

As he stared at her, Lorena could see through his transparent eyes to his brain that had only one goal. *Kill this prey.*

With a shaking hand Lorena raised the pistol, took aim, and fired. The wolf flinched and yelped but didn't leave. She had missed again.

The world narrowed down to Lorena and her adversary. It was as if they were only two beings left on earth. They were two knights in a battle to the death for supreme rights to a disputed mountain kingdom.

Three bullets left.

The wolf took another small step and then another. He snarled showing his ferocious teeth and made a low growl, his yellow eyes unblinking. He began a slow, steady walk, stalking his prey, half circling her, searching for an opening.

She raised the pistol, trying to steady her hand, and fired again. This time the wolf didn't even flinch. He stopped and crouched down lower to the ground. His lip curled with another ominous snarl.

Two bullets left.

Lorena shook with fear. A thousand thoughts cascaded through her mind, coming all at once. *The lord is my shepherd.... No one will know I died here... I shall not want.... Oh, my children... He maketh me lie down... Oh God, I didn't count. How many bullets have I fired?*

After a few moments the wolf continued his circle.

As he stalked Lorena, he narrowed the half circle, getting closer and closer, getting near enough for a final leap.

Lorena pushed back against the boulder, and went to her knees. ... *Can't reload now... and restoreth my soul...* She cocked the hammer and pointed the gun. This time she grasped the pistol with both hands. The wolf growled and coiled, getting ready to leap.

Thoughts of running flitted across her mind. *No, Lorena, stay put, and end it here, one way or the other.*

In a flash of gray, the wolf sprang.

Lorena saw only the underside of his belly. Her mouth opened wide and she gave a silent scream. At the same moment she threw her left arm in front of her face and pulled the trigger.

The wolf yelped, somersaulted in mid-air, and fell to the new fallen snow, bloody and beaten. With a whine and a whimper, he crawled away into the darkness.

Lorena sank to the ground. Her heart was pounding so hard she thought her chest would break.

Blaze appeared and limped to her. The horse nuzzled her and whinnied softly. Lorena got up, fell on the horse's neck and cried.

When Lorena recovered enough to control her movements she tried to re-load the gun. *Oh, God. I only had one bullet left.* Her hands were trembling so hard the new bullets dropped into the snow, and she soon gave up.

"That was too close," she said aloud to Blaze, her voice quivering.

After the terrifying encounter, Lorena didn't dare sleep. She sat, her back against the boulder, and waited impatiently for morning. She wrapped her bedroll blanket around her but even that could not keep out the deadly cold. She feared for her wounded horse.

When the half-light of dawn came, Lorena got up and moved her arms and legs to get the stiffness out of her joints. The snow had stopped sometime in the night, but left the mountain virgin white, obliterating the signs of yesterday's fight.

When Lorena was limber she examined the horse's leg. The wolf had left a jagged wound that had bled profusely. It was now caked but moist, and it looked vulnerable, as if at any provocation it would bleed badly again.

Lorena reached into her saddlebag and pulled out a spare petticoat. She ripped off a long piece and, using it as a bandage, she wrapped the injured leg as best she could. Afraid riding the wounded beast would be too much for him, she took his reins and led him. Both of them, limping severely, started up toward the top of the mountain.

After a few steps she saw a bloody trail. She followed it for a few yards and then she saw him. The wolf had frozen overnight and lay on his stomach, stiff. His front paws were stretched out as if he were caught forever in a leap, his glassy sightless eyes staring up at his home on the mountain.

Lorena felt terrible about his death. She patted the frozen hair on his head. "I guess there'll be a few hungry pups on the mountain tonight."

Reluctantly Lorena left her former adversary. As she trudged upward she felt an odd feeling. She searched her mind and slowly began to realize, as sad as the animal's death was, there was a part of her that rejoiced in her triumph. She was the victor in a fight to the death.

****

As Lorena went higher the temperature dropped steadily and snow began to fall again. At first it was soft and delicate, melting as soon as it hit the ground. Soon it increased until it became a white vortex, the wind whipping it around her and stinging her face.

Lorena stumbled toward the crest of the mountain, her clothes catching on half hidden rocks and bushes. "Damn this outfit, if I'm going to act like a man I better dress like one. I'll have to get some working clothes when I get to civilization."

Towards noon Lorena reached the top of the mountain. A shrieking wind was waiting there for her. Instead of getting warmer, the sky darkened and, although the snow decreased slightly, the wind turned the air terribly cold. The force of the wind pushed against Lorena and Blaze. It was as if nature itself was telling them, *Get off my mountain, go back, go back.*

After struggling against the fierce wind and stinging snow, her heart pounding and her head thumping, she stood at the apex of the mountain and looked all around her. She could see little but the snow, coming at a slant, the wind pushing her back. All at once all fear left her and she felt a great rush through her body as she experienced the exhilaration of conquering the mountain. She laughed uncontrollably, made a fist as if she were shaking it at an enemy, then setting her jaw she started down the rapidly disappearing trail.

After a few moments, Lorena slowed down and began walking ahead of the horse. Leaning forward on the wind, blinded by the white wall of snow around her, she worried constantly that one of them might fall off the mountain.

The exhilaration of conquering the mountain gone, a small spot of anxiety started in her chest and spread, until her entire body was filled with fear. *I'm cold and hungry, and I have no idea where I am.* Depressed, she sat down in the snow and hung her head. Blaze stood next to her, snuffling about in the snow, looking for grass.

"I'm so tired. Maybe if I just lay down a while I'll be all right." She lay down on her side in the snow and felt drowsy, then peaceful. "I'll sleep, just for a little while."

****

"NO!" The voice that woke her was so loud that for a moment she wasn't sure whom it was that shouted. Then she realized it was herself.

Lorena forced herself to stand. "I'm not giving up. I beat the Yanks, I beat the wolves, and I'll beat this mountain too."

She stomped her numb legs on the ground, wrapped Preston's jacket tightly around her, took the horse's reins and started down the mountain again.

For just an instant the wind ceased and the snow stopped swirling. It was then she saw them, twin beacons of light shown from the valley below. The wind picked up again and they disappeared.

Gone. I guess it's just my imagination. No, there they are again. They're lights, and they're real. Hope sprang up inside her; ignoring her pain and discomfort, Lorena pushed down the mountain as fast as her aching leg and the wounded horse would let her.

The wind continued to whip around her and white flakes stung her face. Lorena put her head down, leaned on the wind, ignored the snow, and slogged on down the mountain, praying what she saw was a sign of civilization.

After what seemed like an eternity, she reached level ground.

She could see the lights clearly but they looked as far away as ever.

After what seemed like hours of struggling through the snow and wind, she could finally make out the outline of a cabin. Overjoyed, she redoubled her efforts. Walking, stumbling, falling, and getting up, she made her way to the structure. Blaze staggered behind her, stepping as high over the drifts as his wounded leg would let him. Unable to tell where solid ground was, and limping badly from his wound, he stumbled repeatedly. Lorena feared with all the exertion he would re-open the wound. "Can't stop now Blaze. Keep moving."

As she approached the dwelling, she could see

the lights came from two lamps in the windows of a small cabin. Nearing the door, she saw a faded blue sign swinging wildly and battering the side of the cabin. She squinted and tried to read it.

Aunt Anna's Eatery.

"Thank God, shelter *and* food."

Lorena reached the cabin, went up three stairs to the porch. The horse clattered up the stairs with her.

Anxiously she tried the door. It was locked. She banged on the solid oak door with her fist, and prayed someone would hear her. No one answered. Frustrated, Lorena tapped hard on the window next to the door. Finally she heard a voice from inside.

"We ain't open fer business yet."

She went back to the door and banged again, harder.

"All right, all right, I'm coming! I'm coming!"

The door opened and Lorena came stumbling in, bringing with her the cold, a flurry of snow, and a wounded horse.

Chapter 25

Although the room was warm Lorena still felt chills and trembled involuntarily. She wrapped the bear fur around her tightly and leaned toward the roaring flames in the fireplace. The hot bath and the two shots of whiskey Anna gave her did wonders for her spirit.

She looked about her at a room that was spare and masculine. Opposite Lorena were two leather chairs, and a sofa covered by a black and white cowhide. No pictures adorned the walls.

Lorena sat snugly in a rocking chair, a deer head looked down at her from the far wall with a bland expression. Through an open door she could see the kitchen with a large stove. On the other side of the kitchen was an additional room with a long table and benches.

Anna came from the kitchen holding a steaming coffee pot. "Have some more coffee, child?"

Lorena's eyes lit up. "Oh, yes, thank you."

Keeping the fur snugly around her, Lorena held out her cup and the woman carefully filled it.

When she was done, the woman went to the kitchen put the pot on the stove and returned.

"I put yer horse in the barn and yer clothes in the wash basin. The poor beast's bandage slipped off so I put a new one on him. Put some liniment on him too, fer the soreness." She paused and reflected. "He's not in good shape. What the devil got him, a puma?"

Lorena shivered but this time not from the cold. "No! Wolves!"

The woman shook her head and looked out the window. "They're bad this time of the year; always hungry. I hope the horse makes it. He lost a lot of blood, and he's exhausted."

Lorena shivered again and said a silent prayer for Blaze. *He's got to make it. He's my ticket home.* Lorena stared through the window at the falling snow against the dark sky and felt a grateful glow. *If I hadn't seen the lights—* She couldn't finish the thought.

The woman went back to the kitchen bent over and began stirring a large kettle of stew. The aroma of the cooking permeated the room and made Lorena's mouth water. She watched the woman with interest, all the while feeling the warmth of being welcomed.

Her new friend was a large person, with broad shoulders and broader hips. She had streaks of gray running through her dark brown hair. A lock of her hair kept falling over one eye which she brushed back constantly with a practiced move of her hand. When both her calloused hands were busy, she got the hair out of the way by pursing her lips to one side and blowing. Her homely face was deeply lined, which reminded Lorena of her grandmother, and gave the woman a motherly look. That same face showed a combination of geniality and shrewdness.

Lorena watched her move with the energy of a young person.

The woman moved back to the door and leaned against the frame. "If you saw my sign outside you'd know my name is Anna." She smiled broadly. "Anna Smith. What's yours?"

"Lorena Boykins, I mean, Oakwood." Lorena shook her head. So much had happened to her, even her married name sounded strange.

Anna smiled at Lorena and put her hands on her hips. "Well, which one is it?"

Lorena laughed. "All this has made my brain addled. It's Oakwood, Lorena Oakwood."

"It ain't none of my business, Lorena, but what the hell were you doin' out in this weather half undressed?"

Lorena smiled wistfully. "It's a long story." Her face turned grave. "But what's really important is, I have to get back to Atlanta."

The woman turned back, picked up the spoon

and began again to stir the stew. "Well, we're in the Tennessee Mountains, a long way from Atlanta, and with this weather and all, it'll be a while 'til you can get through—"

The front door banged open.

Lorena jumped, her eyes wide with surprise.

Through the open door several men stomped in, shaking the snow off their boots, and interrupting the conversation. A deep, masculine voice cried out, "Hey, Anna, get the grub out here, we're hungry."

Anna laughed at Lorena's puzzled look. "This here's a eatin' place. All the men who work in the silver mine, and ain't got no wives, show up here every day 'bout this time. Let me feed 'em and I'll come back—"

Lorena got to her feet, ignoring the wince of pain in her hip. "Oh, let me help, I know my way around a kitchen." She laughed. "Besides, I'll be warmer in there."

"It'd be better if you knew your way around rough men."

"Lorena made a wry face. "Unfortunately, I've learned that too."

There was a surprised look on Anna's face as she shook her head, walked to a stack of dishes, picked them up, and went into the dining room.

****

It was late in the afternoon when the stew was gone, and the last man had been shooed out.

The two women cleaned up and retreated to the living quarters. Anna dropped down on the sofa with a tired grunt and Lorena sat down on the rocker holding a bowl of stew.

After a few moments Anna turned to Lorena. "The men stayed later than usual," she said, a wise look on her face. "I guess a pretty face keeps the men here longer than my food."

Lorena put her spoon in the bowl and laughed. "They wouldn't stay two minutes without the hot meal."

"Well, in any case, you sure seem good fer business, Lorena. I ain't had that many men in here since I opened this place."

Lorena put the empty bowl down on the floor next to her chair. "Never mind that, Anna, your stew is delicious."

Anna smiled. "It ain't the food them men was gawkin' at."

Lorena blushed and started rocking.

Anna lit a corncob pipe, puffed a few times and watched the wispy gray smoke spread upward toward the ceiling.

Lorena breathed in the aroma and was reminded of home. It smelled like the tobacco her father used to smoke.

"You're welcome to stay with me 'til the weather breaks," Anna said. "It'll take a month or so 'til yer horse heals anyway."

A disappointed Lorena didn't answer and Anna puffed in silence for a few minutes.

"It gets lonely here in the winter."

Lorena looked at Anna with interest. "Why do you stay here by yourself, Anna?"

Anna looked incredulously at Lorena, then threw her head back and laughed heartily.

"I ain't 'zactly been an angel 'afore I came here. In fact," she laughed, "my name ain't even Smith."

Lorena looked at Anna and a picture of the girls at the Lucky Dollar flashed across her mind followed by Preston's face. A feeling of melancholy moved over her. She pushed it away.

Anna shook her head. "I had a husband and a house once." She leaned back took a puff on the pipe, pursed her lips, and blew the smoke to the ceiling."

"That was in Frisco. I was on the streets makin' a living as best as I could when I met this here sailor. After three days he asked me to marry him. I was young and stupid so I jumped at the chance. Well I didn't know it then but I was better off walkin' the streets. When he wasn't away on a ship, he was drunk. When he got drunk enough, he started beatin' me. And when he wasn't beatin' me, he was drinkin'."

Anna's eyes were distant and her face muscles developed tics as she re-lived desperate days.

"One night he beat me so bad both my eyes were blacked shut. Finally he got tired of hitting me and he kicked me a few times. Eventually he got exhausted and stopped. After a while the drunken bastard upped and fell asleep."

Anna's face contorted, mirroring a deep well of pain and rage, and she stood up. "When I was sure he was out I went to the kitchen, got a knife, and—"

Lorena watched with apprehension as Anna's long pent up feelings exploded.

She made a fist and struck out blindly into the air, her eyes tiny yellow slits of venom. As quickly as she started, she stopped.

After a few minutes of staring with hate into the past she sat down, spent. Then she looked up, smiled weakly at Lorena and shook her head sheepishly. "But that was all a long time ago in Californy. No, I'm safe here. I can't leave, but I'm safe. And 'round these mountains, no one asks yer name or nothin' else 'bout you." Anna colored deeply as if she were ashamed to have revealed so much of her past to a stranger. "I ain't never told anyone else 'bout this...."

Lorena nodded knowingly. "I've already forgotten it, Anna."

There was silence for a while, and then Anna pointed to a door and said gruffly, "When you're ready for bed, that'll be your room."

Lorena nodded, got up and went to the window.

For a long time she stared at the snow covering the ground. She looked up at the mountain she had crossed. The heavy snow laden clouds had passed, and a full moon lit the sky reflecting its cold silver light off the snow, making the night almost as bright as day. The sky was full of stars and Lorena looked for the North Star and thoughts of Preston filled her mind. A lone wolf howled. She shivered and gripped the window-sill glad to be inside safe from the cold, and the wolves.

Lorena turned to say something to Anna, but the woman had her eyes closed and her head crooked to one side. She was breathing slow and even, her pipe hand hanging down near the floor.

Lorena smiled, took the pipe from Anna, put the woman's hand in her lap, and tucked the fur blanket gently around her. She stared down at her new friend's plain, honest face and thought how lucky she was to have picked this woman's cabin.

Lorena opened the door to her room. It was cold. She left the door open to get some of the heat from the fire and sat down on the bed. It was hard and unyielding. She lay down and pulled the blanket over her. For a while she tossed and turned but soon her eyes grew heavy. A blissful warmth crept over her, cobwebs filled her head, and she was soon fast asleep.

She dreamed Preston was lying in the snow,

clad only in army pants and a thin silk shirt. A cold, fearsome wind made his sleeves flap against his arms.

Lorena was trying to reach him and cover him with a fur blanket. But someone was in the way. Someone wouldn't let her go to him. Then she knew. It was John Oakwood.

With a disapproving look John ordered her away. Head hanging, she walked the opposite way, turning back often to see if she could help Preston somehow. But Oakwood shook his finger at her. He wouldn't leave. Suddenly John turned his back to her and strode toward Preston, a pistol hanging from his hand.

Lorena woke with a start.

****

Lorena slept most of the next morning. After she woke she lay in the bed listening through the door to Anna singing softly as she prepared the noon meal. Lorena stretched, got up, and walked to the window. Sometime during the night the snow had begun again. The day was dark and the wind-whipped snow came down at a sharp angle making small drifts. She watched for a while, fully grateful she was not still out on the trail.

The front door opened and Lorena heard someone speaking to Anna in whispered tones. There was a gentle knock and the door opened part way. "Lorena," Anna said softly, her face showing a great sadness as she stepped in the room, "I think you'd best come with me."

"What is it? Lorena said with a heavy foreboding.

"It's your horse."

Lorena grabbed her clothes and boots and quickly put them on. She ran out the door and jumped the three steps into the snow. The two women slogged their way out toward the barn, the wind whirling the snow around them.

Lorena saw Blaze standing alone in front of the barn not moving. Anna had thrown a blanket on the horse and tied it around him. Blaze saw Lorena, whinnied at her and tried to take a few steps toward her limping badly.

Lorena's heart sank and she started to run to him. Just as she got close, Blaze's rear legs gave way and he flopped down on his rump.

Instantly, Lorena's eyes moistened and she froze.

The horse turned his head and looked about with wild eyes and flaring nostrils, then his forelegs crumpled and he went down, falling hard on his side.

"Blaze!" Lorena gasped and quickly raced to him.

When Lorena touched him the great horse's eyes calmed, and he whinnied softly and raised his head.

Lorena sat down in the snow and gently

guided the horse's head onto her lap. She put her back to the wind to protect Blaze, petted his velvet nostrils, and whispered his name.

The stallion nickered a few times, and then his brave heart gave out.

When she realized Blaze was dead, Lorena gave a primordial wail and sobbed his name. She sat in the snow with the dead horse stroking his mane, a stream of tears running down her face.

Several times Anna tried to get her to leave but Lorena wouldn't go. Anna left for a few minutes, and brought back a large blanket and put it over her. She put her hand on Lorena's shoulder and looked up at the mountain.

"Blaze wasn't the first life taken by that heap of rock." With moist eyes for Lorena's pain she patted her friend's shoulder and went back to the cabin.

For a long while Lorena stayed by the dead horse stroking his neck. Finally in the dead of night, Lorena leaned over, kissed the stallion's cold face and left.

****

The next day the sun never shone. The snow fell incessantly and soon the land was pristine white covering the tracks of man and beast. Anna and Lorena watched sadly as the men dug a pit and buried Blaze.

For the next week, snow fell daily, and

snowdrifts came up to the door. Anna and Lorena cooked, the men came, dug a path through the snow, and ate heartily.

Anna only served one meal a day, but it was enough. She earned an adequate amount of money from the men to be comfortable, and was able to pay Lorena two silver dollars a week.

Lorena recognized the irony of her situation. Now she had plenty of money but no way to get out of the valley. She was stuck here until spring.

Three weeks after Lorena came, during the noon meal, the wind began to blow hard enough to make whistling sounds as it found its way through chinks in the logs. It snowed so heavily that the foreman closed the mine. The men, with nothing to do, stayed long after they had finished their meals until Anna, completely exasperated, shooed them out.

After the last man left, Anna began to count the money while Lorena finished mopping the floor. Anna stopped, dropped two silver dollars in Lorena's half full glass jar and gazed at her friend. "Well, girl, your jar is gettin' pretty full. With all the extra money the men leave, you'll soon be able to buy Georgia."

Lorena laughed. "I don't want to buy it, just rent it for a while."

Anna's deeper, tobacco tinged voice joined Lorena's laughter.

The older woman stopped laughing first and

her face turned serious. "You know, Lorena, I never had any kin live with me, 'ceptin' two sorry husbands." She got a sour look on her face. "Yeah, stupid me, I took another one after the sailor." She shook her head and grimaced. "God damn, them two were nasty.... But anyway, I sure do like havin' you here. You're like family, just like the kid sister I never had. If you've a mind to stay....

Anna, a little embarrassed, got up, walked to the window, and stared at the wind-whipped snow.

Lorena compressed her lips and shook her head sadly. "Anna, I would love to stay with you, but I have a husband and two children—

Anna whirled around. "I know, I know. I can't believe that bastard Sherman took you away from them. When you first told me I couldn't accept it as gospel, but now that I know you—

"It's true all right." Lorena's eyes narrowed and her voice turned bitter. "I'd like to put that bastard through half of what's happened to me."

"Well, if you ever want to come back, there will always be a place for you. This eatery has done so much better since you bin here, I'd even give you a share of the business."

Lorena went to Anna and hugged her. She was unaware of the tears in Anna's eyes.

Lorena

It's loaded, be careful

Chapter 26

𝕸onths passed and, as it had for thousands of years, spring came. The snow on Lorena's mountain began to melt, poured down into the valley, and the creeks and rivers turned into raging torrents. Soon the grass turned from brown to green and the barren ground of the hills exploded in a kaleidoscope of colors as wild flowers woke from their sleep and sprang from the earth.

It was that quiet time between the end of the day and the beginning of night, and Anna was staring out the window at the scudding gray clouds passing over the purple mountain.

Lorena noticed that Anna had lost some weight. Her cheeks were hollowed, her eyes were shadowed and her skin had a pale translucency.

It was quiet, too quiet, like the hush of a storm about to break. Finally Anna sighed and turned to her friend. "The mountain passes are clear by now, Lorena," she said, with a heaviness in her voice, "You can borrow one of my horses and leave tomorrow morning." The pain of separation was written on Anna's face.

Lorena reached out and touched her hand. "I don't know what to say, Anna. I'd love to stay with you, but you understand... my children, my home—"

"Don't say anything more. I'll miss you," she said, "but the men will miss you more than I will. They're already blue."

They both laughed as Lorena went in to pack the clothes she would need. Anna followed her.

Anna picked up one of her articles of clothing and turned it back and front. "You're a whiz with a needle, Lorena, I never thought you could make any of my clothes fit you."

"My grandma taught me to sew the hard way." Lorena rubbed her buttock.

Anna laughed and picked up another garment. "What really hurts is this outfit Slim, the foreman, gave you. You didn't have to alter his clothes bit."

Lorena smiled. "He just doesn't have your curves, Anna."

Anna laughed until her tears ran down her cheeks.

****

280

The sun had not yet come up the next morning when Lorena dragged two bundles, tied in tandem, down the steps of the cabin. She and Anna threw the bundles onto the horse's back.

The horse Anna gave Lorena was a tough, hardy buckskin, trained to live off the land like an Indian pony. Anna had it gelded, which gave it more stamina. The supplies were heavy and the horse protested by dancing a few steps then settled down, resigned to the new weight.

Lorena put her foot in the stirrup and mounted. The buckskin danced again and snorted his annoyance.

Anna held up her hand and went back into the cabin. After a few minutes she came out the door with a long piece of dried beef jerky wrapped in burlap. She slipped it into one of the saddlebags. "That'll keep you if you get hungry."

Lorena laughed. "I've already got enough food for four people." She looked down at her friend fondly and Anna gazed back lovingly at Lorena.

Anna's eyes were moist and a tear escaped and ran down her cheek. She quickly brushed at it with the back of her hand.

Backing away, and turning, Anna said over her shoulder, "Wait a minute, I have something else for you." She ran back up the stairs into the cabin and in a few moments returned with a small rifle in her hands. "This'll help keep you safe." She handed Lorena a Burnside Carbine.

"One of the deserters from Lincoln's Grand Army of the Republic traded it to me for a few meals. It's loaded, be careful."

Lorena took it and thrust it into the empty rifle holster on the saddle.

She leaned down and took her friend's hand. "Thank you for everything, Anna." Lorena's moist green eyes thanked Anna far more than any words.

Anna couldn't speak anymore and just squeezed her hand. After a few moments she dropped Lorena's hand, turned abruptly and ran swiftly up the stairs and into the cabin.

Lorena watched her close the door and then sadly turned the horse south.

In the cabin Anna stood at the window, tears spilling down her face. She wiped her tears with her checkered apron as she watched Lorena and the horse canter down the trail and disappear from sight.

Lorena

The end of our world

Chapter 27

In the past months Lorena had become hardened to life and thought she could withstand anything, but she was not prepared for the destruction of Georgia.

On the outskirts of Atlanta, Lorena came upon long rows of trenches, fronted by splintered wooden tree branches sharpened into spikes. Remains of tent cities and equipment of all kinds littered the ground. The graveyards behind old churches were full, displaying freshly dug earth with the new headstones outnumbering the old. Headstones, graves and old crypts appeared to have been vandalized. *The dead here lie in grim repose,* Lorena thought.

Once proud homes, windows broken, walls collapsed and burned black by fire stood as mute testimony to a cruel war. Only their chimneys stood untouched. The ground was bare and brown, a far cry from the bountiful land she left months before. *This will be a season of discontent.*

Lorena stared at the ruin with disbelieving eyes. She stopped the horse and slid off. The remains of a campfire were at her feet and she absently kicked at a burnt piece of wood and turned over a scorched wooden canteen. She put her foot on a mound of dirt in front of a serpentine trench, rested her hand on her knee and looked along the ditch. All the flotsam of war lay at the bottom of the trench. Broken rifles and spent shells by the thousand littered the dirt floor among booted and shoeless footprints.

She shook her head slowly. *Georgia will never be the same again. I know these people. There will be hate on the land for years.*

When she reached the interior of the city, she saw what the war had done to the city of Atlanta. Skeletons of burned out buildings lined both sides of bomb-gouged roads. Lorena despaired at seeing so many women in black.

Anxious and terrified to know the fate of her children she kicked her heels against the buckskin's flanks and moved toward home. As she rode she looked right and left and felt overwhelmed. All she could see was devastation. When she came upon another trench containing several unburied horses, some still attached to artillery traces, the buckskin went mad. He reared and plunged at the sight of the dead animals and it took a while for Lorena to get control of him.

She led the horse away from the battlefield and he picked his way through the shell holes, and the rubble onto deserted streets. Lorena stopped the horse and stared at skeletal homes. *Oh, my God,* she prayed, *please let my children be safe.*

As she moved through town, activity picked up. Soldiers in blue were everywhere among the civilians. She was surprised because they were without weapons and were working alongside the people. To Lorena's surprise, it appeared they were helping the populace to rebuild.

She made her way through the rubble as fast as she could. Her home lay on Peachtree Creek at the edge of town. With wreckage blocking the roads it might take hours to get there.

Lorena reached the intact two story red brick city hall and turned up Hunter Street. She stopped and stared. All the houses, as far as she could see, were destroyed. She moved in silence until she reached McDonough Street and turned the corner. Here her eyes met even greater damage. All the houses on this street were in ruins as well as the jail and the City Hotel.

When Lorena finally arrived on Peachtree Street, she froze. All around her was more wreckage. A trail of twisted blackened trees led him down the familiar avenue. Here and there were glimmers of hope, green shoots bravely trying to survive at the foot of damaged trees.

Lorena's heart ached when she pulled up in front of what had once been her home. All that was left of the beautiful old place was the untouched arbor of cedars looming over a scorched skeleton of wood. As in other ruined buildings, only a pile of bricks that was once a fireplace stood standing.

This scene would be replayed all along Sherman's path through Georgia. The lone standing fireplace bricks would be called, Sherman's Sentinels by the defeated populace. The twisted train tracks, that once brought Atlanta travelers and goods, were given the dubious name of Sherman's Neckties.

It's the end of the war and the end of our world.

Suddenly Lorena panicked. *My children!* She turned right and left looking for someone, anyone who could give her information.

Down the street, on both sides, people were tearing down wreckage and rebuilding. Ex-Confederate soldiers, still dressed in parts of their uniforms, were working together with civilians while children scurried about getting nails and tools for the adults. There were no Yankees on this street.

Lorena urged the buckskin forward and made her way toward the workers. She looked at the people rebuilding the homes. There was no joy here, they all appeared angry and sullen.

She looked for a familiar face but could find none. A feeling of panic came over her and she kneed the horse. She might as well have asked him politely, the tired buckskin would move no faster than a walk.

She finally reached Peachtree Creek. The horse went into the water and stopped in the middle of the creek to drink. While he slaked his thirst Lorena stared at the great sycamores dipping their long branches into the swiftly moving water. She felt lost and alone.

When the horse finished his drink he nodded his head as if he knew Lorena was impatient to get started. They forded the rest of the creek and the horse scrambled up the far bank.

When they reached level ground, Lorena noticed several people standing next to a burned house, deep in conversation. As she approached they stopped speaking and turned toward her. When she reached the group she stopped the horse to speak to them. Out of the corner of her eye she noticed someone familiar. She stared at a stooped and bent figure picking up a piece of lumber. *There's something about him.... My God, it's Doctor Garret.* "Doctor Garret! It's me, Lorena, Lorena Oakwood."

Garret let go of the wood, stood up and stared at Lorena. He shook his head.

Lorena dismounted as the doctor came toward her with a quizzical face. He stepped close to her and studied her eyes. Suddenly recognition came to him. "Lorena!" He recognized something about her, which neither the sunburn nor the lines of tragedy on her face had changed.

She flung her arms around him and held on to him tightly, desperately trying to reach back to the past.

The doctor gently pulled her arms from around his neck and held her at arms length. There was a mixed look of puzzlement and anger on his face.

"Lorena Oakwood, where have you been, girl? We've been looking for you. We thought you were dead."

With her eyes on the ruin in back of the doctor, Lorena's face turned to stone. Her voice was bitter. "I am neither girl nor woman, I am only hate. I might well have been dead. It was that bastard Sherman. He sent me— Oh never mind about that now."

Lorena's face turned somber. "Where are my children? What's happened to John?"

The doctor's face clouded over. There was a terrible truth in his eyes. "Lorena, you don't know? He gripped her shoulder.

Lorena took a step back, horrified.

"Courage, girl."

Lorena's insides shrunk, a feeling of guilt and terror engulfed her. Her fist went to her mouth.

The doctor cast his eyes down. "John was with Hood. When the army's rear was threatened, He was dispatched to command the militia. General Oakwood died at the head of the Georgia Militia at the battle of Griswaldville."

A great sadness came over Lorena. All her thoughts and dreams of coming home to John with a new understanding were gone in an instant.

"Your boy is fine. He's with his grandfather."

A new feeling of anxiety came to Lorena. She felt a sharp pain in the pit of her stomach. "And my girl?"

Dr. Garret shook his head slowly, a look of infinite sadness on his face. It was the same look Lorena saw when he lost his own son. Garret couldn't speak and turned away.

Lorena grabbed his shoulder and spun him around. Her eyes were wild and her fists clenched.

"Tell me!"

Garret's eyes glistened and he turned away again. "Sarah's dead, Lorena! General Williams was there and saw it all. He said she was walking with your servant when a bomb fell—

The world tilted, and then turned black.

When Lorena woke, she was looking up Dr. Garret and several other faces behind him. He was on one knee fanning her with his white plantation hat.

He turned away from her and looked up at the others. "All right folks, give her a little room to breathe." The onlookers moved back, muttering.

The doctor put his arm under Lorena's shoulder and lifted her.

As she sat up, the horror came back to her and she felt a suffocating pain in her chest. For a moment she hung on to the thought she was in a nightmare and that she would wake with her daughter in her arms.

She searched the doctor's eyes but the grave shake of his head told her this was no dream. Lorena grabbed Garret, her fingers digging into his arm. "Tell me what happened to my family!" she demanded.

The doctor let her shoulder go, unclamped her fingers, and began to speak hesitantly, his eyes looking down. "As I told you, John was appointed commander of the Georgia Militia— on the retreat with Hood— at the battle of Griswaldville." He looked up and pointed across the meandering creek. "If it's any consolation he died defending your home." Doctor Garret shook his head sadly. "There were so many dead. Your daughter— A touch of anger flashed in the doctor's eyes. "Sherman bombed helpless civilians, like your daughter, and Hood spent soldiers lives like so many soiled pennies. They were both crazed with power. Near the end of the battle Hood charged Sherman like a mad bull."

Dr. Garret shook his head slowly. "After the battle, Hood left. With our soldiers gone,

Sherman burned almost all of the town and then forced all civilians to leave Atlanta. Of the 4,500 homes in Atlanta, only about 400 escaped damage. Out of a population of 25,000 people, not a soul was allowed to stay here.

"I tell you, Lorena you have never seen a sadder procession leaving Atlanta. Old men and women, crying children and pregnant mothers, all on foot, carrying whatever they could, leaving their homes, going God knows where. General Hood protested directly to Sherman but it did no good. General Sherman has earned an infamy that will stain his memory forever."

The doctor suddenly looked older. There was a dark shadow in his eyes. "The Yankees even desecrated the Atlanta City Cemetery. Their horses tore up the grass by grazing around the graves. Monuments, even the small caskets of children, were broken and scattered. And worst of all, coffins were removed from vaults and replaced with their own dead soldiers. The bastards even stole the silver nameplates from the caskets.

Lorena nodded her head. "I know," she said sadly, "I saw some of the desecration."

Garrett clenched his fists. "If the Yankees treated all the cities they conquered as they did this one, the population of the South will be an anxious and bedeviled people." He shook his head. Now we have a military governor and we're called Military District number 3. What we' really are is prisoners in our own country"

Lorena stared at the creek. She felt empty but no tears would come. Misery cried out in every line of her face.

The Doctor held his hand out to her. "Why don't you come over to the shade and rest awhile."

Lorena shook her head slowly. There was now a look of resigned acceptance in her face. Deep within her a streak of common sense persisted and rose to the surface. *What is done is done. I will grieve later.* Lorena stood up ramrod straight, tottered a few steps then regained her balance. "No, Doctor. I want to go and see my boy. Where is my son?"

The doctor looked at her curiously. "You've changed, Lorena. I guess experience has turned the child into a woman."

She thought about her life from which fate had stolen everything except courage and determination.

"Yes I have changed, Doctor Garret. Life has thrown me into a crucible and I have come out hard steel. The Yankees taught me to hate, so you'll not find the old Lorena Oakwood anymore." She leaned forward and looked him squarely in the eyes. "And I assure you, no one will ever toss me about again." She went to her horse and patted her rifle then mounted the buckskin and pivoted in the saddle. "Now," she said with authority, "where is my boy?"

Dr. Garret reached up and patted the buckskin on his face. "He's at the old homestead. The Yankees never got to that area. Their house was spared. Your slave— excuse me — your servant brought them there. She's still with them."

Good old Ravetta, loyal after all.

Lorena put the reins on the horse's neck and turned him to leave when she was stopped by the sharp sound of her name.

"Miz Oakwood!"

Lorena turned and stared at Garret.

"Atlanta is full of Yankees, carpetbaggers, rascals, scalawags, bummers, blacklegs, sutlers, gamblers, camp followers and scoundrels. The rest of the world is now divided into two parts," Garret said, nodding his head to add emphasis, "where the Yankees are, and where they're not. I suggest you take your boy and go where they're not."

Lorena nodded and turned back. "Thank you Doctor."

"God bless you, Lorena."

No, God bless Ravetta.

Before she turned away, Lorena noticed Dr. Garret was wearing an odd material on his feet. A pang of anger jabbed her when it dawned on her that this kind, compassionate old man was wearing shoes made from an old carpet. Shaking it off, Lorena left without a goodbye, and urged the tired horse to a gallop toward the creek. The horse's hooves made a rhythmic clacking sound as the animal passed over the wooden bridge.

Lorena rode past her home again, pulled the horse to a stop and stared. After a few moments she urged the animal into the rubble and looked around her at the charred remains.

The blackened chimney stood in the center of a pile of wood and stone. Lorena stared at what was once her garden, planted with loving care, the once delightful flowers trampled by the hooves of a thousand Yankee horses. She walked the buckskin around the back of the house and looked at the barn. All that was left was a wooden shell. *Burned by Yankee Bummers no doubt.* The three horses and two cows they kept were gone. Her face hardened and her eyes burned with hate. "Goddamned Yankee bastards," she said through clenched teeth.

Lorena walked the horse back to what used to be the living room of the house and sat quietly in the saddle for a few minutes until she calmed. She stared at the twisted, blackened stairs and thought of her daughter skipping down the scarlet carpet to greet her in the morning. Tears began to roll down her cheeks for her dead child. Her head dropped and she slumped in the saddle and sobbed uncontrollably.

She stayed that way for a long while. Then slowly she began to lift her head preparing to leave. It was then that she saw some of her charred books in the ashes. Lorena slid down off the buckskin and picked up the first book. "*Blackstone*, John's law book," she muttered. She stared at it for a moment then opened the burnt pages and began to read at random. 'The party of the second part.... Shaking her head she laid it down on the ground as carefully as she would have put it on her coffee table. She picked up a second book and brushed away the soot from the cover. '*St. Elmo by Augusta Evans.*' "Oh, God, how I wished I had you to keep me company on that train from Hell."

It was then she saw a piece of writing paper sticking up from the ashes. Lorena reached down, picked it up and blew off the dirt. The top was burned and Lorena began to read from the undamaged part.

—And my dearest wife, this cruel war has made me realize that the most important thing in this uncertain life is the certain, undying love for family. With the angel of death sitting constantly on my shoulder, I have had to examine my life and found it wanting.

If I should come through this terrible war alive, you can be sure that I will devote the rest of my life to loving you, and caring for our two dear children.

I left the army for six weeks to search for you. Nothing. Father has even hired a detective. So far we have found nothing, not a trace.

Since I don't know where you are, I will leave this letter for you on the fireplace mantle. I know you are still alive because I love you too much to let you die.

Your husband forever,
John

Lorena stared into the charred fireplace too sad to cry. "Oh, John, too late, too late." Her heart was tight with pain. Lorena folded the remains of the letter and put it in the pocket closest to her heart. Then, as if she had a great weight on her, Lorena got into the saddle and, with her eyes closed, sat motionless. After a few moments she gave a great sigh, laid the reins on the horse's neck turning the buckskin. They forded a small creek moving slowly toward John Oakwood's childhood home.

When she got to the private road that led to her father-in-law's house, she was pleased. Everything looked untouched by the war. Large oak trees, alive for hundreds of years, lined both sides of the road like a corridor of leafy sentinels. Wildflowers of every color of the rainbow nestled at the foot of the trees. The fields beyond were covered with clover as soft as a Turkish carpet.

Lorena couldn't wait any more and she kicked the horse as hard as she could in his ribs. This time the buckskin responded by racing down the hard packed dirt road. Lorena, her face a picture of determination, urged the buckskin on. She was almost home.

In the distance she saw someone sitting on the porch swing. *Is that my son? He's so tall. No, that can't be my boy.* As she got closer the lad stood up and she saw that he was standing straight and military, coolly staring at her racing toward him. Her heart began to pound and she beamed with pure delight. *Now I know he's mine.*

With a mighty laugh she leaned forward in the saddle, put her face alongside the horse's mane and raced the buckskin down the road, her red hair streaming in the wind.

Chapter 28

𝔗he morning was gray, wet and humid making the occasion more dreadful. Rivulets of rain made their way down the discolored headstones disappearing into the cold ground. The three mourners made there way under the *Oakwood Cemetery* sign looking for a particular place. Ravetta pointed to a gravesite with two head stones and they stopped there.

Lorena kneeled on the sodden ground in front of the graves, her face haggard with grief. Tears streamed down her cheeks and joined at the corners of her mouth then dropped off to the collar of her mourning dress, the same dress she wore at Preston's burial. Her red hair was tucked conservatively under an ebony hat, her face half hidden by a black veil.

Her son stood next to her dressed in a suit that had grown too small for him. He restlessly pulled at the sleeves.

Ravetta stood behind them, crying softly. She put one hand on Zachery's shoulder and her other hand on Sarah's headstone, her face a picture of grief, tears making tracks down her black cheeks. "Chile," she said to Zachery, "you onderstand we is all made outen de dus' of de earth. And you onderstand dat all of us, like yo' sister, when we is dead we all goes back to dus'."

Zachery nodded his head.

For a moment it was quiet, then Ravetta began to shout. "It's mah fault," she wailed, "ah shoulda protected her. Oh, mah poor baby. Why couldn't it have been me, Lord, why not me?"

Lorena got up, wiped her eyes and took Ravetta's hand. Then she reached over to put her hand on Zachery's arm. Absently she read the headstones.

DEBORAH SARAH OAKWOOD
BORN 1860 DIED 1865
THIS ANGEL LIVES IN HEAVEN AND AWAITS US

JOHN ALLEN OAKWOOD, GENERAL, COBB'S LEGION,
14TH GEORGIA
BORN MAY 31, 1840   DIED APRIL 15, 1865
HE GAVE HIS LIFE IN THE 2ND REBELLION,
FOR LIBERTY

Lorena shook her head slowly. Her face was bitter and pale and rigid, appearing as if touched it would shatter. She looked up at the heavy, moisture-laden clouds. *The Yankees have taken much from me, but this is their last blow. I don't know what I'm going to do, but believe this, John Allen Oakwood, I didn't let the Yankees beat me before, and I won't let them now. You rest easy, John, our son will be safe with me.*

She patted her son's shoulder and watched him reading his father's tombstone with tear-filled eyes. "I know you miss him, Zack. I miss him too." She knelt down and wiped the boy's eyes with a silk handkerchief, her own eyes spilling over again. "I will miss them terribly."

Then Zachery did something he had never done before. He reached out, lifted her veil, put his finger on Lorena's cheek and caught one of her tears on his finger. For a moment he stared at it, then suddenly he threw his arms around his mother's neck and wept bitterly. They stayed like that until both of them exhausted their grief.

When they finally parted, Lorena and Zachery walked together down the long rows of crosses.

"We owe these soldiers something we can never repay," Lorena said in a quiet voice. Then she turned to her son. "We're mostly self-centered beings trying to grab only the joy from life. But sometimes your country calls and you have to step up and make the ultimate sacrifice. That's what your father did and what the rebellion of the Southern States taught us."

Zachery nodded his head solemnly.

Lorena gave him a faint smile. "Zack, you're

the man of the house now, so lead the way home."
She hugged him hard and the two of them walked
to the buggy, arm in arm, a wretched Ravetta
trailing behind.

Chapter 29

"Now, Lorena, do you think you ought to be traipsin' off to God knows where? Zack just lost his father and his sister. Do you think it's a good idea to rush him to a new place so soon?"

"But, Colonel Oakwood—"

"Ah agree with him, mah deah. Lord knows ah don't usually agree with Mr. Oakwood, but in this instance ah do—" Mrs. Oakwood stopped with a puzzled look on her face. "Oh deah, what was it that ah was agreein' with him about?"

Mrs. Oakwood came from a small town near the Florida border. Her husband was born and raised in Atlanta. Colonel Oakwood had seen her some fifty years ago while on a trip to Florida to capture and bring back wild horses for the army cavalry. Instead of horses he captured her heart and brought her home. They were old stock, and never part of the new breed that was to make Atlanta the dynamic metropolis and new leader of the South.

They were both raised in the privileged ante

bellum society of belles and beaus, plantations and cotton fields, and the large slave populations that made it all work. It had been a world of advantage, where young girls had many beaus, festive balls and black nannies to pull corsets so tight it was hard for them to breathe.

Time had treated Colonel Oakwood well, but wasted Mrs. Oakwood's body and mind. However a spark of the old life remained in her luminous blue eyes.

Lorena patted the older woman's hand. "It's all right, Mother Oakwood." She turned back to Mr. Oakwood. "Colonel Oakwood, I want you to know this is not a quick decision. I have thought it over very carefully." She looked away. "If I still had my home, that might be different."

"But you have a home, Lorena. We want you and the boy to stay here, with us. He's been happy here." He waved his arm around in a large circle. "And all this will someday be his."

She stopped and took the old man's hands in hers. "I know how you feel, and I am very grateful to you both." She let his hands go and her face turned hard with resolve. "But my mind is made up, we're leaving tomorrow."

Lorena turned and stared out the window past the lush, green lawn toward the city. "Atlanta will never be the same." She turned back to the old man, a small smile on her face. "It never really was a southern town, but it was filled with southerners. Now it's swarming with Union soldiers and northerners. Why there are fifty lazy Africans and carpetbagging thieves to every honest soul on Peachtree Street. No, I don't want my child growing up with them."

"Oh, God!" Mrs. Oakwood exclaimed and staggered to a couch, "now we belong to the Negroes and the Yankees."

Lorena walked to the old lady and touched her shoulder.

Mrs. Oakwood winced and looked afraid.

And I don't want us to be a burden on John's poor mother.

"They won't bother you out here, Mother Oakwood." She turned to Colonel Oakwood. "I appreciate what you both have done. Zack loves you both and I can send him to you every summer." She kissed them both on the cheek and went to the stairs, stopped and looked back at them. "And I love you too."

Lorena started up the stairs to pack. At the top of the landing she turned and looked sadly at the old couple. They were sitting apart on the couch.

Nothing has changed here. He is still cold and aloof, like his son. And she is afraid of every shadow. So many of us, like them, live long dreary lives, and happiness never comes to meet us. It always seems so near yet eternally eludes us.

Lorena looked hard at Mrs. Oakwood. *That might be me, someday, if I stay.*

Everywhere I look there are Yankees and Negroes
and devastation

Chapter 30

From the private journal of Lorena
Boykins Oakwood

October 31, 1865

The hand the North has laid on us is a
heavy one. Atlanta, the city I loved is no
more. Everywhere I look there are
Yankees and Negroes and devastation.

The Union soldiers treat us as prisoners
and poor relations and most mortifying,
sometimes even have to feed us. This
calamity is taking place on our own
land, in our own country.
My friends are now destitute. As Preston
predicted, many of them have turned to
commerce, for which they are ill suited.
My own servant, Ravetta, took our old

cows to the swamp, where she hid them from the Yankee Bummers, and is making butter and milk. We sell them to the Yankee soldiers and she shares the proceeds with me. I'm almost ashamed to take the money, but if I am to be independent of John's parents, I must.

All of Mr. Oakwood's former slaves are free and many have left the plantations. But some of them have stayed and are now tenant farmers. Mr. Oakwood and the Negroes tolerate each other and survive. It's all become too much for me. I am leaving.

I remember mounting the buckboard and looking at the farewell party. Colonel Oakwood was solemn. He hides his feelings well. John was also an expert pretender.

The Colonel took my hand and held it for a split second longer than was necessary. What's this? An emotion? In the next moment he recovers and backs away.

Ravetta's black face is swollen with grief. Tears run freely down her cheeks. She hugs Zack and her heavy body heaves with sobbing. She begs me to take her. I tell her she is better off here. I signed a deed for her and say she can stay in her cabin by the creek that we built for her. At least the invaders did not destroy that. She can enlarge her new dairy business and, with me gone, will not have to share the money.

Zack and I have looked through the wreckage of our old home for anything of value. We found nothing. I fear my beautiful silver and china will be decorating the table of a Northern family this Christmas. My silk sheets will cover their beds. Veni, Vici, Vinci. To the victor go the spoils.

It's time to go. We packed one of Mr. Oakwood's wagons and my sturdy son took his father's place next to me. I marvel that he has grown up so these past few months.

Ravetta pleads one more time and I gently refuse. She dissolves into tears again, and runs into the house. Mr. Oakwood hands me the buckskin's reins then backs away and I prepare to go. At the last instant I looked up and see Mrs. Oakwood at the window on the second floor. I am not sure but I think there are tears in her eyes.

I apply the whip to the horse, and the buckskin starts off. As we roll down the road I try to picture John and I am ashamed that my mind and heart are full only of Preston Beauregard Harrison Lord. He has been taken from me, but evidently I have not yet let go of him.

As I leave Atlanta and the scarred grounds of battle, my heart breaks for the old South.

My native land, goodnight!

There's your new home

Chapter 31

𝕿he sun rose just over the eastern horizon, a blood red wafer drifting through the fog coming off the ground. Lorena looked back at her son sleeping peacefully in a pallet made of blankets and smiled. She was anxious to get on the road, so, before the sun came up she woke Zachery, broke camp and made an early start.

Her thoughts on the future she was startled by the boy's voice.

"Mother, are we there yet?"

Lorena smiled. "No, darling, but it won't be long now."

The lad looked wistful. "I wish Sarah was with us."

Lorena's heart lurched. "Me too," she said quietly.

"Where will we live Mother?"

"You'll see. We're almost there."

She was worried about her son. Gone was any spontaneity. He was a quiet boy before, but now he was somber and thoughtful all the time, and if spoken to, he had to be recalled from another place.

Jumbled thoughts of John, her daughter and Atlanta invaded her thoughts. She knew she would never return to that place, but she could never escape it either.

Lorena started up a long hill. The buckskin protested but Lorena urged him on with her whip and the clucking sound she learned from Robert in Iowa so long ago. The wagon finally creaked to the top of the rise. Ahead was the purple mountain. Lorena pulled back on the reins and the buckskin stopped abruptly. The household goods in the back shifted and the top ones started to fall. Zachery turned and caught a falling box.

"That was close Mother, better take it easy."

"Sorry, son."

"I'm tired of traveling, when will we be there?"

Lorena half turned in her seat. "We are there, darling." She pointed down into the valley. "There's your new home."

Zachery looked puzzled and then disappointed, but said nothing.

Lorena ignored the look. For a few moments she stared up at the great mountain she crossed last winter. A thousand mixed feelings roiled around inside her. She silently said a prayer, then shook her head and eased the wagon down the hill on a path to the valley trail. With eagerness in her heart she went as fast as the buckskin would allow, until she pulled up at the familiar cabin yelling Anna's name.

Lorena jumped down off the seat just as the front door opened.

Anna let out a whoop and leaped down the porch steps and the two women ran to each other and embraced. Finally Anna held Lorena at arms length and looked at her fondly. There were tears in her eyes and she couldn't speak.

The boy got down off the wagon and stood awkwardly next to the front wheel.

After a few moments, Lorena broke away and stood beside her son.

He moved as close to her as he could.

Lorena patted his shoulder. "Zack, this is your new home. And I would like to introduce you to my very dearest friend, Anna."

Anna held her hand out to him. For a moment the boy hung back. Lorena gently pushed him forward. Still reserved, he took a few steps toward Anna. Slowly he reached out his hand and shook Anna's stiffly. "I'm Zachery Oakwood, General John Oakwood's son," he said in an unsteady voice.

Anna shook his hand and curtsied. "Good morning Master Oakwood."

At the sight of the large woman genuflecting, the boy's face relaxed and he broke into a broad grin.

Anna went to him and hugged him. Lorena, laughing joyously, joined them to begin their new life.

****

From the private diary of Lorena Boykins Oakwood

July 4th, 1875

We've been here for almost ten years now.

It has taken a long while for the chains of my past to unwind from around me. My trials during the Civil War have become blurred with time, but even now the grief for my child, and Preston, and John, rolls on endlessly.

Back then time was not the same. A minute was an hour and a day a lifetime. Now, tempest fugit. Perhaps some day I can write a brief narrative and bring that era back into focus. Or maybe some distant relative or friend will find my journals and publish them, to let the world know what that awful time was really like.

My son, Zack, is almost man now. He has grown straight and strong and is tending to the small spread we live on. I watch him mature and take joy in being part of that miracle.

My daughter, Sarah, had she lived, would by now be of an age to be noticed by the young men of the town. Of course Sarah's gone, but she is still alive in my heart.

Zack is going to a July fourth picnic with a young girl from the church, but I will be there to keep an eye on them.

Anna and I still run the restaurant, but the town has grown so large we had to put on more help and now we serve three meals a day.

I've had a few admirers but they don't interest me. No one could ever measure up to Preston. Of course it's foolish to compare. But I'm not lonely, what with my work, my son and Anna.

All in all it's been a good life. In fact I wouldn't have it any other way. Except—

Sometimes on cold and lonely nights I look up at the unmoving North Star and wonder—

I wonder how everything might have turned out if Preston had lived.

Every night when I am in bed I pray that, if this is my last night, I will wake on the North Star in Preston's arms, and spend eternity there with him. Godspeed.

The End

Epilogue

𝔓ulling alongside the gas pump, the man opened the car door, got out, and stretched and yawned to relieve his tension.

"Anybody home?" he yelled towards the ramshackle store.

He waited for a few moments then slipped off his blue jacket and put it over his arm. Carefully he rolled up his sleeves, pulled a red handkerchief out of his pocket and dabbed his wet forehead.

He yelled once more. "Hey, anybody here?" No answer.

Again the man wiped the rivulets of sweat running down his face, patted his neck, and stuffed the handkerchief into his back pocket.

"Damn," he muttered, "where is everybody?"

The traveler had a lean, intense face with a strong jaw, and a thin mustache that went the length of his lip. He wore a white shirt, with gray pants tucked into black cowboy boots. His black striped tie had a tie clasp with a diamond in the center.

With a deep drag on a black cheroot he tipped his Stetson back on his head, expelled the smoke into the air, and looked around him. The ramshackle store and garage stood on the only flat land in the area. All around were hills and rocky ground. North of where he stood was a huge purple mountain that dominated the region.

Next to an abandoned building were two rusted poles sticking out of the ground with a white sign hanging from one hinge. Written in faded black letters he made out the words, *Imperial Copper Mine.*

The man took a step toward the store. Over the entrance to the place was a sign, *Anna's Groceries.* At one end of the building was a smaller building that looked like an add-on. *Oscar's Garage* was written on the side of the structure.

Before he could take another step, a slender, elderly Negro with white cottony hair, dressed in work clothes, came out of the garage. He sauntered toward the man, wiping grease from his hands with a mechanic's rag. When he reached him he asked pleasantly, "Fill it up?"

"I guess you better. And check that right front tire." He pointed over his shoulder at the mountain. "I hit a rock up there and the car rode pretty rough after that." The man looked back down the empty road. "I didn't see any other gas stations on the way here, so I thought I'd better stop when I saw your place. Better to be safe than sorry."

"Yessuh. Not many stations 'roun' here since the depression started. We's just hangin' on ourselves." The Negro put the handle in the fuel spout and started pumping the gas. He leaned back and looked at the car admiringly. "This a new car?"

The man tapped the fender proudly. "Uh huh. Well, almost new. It's a year old."

"You sure takes good care of it. It looks brand spankin' new."

"I'm gonna get me a newer one soon." He shrugged. "Maybe next year. That is if business improves."

A moment of silence, then, "You travelin' a long way?"

"Yeah, from Pascagoula, Mississippi. Goin' on over to Charlotte on business."

While he waited the man drummed his fingers on the fender of the car, watching the gas swirl through the glass bubble. He listened impatiently to the ding of a bell each time the pump registered a gallon slowly being transferred into the year-old Ford. He stopped drumming and pushed his hand through his coal black hair with a brusque movement. "Uh, is that your name on the building, boy?"

"Yes, suh, I'm Oscar."

Well, Oscar, I'm goin' in your store and get me a sody pop. When I get back we can settle up. Okay?"

Oscar nodded in assent.

The man went up the three stairs to the porch entrance and stopped short when he saw her.

The old woman was sitting in a rocking chair, so still he didn't see her at first. She was wearing a worn ebony hat with a black veil, strands of her gray hair, with streaks of red peeked out from under the hat. She was staring at him oddly with dark green eyes that bore right through him.

"Uh, mornin' Ma'am."

She said nothing but continued to stare.

He noticed her twisted body and that her face was creased and furrowed like an old leather purse. In her lap lay a large, worn book. He glanced at the spine of the old book and saw the name of the author, *Balzac*.

She continued to stare at him intently. He felt strong, emotionally charged feelings coming from her, but couldn't exactly put his finger on what they were.

"'Scuse me, Ma'am, I didn't see you sittin' there. I hope I didn't frighten you."

Her glistening green eyes sparkled and a ghost of a smile played on her pale lips. Almost imperceptibly she shook her head.

The man smiled back, satisfied that he had

gotten some kind of response from her. Turning around, he went into the cool, dark interior of the store. The door squeaked then slammed shut behind him and the man uttered, "Damn."

A few minutes later he opened the door but this time let it ease back, holding it with his elbow to prevent its slamming. He nodded again to the old woman and looked down at the cola in his hand, then back at her. "Can I get you something, Ma'am?"

She looked back at him quizzically, her smile fading.

"No?" He shrugged his shoulders. "Then good mornin' to you, Ma'am."

The man shook his head slowly and went down the stairs back to the car.

Oscar was kneeling at the front tire. He stood up. "'Scuse me suh, but you got a bad flat. In fact I hopes you has a spare, 'cause it looks like this tire is done for."

The man looked down at the tire. Not only was it flat, but he could see a ragged tear along the sidewall with the red tube bulging out the hole like a dirty balloon. In disgust he kicked the tire then yelped, dropped the cola, and grabbed his foot. "Damn," he growled hopping on his good foot, "can you fix it?"

Oscar laughed and picked up the bottle of spilled cola. "Your foot or the tire?"

The man stopped hopping and grimaced.

Oscar handed the bottle to him. "About this tire. The onliest thing I can do is put your spare on. Cain't fix that kind of tear with a patch. I ain't got a tire that would fit your car neither." Oscar pointed to the damage. "You're really lucky you got this far." He looked up at the purple mountain in the distance. "It's a long walk from up there."

The man shook his head and dismissed the thought. "Okay, let's put on the spare, but please do it quickly. I've got to be in Charlotte before dark."

"Yes, suh." The Negro ambled toward the garage for his tools. When he got back he went straight to work.

After a few minutes the man tapped Oscar's shoulder.
"Every time I look over at the porch, I see that old woman starin' at me. You know why?"

Oscar stopped spinning a lug nut. "No, suh. Don't know why suh, less'n you reminds her of someone."

"Who is she?"

Oscar got a wide grin on his face, showing a line of bright, white teeth. "She's my Mom."

The man laughed. "Don't kid me Oscar."

"I'm not joking with you, suh. After the Civil War my natural Momma got married and had me. Then the no 'count she hitched up with took off wit her money, and we ain't seed him since.

Momma finally forgot him and went back to her milk and eggs business, sellin' to all the white folks in Atlanta. She did right well too."

Oscar's mouth turned down, and a look of infinite sadness came into his eyes. "When I was 'bout ten years old, Momma got sick wit the typhoid. The business died and so did Momma."

His eyes glistened. "Afore she went, she writ Miz Oakwood— that's the old woman on the porch— and asked if'n she'd take me and raise me. My momma was her nurse when she was a little girl, and helped her survive after the Civil War, so Miz Oakwood couldn't rightly refuse."

Oscar turned and blew Mrs. Oakwood a kiss.

She ignored him, and kept staring intently at the stranger.

"Her real son, Zack, went to West Point, became an officer, and was serving in France, during the World War. He was gassed at Belleau Wood." Oscar shook his head slowly. "He was never the same after that, always hacking and spittin' up some vile green stuff. He lived for a few years then, mercifully, he died in his sleep. I guess I kinda took his place cause when he died, Miz Oakwood," he pointed his thumb at the old woman as if he were hitch-hiking, "upped and adopted me." He smiled broadly, his teeth gleaming against his black face. "That's how come she's my Mom."

Oscar pointed to the land around him. "When I

first came here, this place had a copper mine and Miz Oakwood had a busy restaurant called *Anna's*. When the hard times came in the late 80's, the mine closed and so did the restaurant. Everyone left, and in a few months this place was nuthin' but a ghost town."

The stranger heard a grunt, and out of the corner of his eye he saw Mrs. Oakwood stand up.

"Now all we got left is this garage and that ol' store," Oscar said pointing to the dilapidated building.

Suddenly there was a loud noise, like the crack of a pistol. Mrs. Oakwood had taken a step, and her book had fallen to the floor.

Both men whirled toward the sound.

The woman started toward the railing. While walking, she held her arms out toward the stranger.

"Preston?"

She staggered a few steps, toward the railing.

Oscar shrieked, "No, Momma—"

The stranger froze and watched in horror as the woman's thighs struck the railing and she tumbled over, her head striking the ground. They heard a sickening crack and the woman lay still.

A stunned Oscar couldn't move but the stranger vaulted a row of bushes and in a flash was kneeling by her side.

He looked down at the woman and his blood went cold. Her neck was crooked at an unnatural angle.

He sat down next to her, reached under and cradled her neck, then gently took her in his arms. Her hat lay on the ground and her long gray and red hair spilled over his forearm.

Her watery green eyes opened, looked up at him and bathed him in a love he had never felt before. A strange feeling surged through him and he felt overwhelmed. An unbidden tear escaped his eye.

She reached up and caught the tear on a gnarled finger. Then she smiled and was young again. .

Lorena moved her lips and tried to speak. Failing that she beckoned to him.

The stranger bent closer to her.

She slowly put her arm around his neck and gently pulled him closer to her and kissed his forehead. Suddenly she found her voice. "Preston," she said softly, "I'm ready to go with you."

Then her eyes closed.